After graduating with deg
Political Science, **Eva Sh**
journalism and as an adv
She began writing histori
it combined her love of a happy ending with her passion for history. She lives in Christchurch, New Zealand, but spends her days immersed in the world of late Victorian England. Eva loves hearing from readers and can be reached via her website, evashepherd.com, and her Facebook page at Facebook.com/evashepherdromancewriter.

Also by Eva Shepherd

Young Victorian Ladies miniseries

Wagering on the Wallflower
Stranded with the Reclusive Earl
The Duke's Rebellious Lady

Those Roguish Rosemonts miniseries

A Dance to Save the Debutante
Tempting the Sensible Lady Violet
Falling for the Forbidden Duke

Rebellious Young Ladies miniseries

Lady Amelia's Scandalous Secret
Miss Fairfax's Notorious Duke
Miss Georgina's Marriage Dilemma
Lady Beaumont's Daring Proposition

Discover more at millsandboon.co.uk.

A WAGER TO WIN THE DEBUTANTE

Eva Shepherd

MILLS & BOON

First published in Great Britain 2024
by Mills & Boon, an imprint of HarperCollins*Publishers* Ltd,
1 London Bridge Street, London, SE1 9GF

www.harpercollins.co.uk

HarperCollins*Publishers*, Macken House, 39/40 Mayor Street Upper,
Dublin 1, D01 C9W8, Ireland

ISBN: 978-0-263-32089-3

09/24

This book contains FSC™ certified paper
and other controlled sources to ensure responsible forest management.

For more information visit www.harpercollins.co.uk/green.

Printed and Bound in the UK using 100% Renewable Electricity
at CPI Group (UK) Ltd, Croydon, CR0 4YY

To the staff at South Library Christchurch.
Thank you for supporting the *Word X Word*
writing group and tolerating the sometimes
noisy discussions, the raucous laughter, and
the occasional silent periods of intense writing.

Chapter One

London—
1897

Like most little girls, as a child Grace Lowerby loved fairy tales. When her nanny had read her those enchanting stories, she would disappear into a fantasy world, one where she was swept into the arms of a handsome prince and danced the night away at a magical ball. She would picture him pledging his undying love and taking her away from harsh reality. With him by her side, no one would ever criticise her again and her grandmother would finally find it in her heart to truly love her only grandchild and everything would be right with the world.

Once she was old enough to read for herself, she did not stop indulging in her love of fairy tales, or imagining herself as a princess, loved by all for her beauty and majestic elegance. It was *The Princess and the Pea* that most captured her imagination. She simply adored the story of the ordinary girl who was revealed to be a princess. One day she, too, would be transformed. The world would no longer see her as the daughter of a woman who had shamed her family by marrying a man beneath her, but as a beautiful princess worthy of admiration.

When she reached the age of eighteen and was presented to Queen Victoria, along with all the other debutantes, she was certain her fairy tale was about to become a reality. She was not a child any more and was no longer so silly as to think she actually was a princess, or that she would marry a prince. Such things did not happen in real life, but she was certain she would have her dream Season and had her heart set on marrying a handsome duke and making her grandmother proud.

And she knew exactly which duke would be her husband: Algernon Huntingdon-Smythe, the Duke of Hardgraves. He was by far the most eligible man available and, despite never having met the Duke, she knew for certain that by the end of the Season they would be man and wife.

In preparation for finding the best possible husband, her grandmother had described every eligible man, their background, their interests, their achievements and admirable features. This was to ensure she could engage in captivating conversation sprinkled with fitting compliments sure to pique their interest.

Of all the men discussed it was the Duke of Hardgraves who had the highest number of achievements and the longest list of admirable features. He was noble, from an illustrious family noted for its chivalry. In other words, he was perfect in every way.

The arrival of an invitation to attend the Duke's ball, the very first ball of the Season, hosted at his Kensington address was all the proof she needed that she was about to embark on an enchanted Season.

Every time she looked at the crisp white invitation emblazoned in gold with the Duke's crest, excitement fluttered through her. She saw it as a private message from the Duke to herself, telling her that he, too, was waiting for their romance to begin.

On the night of the ball, as she stood in front of her grandmother dressed in her flowing ivory silk gown embroidered with tiny pink roses, her nervous anticipation grew with each passing minute. She placed her hand on her chest and stomach to try to calm her pounding heart and rolling stomach.

'Stand up straight, for goodness' sake,' her grandmother commanded, eyeing her up and down. 'And turn around slowly so I can see how you look from every angle.'

Grace moved in a slow circle, loving the feel of the cool, soft fabric draped against her legs and the way it caught the light and appeared to shimmer as she moved. She really did feel every inch like a princess ready to meet her prince, or, to be more accurate, a future duchess ready to meet her handsome duke.

'Yes, you are certainly pretty enough,' her grandmother said, more as a statement of fact than a compliment.

The fluttering of her heart increased. Her grandmother had never called her pretty before. She never made idle compliments. In fact, Grace had never received a compliment from her before, so it must be true. She was pretty.

'Stop that twirling and listen to me.'

Grace did as she was told, delighted by the way the long silky train of her gown continued to elegantly swirl around her feet after she had come to a halt.

'Tonight, you must remember at all times that you are descended from a noble family. Your grandfather was an earl. I am a countess. You can trace your family back to the time of Queen Anne when she created the first Earl of Ashbridge.'

'Yes, Grandmama,' Grace responded in answer to the familiar speech.

'You must forget all about the shame your mother brought on this family.'

Grace could say it would be easier to forget about it if her grandmother did not keep reminding her, but she would never question anything her grandmother said. To even think of doing such a thing merely showed what an ungrateful child she was, one who should know better.

'Yes, Grandmama,' she said instead.

'Now you have the opportunity to redeem the family name and make a good marriage.'

'Yes, Grandmama,' she repeated as the speech continued in its usual vein. 'That is what I hope to do.'

'Hmm,' her grandmother said, which was as close as she ever came to approving anything Grace did or said.

'I intend to marry the Duke of Hardgraves.' Grace's heart seemingly jumped into her mouth. It was the first time she had expressed this ambition out loud and she waited in dread for her grandmother's response.

Her grandmother's eyes grew wide in surprise, causing Grace's heart to thump louder. Then she narrowed them in thought.

'A duke in the family,' her grandmother mused, tapping her chin with her forefinger. She lowered her finger and smiled. A rare event, one that caused Grace to smile in response.

'And why not? Our family is as esteemed as any that will be present tonight, more so than many. You are a pretty little thing and your dowry is certainly generous, very generous indeed.' She nodded her head, looking Grace up and down as if weighing up her ability to perform this task.

'You have to marry a titled man, so why not reach

for the highest position available? Yes, I believe, if you do everything right, there is no reason why you can't marry a duke.'

Grace's heart soared with pleasure at her grandmother's approval. This had to be a good sign that all her dreams were about to come true.

'Remember all you have been taught. At all times your focus must be entirely on the Duke as if he is the most fascinating man in the room, which of course he will be. Smile at him, laugh at anything amusing he says, but not too loudly.' She frowned at Grace in admonition as if she had already broken that rule.

'No, Grandmama,' she said, expressing her shock that she would ever do something so gauche.

'You will have to make a good impression immediately and stand out from the other debutantes, so join his circle as soon as we are introduced. And the moment you do get his attention, all your conversation must be about him. Ask him questions about himself, especially ones that allow him to show himself off in the best light. Compliment him when appropriate and, if he asks you about yourself, keep your answers brief and your eyes lowered, so he can see you will be an obedient and compliant wife.'

'Yes, Grandmama,' she said, lowering her eyes in the appropriate manner.

'Good.'

Her grandmother performed one last inspection,

handed Grace her fan and they briskly left the house, climbed into the carriage and set off across London to the Duke's home.

Grace was rarely allowed out in the evenings, it being inappropriate for a young lady to do so before her coming out, and she so wanted to see all the sights that were unfolding before her. But she saw little of the bustling London streets outside the carriage window. She was too consumed with a mixture of excitement and trepidation.

This was it. Just like Cinderella, she was off to the ball and tonight was the night her life would change for ever.

Their carriage joined the throng lining up to drop off the guests outside the Duke's elegant, three-storey townhouse, which shone out like a beacon in the tree-lined street. Warm yellow lights glowed at every window, music flowed out through the open doors and already a large crowd of elegantly dressed men and women were making their way up the steps, laid with a deep red carpet to protect the ladies' evening slippers.

Grace's hand moved to her heart to calm its jittering, and she smiled at the magical sight.

'Didn't you hear a word I just said?' her grandmother snapped.

Grace immediately focused on her scowling grandmother. She was right. Grace had not been listening. That was so remiss of her.

'Stop smiling like that. A lady does not show her teeth when she smiles. It makes her look like a horse.'

Grace's beaming smile disappeared. 'Sorry, Grandmama,' she said and adopted the correct demure smile.

'That's better,' she said, eyeing Grace carefully. 'You won't disgrace me tonight, will you?'

'No, Grandmama. Of course not.'

'I hope you realise that good looks alone are not enough. Your mother was also pretty and could have had the pick of any man. But she was disobedient and stubborn. She threw all her advantages away and ruined everything. You won't be like that, will you?'

'No, of course not, Grandmama.' Grace was shocked her grandmother thought she even needed to ask such a thing.

'Your mother married beneath her. You won't do that, will you?'

She shook her head, then smiled slightly. 'I will make you proud of me, Grandmama, and become a duchess.'

'Good girl.' She smiled, and warmth radiated through Grace at the unfamiliar sign of approval.

'It's such a shame your dear grandfather won't be here to see it,' she said, touching the edge of her eye to wipe away a non-existent tear. 'Your mother's disobedience broke the Earl's heart, but you will be the one to make things right.'

'Yes, Grandmama,' Grace repeated.

The slow-moving carriage came to a halt directly outside the Duke's home and the footman opened the door.

'Right, chin up, shoulders back,' her grandmother commanded.

Grace assumed the correct posture, took the footman's hand, stepped down from the carriage and, keeping her head high, walked up the path and into the Duke's home.

They made their way to the crowded ballroom and paused at the top of the stairs while they waited to be announced. Grace smiled with genuine joy and, despite her excitement, ensured her smile remained the requisite level of demure.

The ballroom was even more magnificent than she had imagined. The row of silver chandeliers suspended from the high, gilded ceiling were all adorned with countless candles that sent shimmering light over the room. Ferns and enormous bouquets of flowers lined the walls, providing a delightful floral scent, and the music from the orchestra seated on the minstrel gallery above the dance floor filled the air.

Her gaze moved to the fashionably attired guests circulating the room and her smile died. This was something she had chosen not to think about. When she was presented to the Queen at Kensington Palace, there had been many other attractive girls present. She should have realised they, too, would be attending the same balls as her. The room appeared packed with young ladies, many of whom were much prettier than Grace. They were all dressed in beautiful gowns equally as elegant as Grace's and, she had to admit, they all appeared much more confident than she ever could.

'Chin up,' her grandmother snapped out the corner of her mouth, while still smiling politely.

Grace immediately lifted her chin and adopted her own polite smile.

The steward announced them. Controlling her nerves as best she could, Grace walked down the marble stairs, in what she hoped could be described as an elegant and sweeping manner. The Duke was waiting at the bottom, and Grace found it all but impossible to look into the eyes of the man she was to marry.

With as much composure as she could muster, she performed a low curtsy and, summoning up every ounce of courage she possessed, she willed her eyes to rise and meet his, desperate to see how he would react to the sight of his future bride.

His gaze moved slowly up and down her, an assessing expression on his face, one she had often seen on the face of the family's estate steward when he was considering the purchase of livestock. Then, to Grace's horror, he looked away at the next young lady lined up.

Something was very wrong. This was not how their first meeting should go.

Why hadn't there been an immediate spark of recognition between them? Why hadn't he looked at her with interest, affection and even dawning love? And why hadn't her heart taken flight at the first sight of the man she was to wed?

Had she been dismissed as unworthy before the night had barely begun? That could not be.

Her grandmother took her arm and led her away.

'That did not go as well as expected,' she whispered discreetly so only Grace could hear. 'But you've been introduced now. All you have to do is get his attention so that he asks you to dance.'

Grace's forced smile quivered. It was wonderful her grandmother still had such faith in her, but after that first meeting Grace suspected it was misplaced.

The attraction between them was supposed to be immediate, just like in the fairy tales. It shouldn't be something Grace had to orchestrate.

How on earth was she expected to attract the Duke's attention? How was she to get him to ask her to dance? And how was she to become his fairy-tale bride if she couldn't hold his attention even during their introduction?

For the first time since she had decided she was going to marry the Duke, she wondered about the wisdom of her plan.

Thomas Hayward avoided society balls like the plague. When he did attend, it was always under sufferance. And attending a ball hosted by Algernon Huntingdon-Smythe, the Duke of Hardgraves, caused him to suffer even more than usual. There was only one thing that would drag Thomas to the Duke's home and find him standing at the edge of the dance floor, stifling a yawn.

It wasn't for the debutantes, all lined up in their pastel colours, like pretty unpicked flowers. It certainly wasn't for the conversation, which made a wet weekend with his maiden aunts seem amusing and scintillating in comparison. And it wasn't to mix with the aristocracy. He'd experienced enough of his so-called betters at the prestigious and ridiculously expensive school his father had enrolled him in to last him a lifetime.

No, he was here for one reason only, to get the Duke of Hardgraves to sign the documents he'd had in his possession for over a month now and surrender large tracts of his Cornwall estate over to Thomas's family firm.

He shook his head in disbelief as he watched the Duke, surrounded by those pretty, pastel debutantes and their equally ambitious mamas. They were drawn to the unmarried Duke like proverbial moths to a flame. If they could see the state of his finances, Thomas wondered if they'd still be as enamoured by the imbecile.

Probably, Thomas admitted with despondency. He'd

learnt the hard way at school that a title counts for more than intelligence, skill, wit, or any other quality one could name, and was certainly more important than something as uncouth as a healthy bank balance.

He pulled his fob watch out of his jacket pocket and flicked open the cover. It was still only ten o'clock. It was painfully obvious what the Duke was doing. He was hoping to make Thomas suffer, just as he had attempted to do at school. Nothing gave the Duke more pleasure than to put the son of a wealthy industrialist in his place. The Duke had failed to do so at school, again and again, but apparently that did not stop him from continuing to try.

They had been rivals from the moment Thomas had arrived at boarding school, a sad and lonely seven-year-old missing his family dreadfully. On his first day, the Duke had tried to give Thomas, 'that no-account upstart', what the Duke called 'a hiding he would never forget'.

Neither of them did forget that fight, but not for the reasons the Duke had expected. But that resounding defeat had taught the Duke nothing. Throughout their school years, he had continued in his fruitless quest to beat Thomas at games, at lessons, at everything, anything, something. And he never did learn that one simple lesson: being born an aristocrat was not enough. Winning took skill, skills that did not come automatically with a title.

Now he was prevaricating in another futile attempt to put *the no-account upstart* in his place. And once again the Duke would fail. Thomas knew the Duke's precarious financial situation. He would have no choice but to sell the land and Thomas was offering more than a fair price.

He looked around the ballroom and wondered if anyone else had noticed the empty sconces missing precious artifacts or the gaps on the walls where paintings had once hung, all sold off to fund the Duke's gambling and extravagant lifestyle. And if he continued to host lavish events such as tonight's ball, his finances were going to become ever more perilous, particularly if he followed his usual course of action and retired to the card room as soon as possible, where he would undoubtably lose more of the money he didn't have.

Thomas shook his head slowly in amazement at the folly of men such as Huntingdon-Smythe. They still thought they lived in a world that no longer existed. They had not adapted to the modern world and believed owning vast amounts of land and a large country home was enough to ensure you remained a wealthy man. Like their ancestors before them, they thought all they had to do was sit back and let the money created by other people's labour roll in.

He took another look at his watch. This was becoming beyond tedious. He'd wait another half an hour, then the deal would be off. There was other land that would serve his needs, even if it was the Duke's land he really wanted.

It perhaps did not make good business sense to offer so much more than the rival railway companies for the Duke's land, but, after all the Duke had put him through at school, taking his land was going to give him so much satisfaction it was worth spending the extra pounds.

He released the yawn he'd been trying to suppress and looked around the room. The group of fluttering debutantes surrounding the Duke continued to grow, the band continued to play and time continued to slowly tick by.

He could, he supposed, pass some time dancing. There were certainly plenty of attractive females in the offing. But really, what would be the point? Despite the elegance of the ornate ballroom, despite the expensive gowns and the murmur of polite conversation, this was little more than an auction room, where everyone was attempting to get the best marriage offer available.

All those young women were in search of husbands and he was most certainly not in need of a wife, and, if he was, he would not find one among this privileged, self-entitled lot.

While several of the attractive young things had sent glances in his direction to express their interest, they had been quickly called to order by their ambitious mamas. They were after a man with a title for their daughters and that excluded him from the ranks of desirable husbands.

Only those whose families were desperate for money would be pushed in his direction and the last thing he wanted in a wife was a vacuous ninny who was prepared to lower herself by marrying a member of the nouveau riche to save an aristocratic family from the horror of having to earn a living.

He watched in sardonic amusement as yet another debutante attempted to join the coterie swirling around the Duke. From across the room an elderly woman was urging her on with the flicking of her hands and angry glares. As pretty as the debutante was, with her artfully styled blonde hair and big blue eyes, she looked far too sweet and uncertain to enter that particular fray.

The huddle of debutantes compacted closer together, like a rugger scrum around the ball, blocking in the Duke and preventing the newcomer access.

The poor thing looked so out of her depth. Despite his disdain for the aristocracy, Thomas couldn't help but have pity for her. She flicked another look in the older woman's direction, then lifted her chin, squared her shoulders and smiled coquettishly. It did her no good. She remained on the outskirts of the circle, blocked by an impenetrable row of silk and satin backs.

A small gap opened behind the Duke and the little blonde moved quickly to fill it. Thomas had to give the newcomer points for her fast movement. Like a good tactician she had seen a weakness in the opposing side and had not let that opportunity pass her by.

She was in, for all the good it was doing her. The Duke's back was to her. She was all but invisible to her quarry. Thomas considered what her next move might be. Whatever she tried, it was not going to be easy. She was either going to have to somehow manoeuvre the entire pack of young ladies so they circled around the Duke, placing her in the front, or get the Duke to turn around. Both were tricky strategies requiring a level of dexterity he suspected was beyond this obvious novice.

Thomas once again glanced down at his watch and saw that the Duke's time was up. He looked over at the trapped debutante and wished her every success with whatever ploy she chose. He did not particularly care if the Duke noticed her or not, but he was grateful that for a few moments she had provided him with some much-needed entertaining diversion.

The Duke looked up from his harem, but it was not Thomas who had caught his eye. The Earl of Sundervale was summoning the Duke from the other side of the ballroom and pointing towards the card room.

Thomas gritted his teeth. That did it. He would not wait a minute longer, not while the Duke gambled away what little money he still had with his cronies.

Not bothering to say a word of explanation to the twittering debutantes, the Duke turned and pushed his way out of the throng. In doing so, he somehow brushed up against the little debutante. Thomas heard her small squeal as she skittered on the highly polished parquet floor on her satin slippers.

Her hands flew up into the air, circling as if looking for something, anything to hold on to as she fought to steady herself. Thomas winced as she hit the floor with an unseemly thud, landing in a pile of lace and embroidered silk.

Oblivious to the mayhem, or not caring, the Duke strode off, while the throng of debutantes erupted into giggling, their mockery barely disguised by their fluttering fans.

It seemed upstarts such as himself were not the only ones who could be made victims of a pack of aristocrats after blood. When the opportunity arose, they'd also turn on their own.

Ignoring the retreating Duke, Thomas strode across the floor, placed himself between the fallen young lady and the giggling pack and offered his hand to the blushing debutante.

Her head remained lowered as she placed her hand in his.

'Thank you,' she murmured, her face so red he could almost feel the heat radiating off it as she rose to her feet.

Thomas rarely danced at society balls, but for this poor creature he would make an exception. He hated bullying, having experienced such cruelty at school, and it was something he would never countenance. He needed to get this young lady away from those mocking debutantes and try to redeem her dignity or they would make the rest of her Season a living hell.

'If your dance card is not full, I would be honoured if you would grant me this waltz,' he said, bowing his head as if her embarrassing fall had never happened.

The giggling halted, but the debutantes continued to stare at them over their fans, their looks gleeful, as if anticipating more entertainment.

She gave a small nod, not meeting his eye, and he led her away from the pack.

'I thought you said her name was Grace Lowerby,' he heard one debutante say. 'More like Graceless Lower-Born,' she added, causing giggling to erupt again.

'Ignore them,' he said. 'Lift up your head and pretend nothing they are saying can possibly affect you.'

She gave a small gasp that sounded like a suppressed sob. He hoped and prayed she would not start crying. To do so would give those bullies their victory and only have them baying for more.

He placed his hand on her slim waist, lifted her limp hand and placed it on his shoulder, and looked over her still lowered head as he waited for the waltz to begin. From the far side of the room, he caught the eye of Algernon Huntingdon-Smythe, watching them with studied interest.

Thomas knew that look well. The Duke was nothing if not predictable. Like a spoilt child, for whom a toy only became interesting when another was playing with it, the Duke now wanted the young woman in his arms.

He pulled her in slightly tighter, wrapped his arm further around her waist, and smiled down at her as if she was all he desired in a woman. He had no doubt what would happen next. The Duke would pursue her, determined to have what he thought Thomas wanted. She would get her revenge on those merciless debutantes and there was nothing Thomas enjoyed more than getting the better of bullies.

Chapter Two

It was all over before it had even started. After such a display, Grace knew she would never win the heart of the Duke, or any other man. From now onwards she would be known as the gauche woman who had taken a humiliating fall and no one would want to be associated with her.

Graceless Lower-Born.

Lady Octavia's words echoed in her ears. It was exactly what she was, graceless and lower born, and her dreams were now completely shredded. And worse than that, her grandmother was going to be furious. It was up to Grace to restore the family to its rightful place in society. She *had* to marry well. She *had* to have children who were titled. And now that would never happen.

Any vitriol that came her way from her grandmother would be well deserved after such a shameful performance from *Graceless Lower-Born.*

If only this man hadn't made things so much worse

by asking her to dance. She would much rather have fled the ballroom, found somewhere quiet and private to cry out all the tears she was holding back and brace herself for the onslaught of her grandmother's disapproval and disappointment.

Instead, here she was, in the middle of the ballroom, where everyone could see her and laugh at her disgrace.

Her cheeks continued to burn as she stared at the buttons on her dance partner's waistcoat. Lift your head up high, he had advised her. Grace doubted she would ever lift up her head again, certainly not in public.

As soon as this dance was over, she would run away, maybe join a convent or sail off to some far-flung country where nobody knew her. She wasn't entirely certain what course of action she would take, but one thing she knew for certain: she would never, ever attend another ball.

She just had to get this dance over with first. Still staring at the buttons on her partner's maroon waistcoat, she focused on the tiny stitches of the silver embroidery and the delicate buttons. How she had ended up in this stranger's arms she had no idea. Her mind was a blank from when she had hit the floor until she was moving around the dance floor.

Had he asked her to dance? He must have. But who was he? She ventured a look at his face, gasped and once again stared back at his waistcoat buttons. The sight of him did nothing to assuage her discomfort and her cheeks did the seemingly impossible and burned even hotter.

She was in the arms of the most handsome man she had ever seen. Dare she admit it, even more handsome than the Duke, whom she had considered the epitome of the dashing, fairy-tale prince.

She flicked another quick look upwards, then just as quickly looked down. While the Duke was blond with blue eyes, this man had black hair, deep brown eyes and what some would consider unfashionably olive skin. And there was something else about him, something almost wild, that was decidedly attractive, albeit also decidedly unsettling. She dared yet another peek.

He was no dashing prince from a fairy tale, but she could picture him in a tale of pirates on the high seas, the wind blowing through that coal-dark hair, or one of highwaymen holding up passengers with his pistols raised. She could see him causing maidens to swoon as he ripped the jewels from around their necks, because he was certainly causing her to become light-headed.

This devilishly handsome creature had seen her fall and, instead of laughing, ignoring her, or dismissing her as being too graceless and low-born to bother with, he had actually asked her to dance. She hoped he was a duke, a viscount or an earl. Then he would be perfect. This would be perfect. He could be the man of her dreams. The one who had saved her and would now sweep her away into her very own fairy tale.

She slowly lifted her head again and this time attempted to smile. She gave up on that immediately, her quivering lips making it an impossibility.

'Allow me to introduce myself,' he said, his deep voice decidedly piratical, causing a little shiver to run up and down Grace's spine. 'I am Thomas Hayward, at your service.'

She waited for him to continue, to inform her of his title. He said nothing. Did that mean he possessed no title? Her grandmother had made her read and reread *Debrett's* until she had committed to memory every member of the British peerage and their lineage, but she could not recall the name Hayward.

All her hopes deflated. He had no title. It was nice that he had rescued her, but it was to no end. Her grandmother would be further incensed. Not only had she made a complete fool of herself, but then she had gone on to waste her time dancing with a man she could never wed.

But there was nothing for it now. She *was* dancing with him and the least she could do was be gracious to a man who was kind enough to dance with an ungainly bumbler such as her.

'I'm pleased to meet you,' she said. 'I'm Miss Grace Lowerby.' She nibbled on her top lip, then remembered that was yet another uncouth action her grandmother had warned her she was prone to and immediately released it.

'I'm the granddaughter of the Earl of Ashbridge,' she added, so he would know she wasn't entirely Lower-Born, even if she had proven herself to be Graceless.

'I'm pleased to make your acquaintance, Miss Lowerby,' he said as he swept her around the floor. He really was a rather sublime dancer. This was the first time she had actually been in a man's arms, the dancing instructor at her finishing school excluded. And it did feel rather nice. There was something safe about being held by him and, as he was an untitled man, she had no need to impress him. That was some consolation, she supposed. She could just relax and enjoy the dance before she had to face the inevitable wrath of her grandmother.

'Are you a friend of the Duke?' she asked, clinging on to the last vestige of hope.

Maybe that was the role he would play in her quest to capture the Duke's heart. He would be the friend who helped her grow close to the man who would soon be her husband. Maybe, just maybe, all was not yet lost.

He laughed as if she had made a joke, which she most certainly had not.

'Friend might be an exaggeration,' came his unexpected reply.

Grace tried not to be too disappointed. While he

might not be the Duke's closest friend as hoped, they were surely associated in some way. After all, he had been invited to this ball. And even an associate could play a role in a fairy tale, couldn't he?

They continued to dance in silence for a moment until Grace remembered her manners. 'Oh, and thank you for, you know, for…' Her voice trailed off as her cheeks burned a hotter shade of red.

He shrugged as if her complete mortification was something easily forgotten. 'I'm sure no one apart from me and those debutantes noticed.'

'And the Duke of Hardgraves,' she added quietly.

'No, I don't believe he saw what happened.'

'How could he have not noticed?' she blurted out, her voice affronted. 'He had inadvertently caused me to fall and had been right beside me when I…when I…' She shrugged, something else her grandmother told her never to do, but in the circumstances, it was surely the better option than once again restating her humiliation.

'I believe the Duke was more interested in departing to the card room.'

She frowned. That couldn't be true. The Duke was a noble man, both from birth and breeding. He came from a long line of aristocratic men who were noted for their chivalry and courtly manners. Her grandmother had regaled her with tales of how his family were once knights of yore, fighting in battle beside their King. Surely if the Duke knew what he had done he would have been conciliatory and charming and she would now be dancing with him instead of Mr Hayward.

'I suppose you're right. If he had seen what happened, he would not have just walked away.' Yes, that explained it. A noble man would always help a lady in distress, even one who has shown herself to be a clumsy dolt. This was good. The Duke hadn't seen. All was not lost.

'Perhaps,' he replied somewhat ambiguously.

'But you saw?'

'Yes.'

'So if you saw, everyone else in the ballroom must have seen as well,' she said, cringing inside. 'Even if the Duke did not.'

'No, I saw what happened because I was watching you.'

Heat once again rushed to her cheeks and this time consumed her body, but it was heat of a different order. It wasn't embarrassment. She wasn't sure what it was, but knew it was in reaction to the realisation that this sublimely attractive man had been watching her.

'So why were you trying to get the Duke to notice you?' he asked.

Surprise replaced her unfamiliar reaction to the thought of him watching her. How could he even ask such a question?

'He's a duke,' she said, stating the obvious. 'The only Duke present here tonight. Well, I mean, the only unmarried Duke.' It would horrify her grandmother to hear her say such a thing so boldly, but as Mr Hayward would never be a marriage prospect Grace could see no reason for going against all her etiquette lessons, just this once. And he did ask. It would surely be impolite not to answer.

'And do you know the man?'

'No, I was introduced to him for the first time tonight, but my grandmother does and she says he is a man of impeccable character. He can trace his family back to Tudor times, you know?'

'Yes, so he has told me, many, many times.'

'So you *are* friends with the Duke,' she exclaimed. She was right. He *would* be the close friend who would act as the go-between and bring her and the Duke together, although she suspected go-betweens were not supposed to be so handsome that their good looks were somewhat of a distraction.

'We went to school together,' he replied, the tense look on his face not quite as effusive as she would have expected from her future go-between. 'It was the Duke who gave me a lifelong abhorrence of bullies such as those debutantes and taught me how to deal with them.'

She smiled at him. A genuine, satisfied smile. The Duke had helped him. That was just how her grandmother described him, as someone gallant, honourable and admirable.

'And one of the things he taught me was you can never show fear in front of a bully,' he continued. 'They feed on it. With those debutantes, you need to ignore everything they say to you, no matter how painful. If they think they have hurt you, it will only make their behaviour towards you even worse. If they believe you are unaffected, they will lose interest.'

She looked over at the group of debutantes, watching her from the side of the ballroom and her body tensed at the thought of the cruel things they were no doubt saying.

Graceless Lower-Born, dancing with an untitled man, is that the best she can do?

'Relax,' Mr Hayward said. 'Lift your head proudly and I'd recommend laughing now as if you are having a glorious time.'

She looked up at him, into those deep brown eyes. Despite everything, she *was* having rather a pleasant time. It was nice being in his arms, very nice indeed. And while he did not have a title, he was undeniably the best-looking man in the room. That was sure to be something those debutantes would not have missed.

She did as he suggested and gave a little laugh, then the ludicrousness of her false laugh struck her and her laugh became genuine. She was laughing at herself for laughing and at the absurdity of her situation.

'That's better,' he said. 'And the debutantes are not the only ones watching you.'

She bit her bottom lip in an attempt to stop herself laughing. Such behaviour would not have been missed by her grandmother. As she well knew, a young lady should never laugh loudly in public. She had already committed so many unforgivable faux pas tonight. She did not need to add to the growing list her grandmother was no doubt tallying up.

The thought of that lecture brought the laughter to a complete halt as dread gripped her.

Once this dance finished, Grace could see herself being dragged out of the ballroom, driven home immediately and, once home, made to stand in silence in front of her grandmother as she was regaled with a list of criticisms and recriminations, of how she was such a disappointment, how she was no better than her mother, how she had proven tonight she was the daughter of a man who was a no-account nobody. Maybe her grandmother would give up on her entirely and she would be cast out and made to fend for herself.

She closed her eyes and prayed that she would not start crying and further humiliate herself.

'There is no need to look so upset, Miss Lowerby. You have now achieved your goal and have the undivided attention of the Duke.'

Her eyes sprang open and she stared at him. He must be jesting and it was a cruel jest she would not have expected from a man she had taken to be kind and considerate.

'I suggest you don't make it too obvious, but if you look towards the French doors under the minstrel gallery you will see he is watching you.'

She flicked a hasty glance in that direction and nearly tripped over her feet once again. Mr Hayward's arm immediately moved further around her waist, holding her steady. She was unsure whether it was Mr Hayward's touch or the sight of the Duke watching her, but she was suddenly decidedly dazed and bewildered.

'I believe you are about to make those debutantes very jealous indeed and get the revenge you deserve,' Mr Hayward said as the waltz came to an end and he led her off the dance floor.

Her heart thudding hard in her chest, she sent another furtive look in the Duke's direction. He was crossing the dance floor and coming straight towards her. She covered her mouth with her gloved hand to suppress a gasp.

'Thank you for that dance, Miss Lowerby,' he said as she continued to stare in the direction of the Duke, her disbelief mounting with every step he took towards her. 'You are about to get what you *think* you want. I just hope it is what you *really* do want,' he added somewhat cryptically just as the Duke reached them.

The Duke bowed low. 'Hayward, are you going to

introduce me to your lovely companion?' he said, his eyes firmly on Grace. She had to be dreaming, but if she was, she hoped she never woke up.

'Miss Lowerby, may I present Algernon Huntingdon-Smythe, the Duke of Hardgraves,' Mr Hayward said, his voice decidedly laconic, as if being presented once more to such a man was not the greatest honour possible for Grace.

She gave her lowest, most elegant curtsy, similar to the one she had performed when presented to Queen Victoria, and she had to admit, this was even more exciting than that auspicious occasion.

'May I have the honour of this dance, Miss Lowerby?' the Duke said, taking her arm before she had the chance to reply. Not that he needed to wait for her answer. She was hardly likely to say no or claim to have promised the next dance to another, not when her future husband had made such a request.

'We need to talk,' Mr Hayward said, his voice moving from laconic to stern.

'Not now, Hayward, I'm about to dance with the enchanting Miss Lowerby. Come to my house party this weekend. We can talk then.'

Enchanting. He had called her lovely and now enchanting. Could this evening get any better?

'I'll be inviting Miss Lowerby and her grandmother as well. I do hope the two of you will be able to make it.'

Grace was hardly able to answer, she was so breathless with excitement. 'I'd be honoured,' she finally gasped out.

'Good, I will see you then, Hayward,' the Duke said and led her out on to the dance floor.

They lined up for the polka and when the Duke placed his hand on her waist she looked over at the teasing debutantes. As expected, they were all staring at her, scowls on their otherwise pretty faces. If one actually could turn green with envy, she was sure they would all now be resembling a row of moss-covered trees.

She almost felt sorry for them. Almost. How could they not be jealous of her success? The Duke had danced with no other young lady tonight, but he was dancing with her.

The music started and they moved off in time with the jaunty tune. This was it. This was the start of her magical future. She was in the arms of a duke. All her dreams were coming true.

Chapter Three

Thomas watched the Duke lead Miss Lowerby around the dance floor. The young lady was smiling fit to burst and the Duke wore that familiar, smirking expression. They both looked as if they had just won a great victory—the Duke because he believed he had bested Thomas by taking the object of his affections off him, Miss Lowerby because she was dancing with the most sought-after man in the room.

She was such a sweet young thing and he wished her every happiness, although whether she would get it with the Duke remained to be seen. And whether the Duke's interest would continue once he discovered Thomas was not pursuing her also remained to be seen.

He cast a look in the direction of the debutantes who had teased her so unmercifully and smiled to himself. They, too, were watching the Duke and Miss Lowerby as they moved around the floor and it was easy to read their thoughts.

Good. Nothing gave Thomas more satisfaction than seeing bullies get their just deserts.

His gaze was drawn back to the dancing couple. He should leave now. The Duke had made it clear he had no intention of signing those papers tonight. Instead, he'd have to attend a damn weekend party. He was tempted to tell the Duke to keep his land, but it would give him far too much satisfaction to watch the man put his signature at the bottom of the document and sign over land that had been in his family for generations to a man he considered a no-account upstart.

And as much as he loathed the idea of spending any more time in the company of vacuous aristocrats talking about the weather or the latest social scandal, Miss Lowerby would be there and he was not averse to her company.

He watched her smiling at the Duke and an image of a gambolling lamb being led happily to the slaughter entered his mind, before he pushed it away. She was not his responsibility. It was not up to him to protect her, especially from something she wanted so badly.

But she was an innocent. He shook his head slowly as he remembered those blushing cheeks. He doubted he had ever seen a young woman turn such a bright shade of red. When he'd first taken her in his arms, she had been unable to even look at him and her body had been rigid with mortification.

But then she had relaxed and he had to admit dancing with her had been rather pleasant. There was something soft and soothing about her. Perhaps she'd even be capable of smoothing the harsh edges off Hardgraves, although he suspected it would take even more than Miss Lowerby's gentle nature to do that.

And there was no denying she was pretty. When that flawless complexion wasn't blushing a shade of bright red it was like fine porcelain and when her petite body wasn't stiff with embarrassment it was delightfully curvaceous. Only a blind man would fail to miss those full, cherry-red lips that appeared to be almost pouting.

It must have been her beauty that had drawn his gaze to her in the first place, even if he had been unaware of it at the time.

If she wasn't a debutante, he'd be interested, very interested indeed. But she was a debutante, an innocent young woman destined to remain innocent until she made a suitable marriage.

He cringed at the thought that it might be the Duke who tasted those sweet lips for the first time, who was able to explore the curves of her delightful body, who had the right to take her to his bed and make her his own.

Again, none of his business.

He looked towards the beckoning door. He should leave Miss Lowerby to her quest of finding a husband and adjourn to one of his usual haunts, where the women were just as attractive and had no interest in becoming anyone's wife, or were already married and seeking some pleasurable diversions with men such as himself.

His gaze returned to Miss Lowerby and the Duke. Yes, he should go. He had already done enough for that sweet young thing. He'd got her out of an embarrassing situation. He'd captured the Duke's attention for her, which had led to him dancing with the young lady and given those bullying debutantes their comeuppance.

Yes, all and all, he'd done more than enough for Miss Lowerby.

The Duke smirked in Thomas's direction as his hand slid further around Miss Lowerby's waist.

A tightness gripped his chest. He drew in a deep breath and consciously released his hands, which had unaccountably curled into fists.

This was ridiculous. It was time to leave. It was obvious the Duke would not be signing those papers tonight and it was obvious he thought he was taunting Thomas by being overly familiar with Miss Lowerby.

Instead of watching this ludicrous display, he could retire to one of the many gentlemen's clubs of which he was a member. Instead of standing on the side of the dance floor, he could be savouring a glass of brandy and enjoying the charms of a beautiful woman who was far from innocent and chaste. Yes, that was where he should be, in the company of a woman who did not indulge in absurd mating rituals like the ones on display in this ballroom, a woman who wanted no more from a man than to give and receive pleasure. In other words, exactly the type of woman he was attracted to and whose company he enjoyed.

There was nothing keeping him at this ball now, yet he stayed, unable to look away from the dancing couple.

Keep your smiles demure and dignified, Grace reminded herself, a ruling that would be easier to abide by if she wasn't so gloriously happy.

Tonight was now beyond magical. She was in the arms of the Duke of Hardgraves, being whirled around his magnificent ballroom. It was almost impossible to believe that after her humiliating tumble that such a thing could happen. She had danced with the most handsome man in the room, now she was dancing with the most eligible. It was a shame they were not the same person, but to expect that would surely be being far too greedy.

The Duke spun her in a circle. He wasn't quite as skilful a dancer as Mr Hayward, but he was a duke—what did it matter whether he was a superb dancer or not?

She looked towards Mr Hayward and smiled in thanks. He did not smile back. Her own smile faltered slightly. No. It mattered not what Mr Hayward thought, all that mattered was that she was more joyous than she would have thought possible.

She looked towards her grandmother, whose smile was even brighter than Grace's. This was all so marvellous. There would be no lectures, no recriminations, she was a success and would be rewarded with her grandmother's approval.

Her gaze took in the cluster of debutantes, standing near the spot she had fallen. They were still glaring at her and she did exactly what Mr Hayward had suggested, raised her chin in an act of defiance and let them know that nothing they could do or say could possibly hurt her.

Then she turned her full focus back to the Duke and sent him her best smile, the one she had been forced to practise until it was the perfect coquettish smile of an available young debutante. Unfortunately, it was wasted as he was not looking at her, but staring over her shoulder.

Panic gripped her stomach. Was his interest waning already? Had another debutante caught his eye? This could not happen. He had said she was lovely, enchanting. He could not have tired of her already. If she was to keep him interested, she had to continue to amuse him and make him see that she was his perfect duchess. But how was she to do that?

The pain gripping her stomach intensified as the lessons she had learnt in finishing school whirled through her mind. How was she supposed to keep a gentleman's interest? She could remember nothing of those lessons the tutors had drummed into their students. Her grandmother's words of wisdom, imparted before the ball, came thankfully to mind.

Compliment him. Focus all conversation on him. Flatter him and keep smiling. The last one would not prove difficult. Now she had to put the others into action.

'The ballroom looks simply divine.'

The Duke made no response.

'It's like being in a fairy tale.'

'Hmm,' was the disappointing response the Duke finally gave. 'I saw you dancing with Hayward,' he added.

'Yes,' she said, there being no other answer to that statement of fact.

'Hmm,' he repeated.

'I believe you and Mr Hayward know each other from schooldays,' she said, fighting to keep the conversation going. That was surely in line with the rules of polite conversation. Her grandmother had said it was important to encourage the man to talk about himself and to remain interested in everything he had to say. The Duke had raised the topic of Mr Hayward and she was also interested in hearing more about him and his friendship with the Duke. Not that it mattered what Grace was interested in, but talking of Mr Hayward would certainly make conversation easier.

'We attended the same school, but we hardly mixed in the same circles,' the Duke said with a slight sniff. 'He's not one of us, you know.'

'I see,' Grace said, not entirely sure what that meant. Was he referring to Mr Hayward's lack of title? And if that was the case, would the Duke consider Grace to be not *one of us* either? Or was he including her in his circle? In which case, he had paid her a compliment.

'His family's new money, you know,' the Duke continued. 'Grandfather or something was a baker, or maybe a butcher or a candlestick maker.' He gave a bark of laughter at his own joke.

She forced herself to keep smiling and even managed the required titter at the Duke's witticism, trying not to wince at the implication of his words. Did the Duke know that her father had been a piano teacher and was that more amusing than a butcher, baker, or candlestick maker?

'It's wrong, so wrong that a man like that should have attended such a prestigious school,' the Duke went on, almost as if talking to himself. 'It should be reserved for the sons of the very cream of society, not the riff-raff.' He gave a derisive laugh.

He looked down at Grace and she made her practised smile, pleased he was talking to her, even if the conversation was making her uncomfortable.

'But you can rest assured we put him in his place quick smart,' the Duke added. 'We let him know, no matter how much money his father had, he would never be good enough for us.'

The tightness gripping Grace's stomach moved up to include her chest and shoulders. Hadn't Mr Hayward said the Duke taught him how to deal with bullies? The Duke could not be a bully, could he? Her grandmother had said he was admirable, honourable and a man worthy of his position in society. No, he could not possibly be a bully. She must have misunderstood. And he had invited Mr Hayward to this ball and to his house for the weekend. He wouldn't do that if there was any animosity between the two men.

'Did you enjoy dancing with him?' The Duke's piercing look suggested this was no innocent question and Grace was unsure how to answer.

'He's a very accomplished dancer,' she said tentatively.

The Duke sniffed. 'I suppose even a tradesman can dance.'

Grace did not know what response was required. She had never danced with a tradesman so did not know. All she knew was she had enjoyed every minute she had been in his arms. Nor had she had to worry so much about every word she said the way she was with the Duke.

'I'm so looking forward to the weekend party at

your estate,' she said, changing the subject on to a less confusing one, one about which she could be completely truthful. 'I hear your estate in Cornwall is one of the finest in the country.'

The Duke thrust out his chest and smiled at her. She smiled back, knowing she had said the right thing.

'It's one of the largest in the county, with more than ten thousand acres, and has been in the family since the fifteenth century, since the time of the first Duke of Hardgraves.' He barked another laugh, but this time did not sound amused. 'The Haywards' estate might be bigger, but they bought it, you know, furniture and all, from some aristocrat or other who had fallen on hard times.'

Grace suppressed a sigh. She had failed to turn the conversation away from Mr Hayward and now she was once again unsure what she was supposed to say. So she took the safest option and just smiled.

'They're absolute scavengers, you know. Can't be trusted.'

Grace continued smiling, although the smile was becoming somewhat strained.

'I so love the polka, don't you?' she said in desperation.

'Hmm,' came his dismissive response. 'Oh, look,' the Duke added, his voice once again animated. 'The cad has finally turned tail and run.' He barked out another laugh while looking over her shoulders.

He spun her around so she could see what he was talking about. Mr Hayward was walking towards the door. He was leaving. A peculiar sense of abandonment washed through Grace. Why she should feel that way she did not know. She hardly knew Mr Hayward and she was now dancing with the man she hoped one day to marry. That was all that should be concerning her. And hopefully, with Mr Hayward's departure, the Duke might speak of other things.

'He had been watching us the whole time, you know,' the Duke said with an air of satisfaction.

'No, I didn't realise,' Grace said as her heart gave a strange jolt. Mr Hayward had been watching her dance with the Duke, just as he had been watching her when she took her unfortunate tumble. All that time, she had been under the gaze of those dark brown eyes.

'The bounder knows when he's beaten, what,' the Duke said, his voice triumphant.

Grace had no idea what he meant, but assumed a smile was required, so that was what she gave him.

The dance came to an end. The Duke led her off the dance floor to where her beaming grandmother was waiting.

'Your Grace,' her grandmother said with a low curtsy.

The Duke gave a small bow of his head. 'If you'll excuse me, ladies, I believe the card room is calling.' With that, he turned and strode away.

His curt goodbye did not dampen her grandmother's excitement.

'Oh, my dear, dear girl,' she said, causing Grace's heart to swell. Her grandmother never used such terms of affection. Such approval was so reassuring and wiped away any remaining confusion caused by her conversation with the Duke or the thought that Mr Hayward had been watching her.

Her grandmother lightly brushed a curl beside Grace's cheek, her face becoming serious. 'You have done so well tonight and redeemed yourself admirably from that early unfortunate incident. That…' she swept her hand towards the site where Grace had taken her tumble '…is something we will never mention again. Nor will we talk about you dancing with that Hayward fellow.' Her grandmother's smile returned. 'Because tonight you are a triumph. The Duke has danced with no other this evening. Only my granddaughter.'

'And he is to invite us to a house party next weekend.'

Her grandmother's eyes grew enormous, as did her smile, which revealed both sets of teeth, a behaviour Grace had repeatedly been told never, ever to do.

'No young lady does that...not unless she wants to look like a horse.'

Should she remind her grandmother of her words? No, of course not—to do so would require a great deal more courage than Grace possessed.

'My dear girl, I could hug you right now.'

Grace's smile grew so large she was in danger of doing her own horse impersonation.

Her grandmother had never hugged her. Well, she still hadn't, but had said she wanted to. Throughout her lonely childhood she had longed for her grandmother to take her in her arms and show her some affection. Maybe, just maybe, she would do so on her wedding day when she became a duchess.

'And Mr Hayward has also—'

'I said we do not speak of that man,' her grandmother said sharply.

'No, Grandmama.'

Grace had merely been going to inform her grandmother that Mr Hayward had also been invited to the weekend party, but she would do as her grandmother instructed and not speak of that man again.

That did not, however, mean she would not continue to think about him.

Chapter Four

From the moment the invitation to the Duke's estate arrived, the entire Ashbridge household was dedicated to preparation for the weekend to come.

Grace was made to stand in front of her grandmother for hours on end as she tried on every gown in her wardrobe, along with her day dresses and tea gowns, so only the most flattering could be packed. Her lady's maid was instructed to work on Grace's hair, creating several different fashionable styles, and made to do so again and again, so her technique was perfected.

Each piece of jewellery was taken out of her jewellery box, assessed for its worth and how much it would add to Grace's attractiveness and status.

Clothing for every possible occasion was also packed so Grace would be ready for all eventualities, including horse riding, tennis, croquet and walks in the countryside. No matter what the Duke wanted to do, whether it was planned or spontaneous, Grace would be prepared.

The servants who were to accompany them were given strict instructions that they were to conduct themselves at all times as if they were already from the household of a duchess. Their uniforms were inspected and reinspected, so that no thread, button, pleat or trouser crease was out of place.

Her grandmother had even contemplated taking their carriages so they would arrive in vehicles bearing the Ashbridge crest, reminding the Duke that Grace had a titled background and came from one of the best families in England.

It was only the thought of several uncomfortable days in a jolting carriage that made her change her mind and opt for a more convenient trip by train.

As the days had ticked off and the weekend drew closer, Grace's dread of what was to come increased until, by the time Friday arrived, any possible joy had been stripped away. The weekend had turned into an ordeal that had to be endured with as much fortitude as possible.

Finally, she found herself seated across from her grandmother while the train rocked them through the countryside. Grace tried to keep her apprehension covered by a joyful expression and polite smile. And it seemed to be working, as her behaviour was yet to receive any criticism.

'This is rather exciting,' she said in her most buoyant manner.

'Hmm, I still think it would have been better to arrive in our own carriages,' her grandmother said, looking disapprovingly at the rich upholstery and polished wooden panelling of their first-class compartment. 'But needs must,' she added, as if sitting in these luxurious surroundings was a great hardship.

'Your grandfather would be so proud of you.' She touched the edge of her eye with a lace handkerchief as if to wipe away an imaginary tear, something she always did when she mentioned her late husband. 'Your mother's marriage drove that poor man to an early grave, but this weekend you can undo all the damage she did.' She smiled at Grace. 'I am so proud of you.'

Despite her nerves, Grace forced herself to smile back. She so wanted to make her grandmother proud, but she wasn't married to the Duke yet and so many things could still go wrong. Throughout the week Grace had envisaged the disastrous scenario of being completely ignored by the Duke, or, worse, him courting another. Her grandmother would be livid and Grace knew she would be blamed entirely. Then she would have to face the shameful train ride home listening obediently while her grandmother recounted everything Grace had done and said that had made the Duke reject her.

The thought that Mr Hayward would be present was some consolation and went some way to preventing her rumbling turbulence from becoming unbearable.

Why she felt so comfortable in his company she could not fathom. She would expect a man as handsome as him to unnerve her as much, if not more, than the Duke. Perhaps it was simply because he had no title and was therefore not a man she needed to impress. She could be herself, not worry about saying the right thing, smiling in the correct manner, or behaving with the expected level of demureness. Something she rarely, if ever, had the opportunity to do.

While her grandmother read her book, Grace attempted to soothe her nerves by watching the scenery pass by outside the window, taking in the farms, villages and the busy country stations.

After several hours they arrived at the small station closest to the Duke's home and disembarked on to the busy platform. Porters rushed hither and thither, collecting their trunks and loading them on to the waiting carriages. The driver helped Grace and her grandmother into one, while the servants rode in another with the luggage.

'It's such a shame we have to use public carriages and not our own,' her grandmother said, sniffing in disapproval as she looked at the leather seat, on which people whom she did not know had sat.

As the carriage took them closer and closer to the Duke's home, the tension in Grace's body increased. She would soon have to put on the most important performance of her life and she was unsure whether she was up to the task.

They turned off the country road and drove through the large black-and-gold wrought-iron gates signalling the entrance to the Duke's estate. Then the wheels crunched on the gravel as they travelled up the long drive, under a canopy of oak trees.

'Magnificent, simply magnificent,' her grandmother declared, as the house came into view.

Magnificent was no exaggeration. The three-storey ochre-coloured stone home stood beside a lake and appeared to float on the shimmering water. The countless windows glinted in the early-evening light and large Corinthian columns stood proud beside a portico in front of the grand entrance.

It was a house designed to make a statement. And it was doing just that. Her grandmother's Suffolk estate was so large that as a child Grace had often got lost as she wandered alone through its warren of corridors, but the Duke's home made the Ashbridge estate look small and insignificant.

'And if you do everything right this could all be yours,' her grandmother said, smiling at Grace.

She swallowed down a lump in her throat and attempted to smile back. It had been nerve-racking enough trying to gain and keep the Duke's interest during the ball at his townhouse. To do so when surrounded by this grandeur was going to demand a level of confidence she was certain she did not possess.

'Never forget, you are the granddaughter of an earl,' her grandmother said, sensing Grace's trepidation. 'Your family harks back to the days of Queen Anne. There is absolutely no reason why you cannot become a duchess and all this cannot be yours.' She patted Grace's hand. 'Right, put on your prettiest smile, keep your chin up, your eyes lowered and your shoulders back.'

Grace did as commanded as she stepped down from the carriage. But it was all for nought. The Duke was not there to welcome them.

She lifted her gaze to her grandmother who was far from pleased. The Duke's absence was not a good sign. Did it mean he did not consider them important enough to greet in person?

A servant bowed to them as they entered the great hall and, while he was discussing the arrangements for their bedchambers with her grandmother, Grace took the opportunity to take in the grandeur of the room.

Like the house itself, it was designed to impress. Light shone through the large glass dome two storeys above her head. The cream walls edged in gold and the marble floor gave an opulence to the large space, while the columns added an extra touch of elegance.

The only note of discord in the otherwise harmoniously designed room were the spaces on the walls where paintings had presumably once hung and the empty sconces in the walls that Grace assumed had once housed works of art.

They must have been taken to be cleaned or repaired, Grace assumed.

She followed her grandmother up the sweeping staircase and along the corridor that led to her bedchamber.

'We're late,' her grandmother said to Grace's lady's maid as if it was somehow her fault. 'We should have taken an earlier train.'

'Yes, my lady,' Molly said apologetically, as if she had been the one to decide the timetable, not her mistress.

'Make haste in dressing my granddaughter,' her grandmother continued. 'But ensure she looks more beautiful and elegant than she ever has before.'

Grace and Molly exchanged looks, both wondering how they were to achieve the impossible, but both knowing somehow they would have to do so.

As soon as the door closed behind them, Molly set to work. Grace was bathed and scented, her hair styled to perfection, her corset pulled in so tight she wondered if she'd be able to breathe and the Ashbridge family jewels of diamonds and sapphires draped around her neck, hung from her ears and even placed so they would adorn her hair.

When Grace was ready for inspection, her grandmother was summoned.

While her grandmother looked on critically, Grace turned in a small circle, hoping the pale gold gown embroidered with tiny butterflies in silver thread, with matching elbow-length gold gloves, would get the nod of approval and she would not have to go through the process of undressing and dressing in another of the myriad gowns that had been packed.

'Yes, perfect,' she finally declared, and Grace and Molly both released their held breaths.

'I believe our late arrival might be for the best,' her grandmother said as she hurried Grace out of her bedchamber. 'You'll be able to make an entrance and the Duke will have to notice you. Now, remember, don't talk too much.'

That was an instruction Grace was sure she would be able to follow, the constriction of her throat making the idea of trying to form words seem an impossibility.

They reached the door of the drawing room. Her grandmother stopped and grabbed Grace's arm, her brow furrowed. 'Tonight is the most important night of your life. Under no circumstances are you to appear anything other than a refined young lady of good breeding. Do you understand?'

'Yes, Grandmama,' Grace said, wishing she had the courage to pick up her long swirling train and run as far away as possible.

'Do not, I repeat, do not do anything unrefined. You won't get away with embarrassing yourself a second time.'

'No, Grandmama.' Grace knew she was referring to that incident that was to be never mentioned again, and colour flooded her cheeks at the memory of just how humiliating that had been.

'And if you must blush, do it prettily to show that you are coy and chaste. Do not under any circumstances turn into something resembling a beetroot the way you did at the Duke's ball.'

'Yes, Grandmama. I mean, no, Grandmama.' Grace was unsure what she meant, she just wished her cheeks and stomach would settle down and this awful trial would be over.

'Right. Let's go and capture the heart of the Duke,' her grandmother said and nodded to the footman to open the door.

They entered the drawing room and Grace fought to do as she was instructed. She continued smiling while her stomach churned, tried to look dignified while her heart pounded fiercely against the wall of her chest and fought to stop her cheeks from blushing and turning her into that forbidden beetroot.

'There he is,' her grandmother said quietly while still smiling.

Grace looked in the direction her grandmother indicated and saw the Duke standing beside the mantelpiece, a crystal glass in his hand, surrounded by a ring of talking and laughing gentleman along with several young women, all adopting the same well-practised smile as Grace.

She was presented with exactly the same challenge that had confronted her at the Duke's ball. Her grandmother would expect her to somehow join that group, to dazzle and shine, and, of course, to remain firmly on her feet at all times. It was all too much.

Her gaze flittered around the room, searching for somewhere, anywhere, she could hide. Her wandering gaze halted at Mr Hayward. He was watching her. Her nerves stilled slightly. If only she could rush across the room and take refuge in his strong arms.

He nodded his head in greeting and her forced smile became genuine. It was truly delightful that he was here tonight. It was as if she had a friend, someone who would not be judging her, not putting demands on her, someone who would rescue her rather than condemn her if she failed to behave with the requisite level of elegance demanded of a debutante.

He excused himself from the group of men with

whom he had been talking and crossed the room towards her. Her anxiety turned to anticipation and excitement, even though the fluttering in her stomach and warmth flushing her cheeks and body remained the same.

She had been thinking of his dark good looks constantly over the time they had been apart, but it was now apparent her memory did him a disservice. He was more handsome than she had remembered. He was dressed in the same style of black swallow-tailed evening suit as every other man in the room, but on him it looked so much better. Despite the formality, he still bore the appearance of a man who would be more at home on the prow of a pirate ship and his crisp white shirt and cravat added to this image, contrasting with his olive complexion that suggested a life spent outside and not in the confines of drawing rooms.

'Miss Lowerby,' he said with a bow. 'Lady Ashbridge,' he added as he bowed to her grandmother.

'Mr Hayward,' her grandmother said in a distracted voice, still looking towards the Duke. 'I am surprised to see you here this weekend. What brings you to the Duke's estate?'

'I have business with Huntingdon-Smythe.'

Her grandmother turned to frown at Mr Hayward. Grace did not know whether it was the shameless mention of business or calling the Duke by his given name that had caused such offence, but her grandmother was doing nothing to hide a look of distaste.

Mr Hayward smiled as if offending her grandmother was an enjoyable pastime. 'I intend to buy a substantial amount of the Duke's land to extend my family's railway lines to this part of Cornwall.'

Her grandmother's eyes grew larger in shock, before she once again smiled. 'That's very progressive of the Duke to want to open up this area to such modern means of transport. Very progressive indeed.'

Mr Hayward laughed. 'That's one way of looking at it, I suppose.'

'Well, please don't let us keep you,' her grandmother continued. 'I'm sure you have…' she paused, her nostrils flaring '…business to conduct with other guests.'

Mr Hayward bowed and departed. Grace's heart sank. She did not want him to abandon her. Now she was all alone, alone and expected to perform some sort of illusive magic trick and make the Duke fall under her spell.

'All the time that Mr Hayward was speaking to us the Duke was watching you,' her grandmother whispered through smiling lips. 'I had to get rid of that man as quickly as possible. It would not do for the Duke to think we consort with such types.'

Grace took a furtive look in the Duke's direction. If he had been looking at her, he was not doing so now.

He was watching Mr Hayward and, like her grandmother, it was with a look of disapproval.

'Keep smiling, Grace,' her grandmother whispered. 'I'm sure he'll approach you soon.'

Grace did as she was told, feeling somewhat silly that she was smiling at nothing.

The Duke did not approach. He remained the centre of a group of fluttering debutantes, many of whom she recognised from the ball. Grace kept smiling, her jaw starting to ache. Nothing continued to happen.

'I don't think he's coming,' she said quietly to her grandmother, still forcing herself to maintain that smile.

'No, I believe you're right. But his focus had been intent on you while we were talking to Mr Hayward.' Her grandmother looked over at Mr Hayward, who was in conversation with a man Grace did not recognise.

'Come with me.' Her grandmother took her by the arm and the nerves flittering in Grace's stomach burst into manic flight. She was about to be thrust on the Duke. Last time she had done that she had ended up slipping over on the ballroom floor and landing in an undignified heap. That could not happen again. It simply could not happen.

She fought to remember her instructions. Smile. Don't laugh loudly. Don't show any teeth. Compliment when appropriate. And do not, under any circumstances, do anything awkward and clumsy like falling over in front of these elegant, sophisticated people.

But they did not head in the direction of the Duke but towards Mr Hayward.

What on earth was her grandmother up to?

Mr Hayward turned to face them. One questioning eyebrow briefly rose as if he was wondering the same thing. Then, as etiquette demanded, he introduced Grace and her grandmother to his companion, who, after a brief exchange of polite conversation, excused himself.

'I was fascinated to hear about your business dealings,' her grandmother said, surprising Grace and, by the look on Mr Hayward's face, surprising him as well.

'And what is it about the railways that particularly interests you, Lady Ashbridge?'

'Oh, all of it,' she replied, not looking at Mr Hayward, but to where the Duke was standing.

'Would you like to hear about the problems with different-sized gauges? Or perhaps you are more interested in the various methods for the transportation of goods. Or maybe you would be excited to hear how the railways will open up more of Cornwall for working people wanting to travel to the seaside for day outings?'

'Yes, yes, that's all fascinating,' her grandmother said, not looking at a bemused Mr Hayward. 'Now, if you'll excuse me, I believe Lady Beatrice is trying to attract my attention.'

Grace and Mr Hayward watched her grandmother bustle across the room and join several older women. This was all very peculiar and Grace could only wonder if the pressure was affecting her grandmother as much as Grace and making her somewhat demented.

'Who would have thought Lady Ashbridge would harbour such an interest in railways?' Mr Hayward said, a knowing look on his face as if this was not a surprise at all.

'Yes, that is unexpected,' Grace said, still watching her grandmother. While she nodded along with whatever the older women were discussing, her eyes were firmly on the Duke. Grace followed her gaze, gave a little gasp at what she saw and immediately turned to Mr Hayward as if seeking sanctuary. The Duke was staring straight at her and his glowering expression was not that of a welcoming host.

'I believe you have once again caught the Duke's eye,' Mr Hayward said, his tone suggesting this was not necessarily a good thing.

Grace gave a tremulous smile, her nerves fizzing not just inside her stomach, but throughout her body.

'I assume your grandmother is hoping you'll do more than just catch his eye this weekend.'

Did she detect a note of bitterness in his voice? If she did, she could not think of that now. She had to prepare herself for the possibility that the Duke might approach her.

Smile, laugh, but not too much. Compliment him... talk only of him.

'And I believe your grandmother has discovered the perfect bait so you can do just that,' he added somewhat cryptically, then he smiled at Grace. She so loved that smile, which helped to soothe her jittery nerves. 'But it is of no matter as it is delightful to see you again, Miss Lowerby,' he added.

'And it's delightful to see you again,' she responded with all honesty and a heartfelt smile.

'Are you looking forward to the weekend?' he asked.

It was time to put all honesty aside and give the expected responses. 'Oh, yes, I've heard there's to be horse riding, croquet and so many other activities.' *And during all these activities I will be expected to shine and impress and show the Duke I am born to be a duchess.*

'So I believe.'

'Do you intend to take part in any of these activities?' she asked hopefully.

'No, I will be leaving once the Duke has signed over his land.'

'Oh,' she gasped. 'That is a shame.'

'Not to worry, Miss Lowerby, I suspect you will be fully occupied this weekend and will hardly notice my absence. Your grandmother obviously expects you to dedicate all your time to landing your prey, hook, line and sinker.'

'Oh, will there be fishing as well? I don't believe we packed for that and, to be honest, I hate fishing. I always feel so sorry for the poor fish.'

His smile turned to laughter, a lovely melodious laughter. 'Miss Lowerby, you are a delight.'

Warmth coursed through her, although she had no idea what she had said that was so delightful, but it was lovely to make him laugh.

'I don't know if there will be fishing, but I do know that everyone in this room is trying to reel in something or somebody.'

'Oh,' she said with some embarrassment, catching the meaning of his words. 'But some of us are better anglers than others,' she added. Grace did not need to look towards the Duke to know he was still surrounded by several pretty young women who were more skilled in the arts of capturing a man than she would ever be.

'You have no need to worry on that account. With your formidable grandmother in your corner I can hardly see how you can fail.'

She looked over at her grandmother, who was nodding at something Lady Beatrice was saying, but watching Grace carefully. Then she looked towards the Duke and, to her horror, she could see he was now crossing the room, straight towards her.

'He's coming,' she gasped out, then blushed, having revealed far too much to Mr Hayward.

'Breathe, slowly and deeply,' he advised. She did what he said, but had only managed one long inhalation before the Duke was at her side.

'Miss Lowerby,' he said with a brief nod of his head.

Her held breath came out with a loud embarrassing gush, causing the Duke to frown. This was not going well, but at least she was still on her feet.

'Your Grace,' she said with a small curtsy.

'I hope Hayward hasn't been boring you with talk of business, acquisitions and accounts.'

'Oh, no, not at all,' she said. 'We were talking about…' She bit her lip. 'About fishing.'

This caused Mr Hayward to smile, and she smiled back at him, until she caught the Duke's look of disapproval and drew her features into a more composed countenance.

'Fishing, eh? Didn't know you fished, Miss Lowerby. My estate has several of the finest fishing rivers in this part of the country, you know. Love it myself. If you wish, I can take you fishing tomorrow.'

Grace's stomach did an unpleasant flip. She had been taken fishing once as a child and had hated it. She had even burst into tears when the little fishy had been pulled out of the water, gasping and flapping around, and had begged for it to be returned to the river where it could swim happily away. And now she would have to prove to the Duke it was something she loved as much as he did.

'That's the beauty of owning ten thousand acres,' the Duke continued. 'You have plenty of land so you can fish, shoot, hunt and ride to hounds.'

Shoot? Ride to hounds?

Every inch of Grace's body tensed as she tried to come up with an excuse, any excuse, to get her out of those repugnant activities. Fishing was bad enough, but as for killing innocent little birdies and chasing terrified foxes across the countryside—those activities were abhorrent to her.

'I'm afraid you can't take Miss Lowerby fishing tomorrow,' Mr Hayward said before she had time to formulate an answer that would save her from such a terrible fate. 'She has agreed to take a walk with me so I can show her where the new rail line is to be installed.'

The Duke's lips curled in disdain while relief swept over her. Mr Hayward had saved her once again, this time from the horror of having to kill defenceless little fish and the embarrassment of exposing her abhorrence for blood sports.

'Has she?' the Duke said, his nostrils still flared. 'Has she, indeed? Well, I hope Hayward doesn't just show you where the railway line will go, but also shows you the extent of my estate, which takes in not just the best fishing streams in the county, but also comprises enormous parts of the coastline, several villages, and heavens knows what else. It is one of the largest estates in the country.'

'Then we will have to take a very long walk indeed so we can take in all its wonders,' Mr Hayward said, causing the Duke to smile at the compliment, then scowl.

'Wonders that have been in my family since Tudor times,' the Duke said, a note of venom in his voice.

Mr Hayward gave a small laugh that did not sound amused. 'And some of those wonders won't be in the family for much longer.'

The Duke fixed his glare on Mr Hayward, his fists clenched at his side. She looked from him to Mr Hayward, who was smiling at the Duke in a manner that was almost taunting, then back at the Duke, waiting for his riposte. He said nothing. She looked to Mr Hayward to see what he would do or say next.

'Speaking of losing land, you have some papers to sign,' Mr Hayward added.

The Duke waved his hand across his face. 'Money and business, is that all you ever think about, Hayward? You need to learn to appreciate the finer things in life, the things that money can't buy.' He looked at Grace and smiled. She smiled back, as was required.

Mr Hayward made a dismissive laugh. 'It's lucky for you it doesn't take money for you to attract these finer things, or you'd be struggling, wouldn't you?'

Grace gasped at this insult as the Duke stared at Mr Hayward, his eyes blazing, his fists curled ever tighter. If this look of aggression was meant to cower Mr Hayward, it had no effect. He continued to stare at the Duke, his face impassive.

'Someone needs to put you in your place, Hayward,' the Duke said through gritted teeth.

'I believe you've said that to me before, many, many times, going right back to my first day at school. When do you think that will finally happen?'

The Duke once again looked at Grace. 'Very, very soon.'

Grace waited for Mr Hayward's response. He said nothing. She looked back at the Duke, who was once again staring at Mr Hayward with undisguised dislike.

With her head moving from one to the other, this was starting to feel like watching a rather unsettling tennis match. Or was it more like watching stags during the rutting season, sizing each other up before an attack? Heat rushed to Grace's cheeks at the thought of such a thing and she was pleased the two men were still staring at each other and neither saw her cheeks turn bright red.

'Your Grace… Mr Hayward,' her grandmother said, joining the group.

Both men turned to face her and bowed their heads, still wearing those implacable expressions.

With her grandmother present, Grace knew it wisest

to adopt the required sweet smile and a look of interest in everything the men said, particularly the Duke. If her grandmother knew of the level of animosity between these two men she would be outraged and there was the danger she would once again forbid her from being in Mr Hayward's company.

Grace's heart jumped within her chest at that possibility. Being in Mr Hayward's company was the only thing making this occasion bearable. It was so wonderful to talk with him, to laugh with him, and when he looked at her with those deep brown eyes, it was as if there was a connection between them, something intangible, something rather marvellous.

She would almost rather her grandmother forbid her from being in the Duke's company than Mr Hayward's.

Her hand shot to cover her mouth, as if she had expressed that outrageous statement out loud and was desperate to take it back. She looked at the assembled group, fearful that they might have read her mind.

The two men and her grandmother continued to chat in what appeared an almost amicable manner. No one had noticed Grace's inner torment, so she resumed smiling, pleased that in her confused state no more was expected of her.

She looked from one man to the other. Despite the supposedly polite conversation now taking place, there was still that undercurrent of deep-seated discord in everything they said. And what was that reference to money couldn't buy the finer things in life? Were they talking about her? She hoped not. Surely that was not how those two men saw her, as something that could be bought.

She watched her grandmother, smiling at the Duke as if he was the most intelligent, wittiest, interesting man she had ever met, and a horrible thought occurred to her.

Could her grandmother be wrong? Was it the title that she admired, not the man? No, that could not be right. As her grandmother had said, again and again, if a man is at the very pinnacle of society, it is because he is a superior man in every way.

That was why her grandmother was so supportive of her desire to marry the Duke, so she would have the best of husbands and the respect of being married to a man every other debutante had set her heart on.

'I'll bid you two ladies goodnight,' Mr Hayward said, drawing her out of her reverie. 'And I look forward to our walk tomorrow, Miss Lowerby.'

Grace curtsied and kept smiling while looking anxiously in her grandmother's direction to gauge her reaction. Her grandmother was certain to lecture her on the folly of wasting time with Mr Hayward when she was supposed to be pursuing the Duke.

'You are to walk with Mr Hayward tomorrow?' her

grandmother said the moment Mr Hayward was out of ear shot. 'How pleasant.'

What on earth was happening? Everyone this evening was acting in such a peculiar manner and Grace could hardly keep up with what was being said and not being said.

'I would recommend making it a very short walk indeed,' the Duke said with a sneer in the direction in which Mr Hayward had departed, then smiled at Grace. 'Remember, you have promised me a dance tomorrow night.'

Grace could remember doing no such thing, but it was of no matter. If the Duke asked, then of course she would accept.

'Dancing,' her grandmother exclaimed. 'How delightful.'

'Remember, keep the time you spend with Hayward as brief as possible.' And with that final instruction, the Duke excused himself.

Grace braced herself for the inevitable lecture that would follow now that they were out of the Duke's hearing and tried to compose a justification for agreeing to take a walk with Mr Hayward.

'Well done, my dear,' her grandmother said, using that surprising term of affection. 'You are playing this perfectly.'

Grace was unsure how she was supposed to react to that statement. She wasn't playing anything, perfectly or otherwise, but compliments from her grandmother were rare indeed so she would merely accept it as the precious gift it was.

'It will do no harm to encourage Mr Hayward. Nothing piques a man's interest in a girl more than knowing that she is sought after by another. It's a shame that Mr Hayward is not another titled man, but needs must.'

'Yes, Grandmama,' Grace answered in her usual quiet manner, while inwardly dancing a little jig. She was not only being allowed to go on tomorrow's walk, but had just been given permission to encourage Mr Hayward, even if she was unsure what encouraging entailed.

'But just remember, only encourage him so far. It is the Duke's heart you have to win this weekend,' her grandmother added in that more familiar admonishing tone.

Grace was tempted to ask her grandmother how far was too far when it came to encouraging a man, but felt it wise to keep that question to herself. It would not do for her grandmother to think she was pleased to be spending time with Mr Hayward. So she would remain ignorant of the finer details of what was expected when it came to encouragement and just try her best.

Chapter Five

'I believe we have a contract to sign,' the Duke said to Thomas after breakfast the following morning.

Finally.

Once Thomas had what he wanted he could escape this infernal weekend party and get away from these people and all their machinations. It would be a shame to miss his walk with Miss Lowerby, but as she was here to win the Duke it would be no real loss.

Would it?

He paused momentarily as he followed the Duke down the hallway towards his study.

No, of course it would not. He resumed walking. She was not his type in more ways than he could list.

She was a sweet, innocent debutante in search of a titled husband. Every one of those qualities made her exactly the type of woman he avoided. Sweet and innocent were not what he was after when it came to feminine company. The women he enjoyed spending time with were those who flouted the rules of society rather than obeying them to the letter the way Miss Lowerby did. And as for a young lady in search of a titled husband, that put him out of the running on two counts. He had no title and he most certainly was not in search of a wife.

No, his departure was all for the best. He would get the Duke's land and Miss Lowerby would hopefully get the Duke. And even if she failed in that quest, such an attractive young woman was bound to capture another titled man. Her dance with the Duke at his ball would have been noted by everyone in society, along with this coveted invitation to his house party. That would have drawn the interest of every eligible marquess, viscount, earl and baron after a suitably compliant wife. When it came to finding a husband, she most certainly did not need his help to achieve her goal.

They entered the study, and the Duke collapsed on to the leather chair behind the large mahogany desk. A desk, which Thomas noted did not contain the legal papers they were to sign. It looked like the Duke intended to play yet another of his games before he succumbed to the inevitable.

With a sigh of irritation, he took the facing chair and gave a quick look around the room. Glassed-in bookshelves lined every wall and each shelf was packed with books, none of which Thomas suspected the Duke had ever read. The room carried the lingering smell of cigars and a hint of brandy. That was more likely what this room was used for, as a place where the Duke could pretend he was a man of substance running a well-oiled estate, when, in fact, it was merely another place for him to drink, smoke and while away his endless free time.

But it was of no matter to Thomas what the Duke did with his time. While men like Hardgraves continued to squander the fortunes they had inherited, men like Thomas would continue to profit.

'Right, let's get these papers signed so I can be on my way,' Thomas said, knowing it would not be that easy.

'Not so fast, Hayward, not so fast.'

Thomas swallowed his exasperation, determined not to let the Duke see the effect he was having on him.

'Weekend parties always involve some gambling, so I have a wager for you,' the Duke said, picking up a letter opener and flicking it with his finger.

'You know I'm not a gambling man,' Thomas replied. If he cared one fig about the Duke, he would advise him that he, too, should cease to gamble if he wanted to keep hold of what was left of his fortune. But he did not care even that one proverbial fig for the Duke, so he kept his opinions to himself.

'Oh, I think you're going to want to take this wager.' The Duke stared hard at Thomas, those beady eyes reminding him of a venomous snake he had seen at the London Zoological Gardens, and he suspected, just like the snake, the Duke was planning to strike.

'Miss Lowerby is a rather comely chit, don't you think?'

Thomas's teeth clenched together. So that was what this was about. That should have come as no surprise.

'Indeed,' he replied, not rising to the bait.

'Quite fancy her, do you?'

'I'm not here to discuss Miss Lowerby. I am here to take your land and I am offering more than a fair price for it. You won't get better anywhere else and, as we both know, you need the money.'

The Duke's eyes narrowed further and Thomas regretted the harshness of his tone and the reference to the Duke's precarious financial position. Like a stubborn child, the Duke was liable to cut off his nose to spite his face if he thought he was being insulted and deny Thomas the land.

'Business, that's all you ever think about, isn't it, Hayward?' He looked Thomas up and down as if this was the worst insult he could make on a man's character. 'If you were a gentleman, you would know that weekend parties are about having fun, gambling and entertaining the ladies.'

Thomas could point out *he* was not here at this weekend party for fun, gambling or for the ladies, but he would be pointing out the obvious to the Duke and to antagonise him further would do nothing to shorten these proceedings.

'So I propose we do all three,' the Duke added.

Or we could do none of them and just sign the bloody papers.

'I have a proposition for you. One that involves Miss Lowerby.'

'What about Miss Lowerby?' Thomas snapped back, annoyed at the terseness in his voice.

A satisfied smile curled at the edge of the Duke's lips, as if he had caused Thomas to reveal more than he intended. But his reaction had nothing to do with Miss Lowerby. He was merely irritated by all this unnecessary game playing.

Wasn't he? Yes, of course he was.

'I propose a wager involving her and my land,' he said, a viciously joyful note in his voice. Thomas had heard that tone before many times at school. It usually meant someone weaker than the Duke was about to be hurt.

Thomas clenched his fists tighter. If the Duke proposed anything that would harm that innocent young lady, he would feel the full force of Thomas's wrath, even if it meant losing the land.

'I believe, despite your best efforts, that the young lady knows quality when she sees it and it is with me that her real affections lie. So if by the end of this weekend I have proven that to be true, then I will sell you my land at a lower price. However, if by the end of the weekend she is smitten with you…' the Duke smirked as if this was an impossibility '…then you will have to pay a higher price for my land.'

Thomas forced his face to remain expressionless. Was the man completely insane? No wonder the Duke was such an appalling gambler if he made bets like this, ones in which even if he won, he lost.

'It will be like a duel that men fought in the good old days when they were allowed to do such things, but instead of swords or pistols at dawn, this will be a wooing duel,' the Duke added, obviously pleased with this imagery. 'One that proves once and for all who is the better man.'

'You're on,' Thomas said, reaching across the desk and shaking the Duke's hand, hardly able to believe the man's stupidity. During their schooldays, Thomas had bested the Duke at both lessons and sports, and had knocked him to the ground on numerous occasions while they were having boxing instructions. Despite that, the Duke could never understand that a title did not automatically make you the better man and it was obvious he still had not learnt that lesson. Now he was so desperate to beat Thomas at something, he would sacrifice his land, even if all he got was the appearance of a win.

So be it. All that would be required of Thomas was to pretend to woo Miss Lowerby, a young lady who had already set her heart on marrying the Duke. Once he had gone through that pretence and inevitably lost her affections to Hardgraves, he would walk away with the Duke's land at a cheaper price than he had originally offered.

The Duke stood up and puffed himself up as if they were about to commence battle. 'Let the best man win the fair maiden's heart,' he said.

Thomas resisted the temptation to laugh in the idiot's face. Not only would losing this bet be to Thomas's benefit, but giving the Duke the impression he was wooing Miss Lowerby would prove no arduous task. In every way, Thomas would come out the winner this weekend.

As arranged, Thomas met Miss Lowerby at the entrance of the Duke's home so he could accompany her on a walk. And as expected, she behaved in the correct manner of a well-trained debutante and kept him waiting a few minutes. But it was rather worth the wait. If he had to pretend to woo a young lady, he could think of none better than Miss Lowerby. She really was rather lovely and seemed to get more lovely each time he saw her.

Dressed in a pale pink day dress and carrying a lacy parasol in her gloved hands she was as pretty as a picture. She smiled at him. It really was a delightful smile, one that lit up her face and made those big blue eyes sparkle.

He smiled back at her, genuinely pleased to see her and looking forward to their walk around the estate, even if all he would be doing was showing her all that might one day be hers if she did achieve her aim of marrying the Duke.

'Shall we?' he said, offering her his arm.

She placed her arm through his and he led her out through the entranceway and into the formal garden, the dutiful lady's maid following at a discreet distance.

'I dare say the Duke has already told you he possesses one of the most opulent estates in all of England and one of the largest,' he said, unable to keep the sarcasm out of his voice. Thomas had lost count of the numbers of times he'd heard that boast, as if it was proof of the Duke's prowess as a man.

'Yes, I believe he has mentioned that on one or two occasions. Although he said that while his is big, yours is even bigger.'

Thomas laughed out loud. He looked at Miss Lowerby to see if that was a deliberate double entendre, but her innocent smile made it obvious she was unaware of how her words could be interpreted. 'We've never actually got out a ruler and compared, but I'm fairly confident that I have the advantage.'

She smiled politely at a joke she did not understand.

'I take it your grandmother did not object to us taking this walk together?'

Her cheeks coloured slightly. 'I'm afraid I have a confession to make.

He raised his eyebrows. 'You, Miss Lowerby? A confession? What could a young lady such as yourself possibly have to confess?'

'Grandmama has instructed me to encourage your attentions.'

Thomas gave a low chuckle. He was not in the least surprised. That canny old woman had no doubt noticed what would be obvious to everyone except Miss Lowerby—that the Duke wanted what he thought might be denied him.

'And how do you feel about that?'

'Oh, I'm very pleased,' she said with a sincere smile, then her blush grew deeper and she lowered her eyes as if she had done something wrong or revealed too much.

'As am I,' he said, surprised at how true that statement was.

She bit her top lip lightly, drawing his gaze to that rather attractive feature. Soft, full and decidedly kissable, with an intriguing line in the centre of her plump lower lip that gave her an unexpected sensual appearance.

'So how are you going to do that?' he asked, forcing himself to look away from her lips.

'Do what?' She looked up at him in confusion.

'Encourage my attentions?' That teasing question was rewarded with another blush tinging her creamy cheeks.

'Grandmama didn't go into details.' She gave a small, embarrassed laugh. 'What do you suggest?'

'It's not really my field of expertise. Weren't you taught about such things at finishing school? My sister told me that learning how to encourage a man's interest is the only thing a young lady is taught at such institutions.'

'Yes, she's right.'

She thought for a moment, then sent him a pretty smile, one that held a hint of mischief. 'Well, I could flutter my eyelashes at you, I suppose.'

'All right. Let's see your best flutter.'

She stopped walking, attempted to pull her smiling lips into a more serious expression, tilted her head in a coquettish manner, then fluttered rapidly, causing him to once again laugh out loud.

She lightly tapped him on the arm. 'You're not supposed to laugh. You're supposed to be enraptured.'

'So what else do you have in your arsenal so you can reduce a man to a quivering idiot?'

'Well, if I had my fan, I could flutter it lightly in front of my face, hiding all but my eyes.'

'Which presumably would also be fluttering.'

'No, I believe that would be overdoing it somewhat.'

'But there must be something other than all this fluttering you can do. You can't spend all your time looking as if you've got something caught in your eye.'

'I believe you are making fun of me, Mr Hayward.'

'I believe you might be right, Miss Lowerby.'

They exchanged smiles, then she blinked rapidly, not to flutter and enrapture, but to break the gaze which they had held for perhaps a moment too long.

'But you're right,' she continued as they commenced walking. 'Fluttering is not all I've been instructed to do. I could laugh at your jokes.'

'I'd have to say something funny first.'

'Oh, no. What you say doesn't actually have to be funny, as long as it's an attempt at humour.'

'All right, let's pretend I've just tried to make a joke. Let's hear your best laugh.'

Smiling, she placed her gloved hand lightly over her mouth and gave a small titter, a titter which soon turned into a small laugh. Then she was laughing whole heartedly, still trying to cover her mouth with her gloved hand.

'Not like that,' she gasped out as she attempted to stop her laughter. 'No teeth,' she said, failing in her attempt and laughing even more loudly.

'Teeth?'

She laughed herself out, then smiled up at him, a cheeky glint of amusement in her blue eyes. 'A young lady must never show her teeth when she laughs or she is in danger of looking like a horse.'

It was his turn to laugh. 'Whoever said that was a fool. I don't believe I've ever seen a horse laugh.'

'No, neither have I.'

'So, your fluttering has failed to enrapture me. You've committed the unforgivable sin of laughing so hard at my unfunny joke that you exposed your teeth. What else are you supposed to do to encourage my affections?'

'Well, I also have to compliment you.'

'I like the sound of that. Off you go, then.'

Her hand covered her mouth again, but not soon enough for a laugh to escape. 'Why, Mr Hayward, everything you say is so clever,' she said, her laughter making a mockery of her words. 'You are such a learned man it quite shames me to know I am so ignorant by comparison.' This was followed by another round of eyelash fluttering, which caused Thomas to join in her laughter.

'Excellent work. I feel thoroughly complimented and I particularly liked the flutter at the end which added a certain panache.'

'Why, Mr Hayward, I believe you are flirting with me,' she said, still fluttering those dark eyelashes. 'That's something else we're supposed to say, but it has to be said in a manner that the gentleman knows that you want to be flirted with.'

'And you did it admirably.'

They smiled at each other, and Thomas had to admit laughing with her, teasing her and flirting with her definitely held their attraction.

His gaze lowered to her smiling lips. But she was wrong. If she really wanted to encourage a man all she had to do was pout those lovely full lips, then he would be entirely lost.

Her smile faded and her lips pursed slightly as if she was reading his mind. A jolt of hot desire shot through him as he imagined his lips on hers, his tongue running along that full bottom lip, of her lips parting as he entered her, tasted her, savoured her.

He looked straight ahead.

Where the hell did that come from?

His fevered mind had turned something that was merely harmless fun into something far from harmless. He was supposed to be pretending to woo Miss Hayward. There should certainly be no actual wooing involved, and most certainly no kissing. He did not want Miss Lowerby. He wanted the Duke's land, nothing else.

'But I have another confession to make,' she continued.

'Another one?' he asked, forcing his voice to remain light. He, too, could make a confession about what he had just been thinking, but that was something he would be keeping to himself.

'Well, it's the same confession, but I didn't tell you all my grandmother said. She told me to encourage you as she believes it will further garner the Duke's interest in me. I am so sorry.'

'You have absolutely nothing to be sorry for.' If anyone should be apologising it should be him. Despite enjoying this walk, he was only here for one reason, to get the Duke's signature on that document and, thanks to her, he now had the opportunity to get the land at a lower price than he had been prepared to pay.

But that was something she did not need to know. And surely no harm would come of this. She would get what she wanted. Her grandmother would get what she wanted and Thomas also would get what he wanted. No, nothing was to be gained by making such a confession.

'Your grandmother is right,' he said instead. 'Nothing gets a man's blood pumping faster than a bit of competition.'

That and very kissable lips.

'But it all seems a bit, well, as if we are using you.'

'I'm happy to be used,' he said, meaning every word. Miss Lowerby was not for him, but she was delightful company. She also had an attractive face, decidedly alluring lips and a temptingly curvaceous body. If she wasn't an innocent debutante, he'd be more than happy for them to use each other in every pleasurable way imaginable.

He coughed lightly. 'So your heart is set on marrying the Duke?' he asked, bringing his wayward thoughts back to reality, one in which Miss Lowerby was an innocent young debutante who had to save her innocence for the titled man she married.

'Oh, yes,' she gushed. 'I know I shouldn't say this, but to marry the Duke would make all my dreams come true.'

Thomas's teeth gritted tightly together and his stomach clenched as if it had taken a punch. Why he should react in such a manner he had no idea. It was what the aristocracy did. They vied to make a marriage that would advance their position in society and no one would advance Miss Lowerby further than the Duke. It was just a shame he was such an oaf who did not deserve a young lady such as she.

'And why would that be?' he asked, annoyed that his tone might be revealing his irritation, but unable to disguise the rancour in his words. 'Is it his wit and intelligence that attracts you? Is it because he is a man of the highest calibre? Is it because he manages his estate with such skill and proficiency? Is it because he demonstrates a high level of integrity in all matters?'

He knew the Duke possessed none of these characteristics. There was only one thing that made him an attractive catch. His title.

He looked down at her, waiting for her answer. Her otherwise smooth brow crinkled in confusion and guilt rippled through him. He should not make sport of her desire to capture a man of the Duke's status. It was what she had been trained for all her life and she would know of no other way to behave.

'What is the dream that you are sure will come true if you marry the Duke?' he asked in a gentler tone.

'It's what I've wanted for as long as I can remember. And it would make my grandmother happy. Very, very happy,' she said quietly. 'And that is what I want, more than anything in the world.'

'And you becoming a duchess is also your grandmother's dream, is it?' That was a question that did not need to be asked.

'Yes.' She nibbled on her lip again and he wished she wouldn't. He did not need a reminder of how tempting her lips were.

'I don't know if you know much about my unfortunate background,' she continued in that quiet, apologetic manner.

He raised his eyebrows in surprise. He doubted there could be anything in this sweet young woman's background that was unfortunate. In fact, he doubted she even had a background. Young ladies such as she were sheltered from everything until they reached the age of eighteen. Then they were thrust into society where they were measured and compared by all the men in pursuit of a wife.

'Unfortunate?' he probed.

'My father was a piano teacher,' she blurted out as if confessing the most heinous of sins.

He waited for her to continue and reveal her terrible past.

'My mother ran away with him against her parents' wishes.' Her expression was imploring, as if waiting for him to grasp the magnitude of this scandal.

'I see.' It was hardly a crime, but obviously in this young lady's eyes marriage to a piano teacher was an unforgivable act of treachery.

'She could have married anyone, Grandmama says, but she threw it all away.' Her eyes continued to appeal for his understanding.

'And where are these terrible parents now?'

'They died in an accident.'

'I am so sorry,' he said, regretting his jesting description of them as terrible.

'My grandmother kindly took me in. So I owe it to her to pay her back for all she has done for me and to make amends for the shame my mother brought on the Ashbridge lineage by making a good marriage.'

It sounded like a well-rehearsed speech, one her grandmother had presumably made many, many times while she had been growing up.

'Do you remember anything about your mother and father?'

'No, not really. I was only a small baby when they died in a carriage accident.' She looked down and blushed slightly. 'When I was a little girl and exploring my grandparents' estate I found a portrait of my mother that had been put away in the attic. She was rather beautiful and had such kind eyes.'

'Just like you,' he added quietly.

She smiled at him. 'Grandmama has said she was stubborn and disobedient, but she didn't look like that in the portrait. She looked gentle and loving. When I was a child I spent a lot of time up in the attic sitting close to that portrait, especially when I'd done something to displease Grandmama. I'd imagine my mother holding me and telling me how much she loved me.' She looked down at her feet. 'It's silly really.'

'I don't think it's silly in the slightest. And I'm sure your mother would have loved you dearly,' he said, fighting off anger at her harsh grandmother who had failed to see that her granddaughter was sad and lonely.

'But I'm not a child any more,' she said with a sudden determined edge to her voice. 'And I am very grateful to my grandmother and owe her so much. When I was growing up she arranged for a series of nannies to look after me.'

Her teeth clamped on to her quivering bottom lip and Thomas wondered whether she was trying to bite back tears. It was so unfair. Every child deserved to be loved and cared for by their family, not handed over to paid staff who came and went at the whim of their employer.

'And since my debut and my presentation to Queen Victoria, Grandmama has devoted all her time to me.' She smiled at Thomas as if the old lady was bestowing a great gift on her granddaughter, rather than using her to pursue her own aims. 'And before that she did provide me with all the tutors I required so no one would ever know that I had a father who was, well, a…'

'Nobody?'

She bit her lip again. 'I'm sorry,' she murmured.

'No need to apologise. If that's as unfortunate as your background gets, then believe me, you have nothing to be ashamed of. Your father made an honest living and your mother presumably married for love. I can see no shame there.'

Her blue eyes grew wide in surprise. He suspected these were two possibilities she had never considered or, if she had, they were ideas too shocking to be spoken of aloud.

'I'm certainly not ashamed of my background, nor do I see it as unfortunate,' he continued. 'My great-grandfather was a baker. His son expanded the business and moved into other areas of commerce. My father expanded those enterprises substantially, as I intend to do. I'm proud of what they have achieved. Although…' he shrugged '…my father and your grandmother do have one thing in common.'

'They do?' Her eyes grew wider as if she could not possibly imagine that to be true.

'My father wanted a title in the family and he got it. My sister Georgina married the Duke of Ravenswood.'

Miss Lowerby nodded. 'She did her duty by the family. Your parents must be very proud of her.'

This caused Thomas to laugh loudly. 'If you had ever met Georgina, you would know she would never do her duty and, if anyone tried to make her do so, she would take a great deal of pleasure in doing the very opposite. My father was, however, lucky. She fell in love with the Duke he had tried to force her to marry, otherwise it would never have happened.'

'Oh, I see,' she said quietly, her brow furrowed as if she did not really see at all. Then she smiled as if it all suddenly made sense. 'Your sister really did get a fairy-tale ending. It does actually happen.'

Thomas groaned inwardly. She really was a romantic, a sweet, innocent romantic, and he was tempted to let her know what marriage to the Duke would really entail and it would be no fairy tale. But what good would it do? Her heart was already set on the Duke and it was hardly his place to change it.

Chapter Six

Grace was unsure whether talking so freely with Mr Hayward was what her grandmother had meant by encouraging his attentions, but it was rather liberating to not have to watch everything she did and said, and surely it would do no harm. It wasn't as if he could ever be a contender for her hand in marriage.

She had never told anyone about those furtive trips to the attic as a child. Her grandmother would be outraged to know she had ever seen her mother as anything other than the source of the family's shame, but Mr Hayward seemed to understand why she had done it. Perhaps that was why she had told him her secret and why she now had no regrets about doing so.

She sent him another smile as they walked along in silence. Even this comfortable silence was rather pleasant. She closed her eyes briefly, enjoying the gentle caress of the soft breeze on her face, the tweeting of the birds flitting between the trees and the occasional bleating of sheep in the distance.

She felt so light in Mr Hayward's company. Unlike being in her grandmother's company, she was not constantly on her guard to make sure she said or did nothing wrong. Nor was it as taxing as being in the Duke's company where she had to pretend to be exactly the sort of young lady he wanted her to be. She could just be herself with Mr Hayward, although, after years of having to be the person she was expected to be, she had to admit, she wasn't entirely sure who that person was.

It was hard to believe she had actually made fun of her finishing school lessons, but it was so good to laugh, really laugh, without having to worry about how she looked and what impression she was making. She was so thankful to her grandmother for allowing her this precious time with Mr Hayward, even if it was for the rather questionable reason of using him to capture the Duke.

And her confessions had removed a weight that she had been carrying. He would now understand why it was so important for her to marry the Duke. It wasn't just for her own sake. Nor was she being bought by his title. It was because of her debt to her grandmother, a debt that could only be paid by making a good marriage.

It would be nice if she already felt comfortable in the Duke's company, but one day, hopefully, they would be able to spend enjoyable time together, just like this.

She looked up at Mr Hayward—perhaps one day he would be walking like this, arm in arm with the young lady he wished to marry and would find the happiness he deserved.

Grace's breath caught in her throat at the thought of this young lady, who, as far as she knew, did not yet exist. Who would she be? Would she be prettier than Grace, more amusing, more accomplished? What sort of young lady would he take as a wife? Grace both wanted and did not want to know the answer to that question.

'Do your parents expect you to make a good marriage, the way they expected your sister to do so?' she ventured, her stifled breath making the words sound awkward.

'Fortunately for me, I cannot bring a title into the family, so I am free to marry whomever I choose.'

'And what sort of woman do you plan to marry?' She forced her voice to remain light, as if this was a question of no real account.

He sent her a quizzical look, and she instantly regretted the question.

'I am sorry, that was forward of me.'

'Not at all. I hope you will always feel that you can ask me anything.'

She smiled, grateful that he had once again made her feel comfortable. 'Well, what sort of woman do you plan to marry?' she repeated, it being the one question she was desperate to have answered.

'If I do marry, and I say if, not when, it will be to a woman who is intelligent and can be a helpmate, rather than one who spends all her days taking tea, gossiping and shopping. She will be a woman I respect and admire.'

'And love?' she asked, her voice little more than a whisper.

He shrugged. 'It's all hypothetical as I have no intention of marrying.'

Grace's breath came easier as that imaginary woman disappeared from her mind, leaving just the two of them walking together and enjoying each other's company.

'You are lucky to have the freedom to choose who you marry and whether you wish to marry or not,' she said, her statement causing her some surprise.

He gave her a considered look. 'Yes, I am, but you also have a degree of freedom.'

'I suppose,' she responded with a small, dismissive laugh. 'After all, I'm not a slave.'

She continued to smile at him, but he did not return her smile.

'No, you are not a slave, nor do you have to marry if you do not wish to do so. Women do have some choices now. My sister has a friend who is an artist, another who runs a successful magazine, another who has established a school for women in the East End of London.'

Her smile died and she stared at him as if he was talking a foreign language. Choices? There was only one real choice for a young lady such as her and that was to marry well.

'You don't have to do anything you don't want to, Miss Lowerby. Remember that. You can make decisions about what sort of future you want.'

'Of course,' she said, unsure what other answer she could give.

Once again they slipped into silence, but this time it was not quite so companionable. What did he mean? She didn't have to do anything she did not want to? She *was* doing exactly what she wanted to. Wasn't she? She wanted to be married and to the best of all possible husbands and that was surely the Duke. And more than that, a good marriage was what her grandmother had always wanted and she deserved such a reward for all that she had done for Grace.

Yes, she hoped to marry a man she loved and while she might not be in love with the Duke, not yet, she was sure, like Mr Hayward's sister, she, too, would grow to love him. She nodded her head to underline this conviction. Yes, that was what she wanted, what she had dreamed of all her life.

They reached a river, over which spanned an ancient arched bridge, moss growing up the pale brown bricks.

They paused and looked down at the gently flowing water and the grass banks speckled with flowers.

'Should we return to the house? Your grandmother might be wondering where we have got to,' Mr Hayward asked. 'As might the Duke.'

She looked over her shoulder. He was right. They should return. But it was so pleasant being in Mr Hayward's company. And, she had to admit, it was rather pleasant to be on the arm of a man so sublimely handsome, so charming and, well, such fun.

Her grandmother had instructed her to encourage Mr Hayward in order to capture the Duke, so to spend a little bit longer in his company would surely be what was expected of her.

'But you told the Duke you were going to show me the land you wish to purchase from him,' she said. 'We are yet to see it.'

He raised his eyebrows slightly. 'It's on the far side of these fields and there's not much to see.'

'Still, I'd like to see where the railway will run.'

'As you wish.'

Arm in arm, they crossed the bridge and walked over a grassy field. As they passed a flock of sheep, they lifted their woolly heads from their grazing, assessed the passing couple as being no threat and returned to their contented munching.

It would be so lovely if they could continue on this walk indefinitely and she did not have to go back to the house where so much was expected of her. But after a few minutes Mr Hayward came to a stop and stood looking at the land that appeared no different from any other part of the field.

'This is it. As I said, there is nothing much to see.'

He was right, but she was still pleased they had spent this extra time together.

'Shall we return now?' he asked.

'What is it about this bit of land that makes you wish to buy it?' She was not especially interested, but was determined to delay the inevitable, even if for a few moments longer.

He pointed towards the horizon. 'It's a direct route to the coal mines owned by my family. At present we're having to put the coal on barges to transport it to the nearest rail depot. When we lay tracks over this land, we'll be able to run trains directly from the mines to the port.'

'So it will be much more efficient?'

'Indeed.'

She looked around at the contentedly browsing sheep. 'But where will the sheep go?'

'As you can see, the Duke does not run a particularly large flock, so this loss of land will hardly make any difference. And sheep are not as profitable as they once were. Cheaper wool is imported from the colonies and inefficient farms such as this can't compete.'

'I see.' She bit her lip, about to ask a question she

should not. 'Is that why the Duke has to sell the land, because it's no longer profitable?'

'Hmm,' he said as if considering how much to reveal.

She tilted her head in encouragement.

'Unfortunately, the Duke has not learnt that the way in which his family has farmed for centuries, or rather, the way in which his tenants have farmed, is outmoded.'

'But wouldn't it be better to change the way you farm, rather than sell off land that you'll never get back? If he keeps selling off bits here and there, eventually he'll have no land and no way of making money.' She looked over towards a group of cottages, presumably where the tenant farmers lived. 'And what will the people who work on the land do if that happens? Where will they go?'

She looked to him for answers. He was gazing down at her with an expression she had not seen before, not from the Duke, not from her grandmother, not from anyone. It was as if he was taking what she had to say said seriously.

'You are completely right, Miss Lowerby. Unfortunately, men like the Duke seldom realise that, or, at least, not until it's too late.'

'Unfortunate for them, but fortunate for men of business like yourself. I hope he is at least getting a good price for what he is selling off.'

'I have offered the Duke a fair price, although thanks to you I'm hoping that by the end of this weekend I will have made an even better deal for myself.'

'Thanks to me?'

'Yes, I believe you might be my lucky star.'

She smiled, flattered that he should see her in this light.

'But would it not be better if I was your unlucky star?' she said with a laugh, so he'd know she was teasing. 'After all, I should be trying to help the Duke get a better price for his land.'

'I can see you have a good head for business. If you do marry the Duke, I'll have to watch out for that if I make any future deals with him.'

If she married the Duke.

Why was that prospect no longer filling her with such excitement? It couldn't possibly be because of Mr Hayward, could it? Surely not. Yes, she enjoyed his company and, yes, he was the most handsome man she had ever met, and she was flattered that he chose to spend time with her, but it was the Duke she had set her heart on.

Mr Hayward was, of course, kind and undeniably companionable and these were qualities she had yet to see in the Duke, but surely a man as eminent as the Duke would possess such virtues as well. Then, of course, there was her surprising reactions when Mr Hayward looked at her, that strange fluttering that erupted in her stomach, that quickening of her heart, the shortness of breath. But surely she would eventually feel that way about the Duke as well.

And none of that mattered anyway. He was wholly unsuitable. She knew that and her grandmother certainly knew it. They would not be standing together looking at an empty field if her grandmother did not see this walk as part of the plan for her to wed the Duke.

And her own plan, of course, she reminded herself. Marriage to a titled man was what she had longed for since she was a little girl. It was what she lived for and now that opportunity was within her grasp. Any other ridiculous thoughts needed to be pushed firmly out of her head.

'Perhaps we should go back to the house,' she said, knowing it was the right thing to say, even if it was not entirely what she wanted to do.

'What? Have you had enough of staring at an empty field that will one day be a railway track?'

He smiled down at her and, despite her confusing thoughts, warmth enveloped her as she looked up at those smiling eyes, then down to those beautiful lips. And they *were* beautiful. What would it be like to run her finger over their sculptured edge, to feel their softness under the pad of her finger?

The lips stopped smiling and her gaze moved back up to his eyes. As if transfixed, she stared back into his deep brown eyes. Her heart pounding loudly in her chest, blood surging through her body, she knew she wanted to do more than just touch his lips with her finger. She wanted to feel them against her own lips, for him to take her in his arms and kiss her. She wanted to feel his body against hers, his arms around her holding her tightly.

'You're right,' he said, his voice husky and unfamiliar. 'We should return to the house.'

'Yes, yes, of course.' She forced herself to look away. What on earth was wrong with her? She should not be having such thoughts about any man other than the man she wished to marry and, even then, not until her wedding night. And she most certainly should not be having them about Mr Hayward. It was beyond shameful and she could only hope he had no idea where her mind had unaccountably strayed.

He took her arm again and they retraced their steps, her lady's maid still trailing several yards behind them.

Grace attempted to steady her breathing, tried to bring her still rapidly beating heart to order and to stop thinking of how her lips had tingled, nor how her body had throbbed as she had stared into his eyes.

Forgetting such unfamiliar, unforgivable reactions would be so much easier if she was not so close to him. So close she could feel the warmth of his body. So close she could even smell the crisp citric scent of his soap and something else, a musky, underlying scent that was, oh, so masculine. She breathed in gently, loving the way that scent filled her up. Despite her commands not to do so, she inched closer to him.

No further words were exchanged as they once again crossed over the arched bridge and finally walked up the gravel path towards the Duke's looming house. As they drew closer Grace could see two shapes waiting for them at the entranceway: her grandmother and the Duke.

Seeing the two of them brought reality crashing down. She instantly moved further away from Mr Hayward and, if it wasn't such a rude thing to do, she would have dropped his arm so no one would suspect the guilty thoughts that had possessed her. If her grandmother had any inkling of what she had been wanting to do only moments earlier, she would be horrified, not just because they were inappropriate for a young lady to have such desires, but because she'd had them for a man who had no value as a potential husband.

As if about to be punished, Grace braced herself, even though she knew her grandmother could not possibly know what she had been thinking or feeling. They drew closer to the house and Grace could see that her grandmother was smiling. Her tight shoulders relaxed. She breathed easier, but that did not mean she should not be on her guard to ensure she never, ever had such a reaction to any man again—any man, that was, except the Duke.

'Did you have an enjoyable walk?' her grandmother said as soon as they reached the top of the steps.

'Yes, Grandmama,' she answered in the expected manner.

'Good. Then you'll have to tell me all about it over a nice cup of tea.'

After saying their goodbyes to the Duke and Mr Hayward, she followed her grandmother into the ladies' parlour. The moment the door closed behind them, her grandmother took hold of her, still wearing that delighted smile.

'It's working, my dear, it's working,' she said, her words coming out in a rush. 'The Duke was beside himself, wondering why the walk was taking so long, where you had gone and what you were doing.'

'And that's good?' Grace asked.

'Of course it's good. He definitely wants you now and I suspect it won't be long before he's asking for your hand.'

Grace forced herself to smile. She should be delighted. Of course she was delighted.

'So should I keep encouraging Mr Hayward?'

'What? No, I think he's served his purpose now.'

'Oh.' Grace tried to ignore the clenching in her chest.

Her grandmother tapped her chin in thought. 'Well,

yes, maybe. If the Duke's interest does start to wane, then encourage him by all means.'

'Yes, Grandmama,' Grace said with a smile.

'Otherwise, have nothing to do with Mr Hayward.'

'No, Grandmama,' she added, clinging on to the hope that the Duke's heart had not been captured, at least not yet.

'Pleasant walk?' the Duke asked as he followed Thomas up the stairs. Was the man going to trail behind him all the way to his bedchamber?

'Perfectly nice, thank you. It's good of you to enquire,' he responded, his voice dripping with sarcasm.

'I'm not an imbecile, Hayward,' the Duke said, causing Thomas to smile to himself. That was news to him.

'I could see the blush on her cheeks and the sparkle in her eyes. It's that look chits get when they're ripe for the picking.'

Thomas stopped walking and turned to face the Duke. The Duke took a step backwards down a stair and raised his hands in a parody of surrender.

'Don't get so upset. I was merely going to say you had the advantage of making the first move. While you may have won this hand, the game isn't over yet. Believe me, I still have a few cards up my sleeve.'

Thomas released an irritated sigh at the laboured metaphor.

'Tonight there will be dancing and by the end of the

evening little Miss Lowerby will be mine,' the Duke added with a supercilious smile.

Thomas could inform him that Miss Lowerby was already his. She had been his since before they had even met, but instead he asked, 'Will the dancing take place in the ballroom?'

The Duke's supercilious smile died, as Thomas knew it would. While the ballroom at his Kensington home was pristine, the one at this estate was reputed to be in a desperate state of repair and would need a great deal of money to bring it back to its former glory, money the Duke would not have until he sold his land to Thomas.

'Not tonight, no,' the Duke said through clenched teeth. 'We are a small group of only twenty or so. The blue drawing room provides a more intimate space.'

And doesn't require all those expensive candles to light it. Candles you can ill afford.

'And I take it after you have made your play, we can declare a winner and you will sign those papers.'

'Don't be so hasty, Hayward. If you knew the ladies the way I do, you would know that wooing can't be rushed.'

Thomas stifled a laugh. Did this buffoon really delude himself into thinking the young ladies pursuing him required wooing? Did he not realise they were chasing his title and cared nothing for the man who possessed it?

'As you wish,' he said instead. 'But by tomorrow a winner must be declared or the bet is off and I will look elsewhere for land to buy.'

He took satisfaction in seeing panic ripple through the Duke at the thought of losing that much-needed money.

'Of course. I'm sure by then Miss Lowerby will see who is the better man.'

'I'm sure she will,' Thomas added and continued walking.

Although that does not mean that it will be the better man she will wed.

Thomas passed the remainder of the day in his room, seeing to correspondence and other business matters and trying to put Miss Lowerby out of his mind, a task that was proving surprisingly difficult. The thought of that sweet, trusting young woman married to that cretin was a torment. But any intervention from him would not be welcome and was sure to prove fruitless.

He paused in his work and looked out the window. There was one action he could take to make her a less desirable catch for the Duke. He could ignore her. Without the incentive of trying to take something Thomas wanted, there was a good chance the Duke's interest would move elsewhere. The man was such a simpleton he was unlikely to appreciate anything or anyone unless someone else wanted it.

But what good would such actions really do? If she didn't marry the Duke, it would be some other titled man and perhaps one even worse than the Duke, if that was possible. And at least she would get to be a duchess. There were certainly advantages to being at the pinnacle of society and, as she said, it was her dream. He just hoped her dream did not turn into a nightmare.

No, he would continue to play along with the Duke's ridiculous plan, endure one more interminable evening, mixing with people he had made a point of avoiding whenever possible and watching the disagreeable sight of the Duke of Hardgraves in the act of wooing the delightful Miss Lowerby.

Chapter Seven

Was it wrong to hope that the Duke's interest did wane, even just a little bit, so that Mr Hayward would once again have a purpose?

That was the question Grace had pondered for the remainder of the day and was still trying to find an answer to when she entered the drawing room for pre-dinner drinks.

The Duke smiled at her from across the room and her heart sank. His interest was not waning, not in the slightest. If anything, it was showing an increased level of vigour. Would that mean Mr Hayward *had* served his purpose? Would she never speak to him again, walk with him, laugh with him?

It should not matter, but the aching in her heart suggested it did matter, a great deal.

The Duke broke from the group surrounding him and headed straight for Grace and her grandmother. 'Miss Lowerby, you are a picture of youthful beauty tonight,' he said, taking her hand and kissing the back.

She made the smile she had perfected with many hours of practice in front of the looking glass. One that aimed to be both coquettish and alluring. One she hoped would hide her inner turmoil.

'Thank you, Your Grace,' she said with a curtsy.

The Duke nodded to her grandmother, but his gaze remained fixed on Grace, as if unable to look away.

'And did you enjoy your walk?' he asked, a challenging note in his tone.

'Yes, Your Grace,' she answered, unsure if that was what the Duke wanted to hear.

'My granddaughter was telling me how splendid your estate is.'

Grace had told her grandmother no such thing, but it mattered not. The Duke had been flattered, that was all that was required, even though it was Grace who should have been the one paying him the compliments.

'Yes, quite magnificent,' she added, causing her grandmother to smile in approval.

'Yes, I have ten thousand acres and some of the finest fishing rivers and game reserves in the county,' he said yet again and Grace nodded, smiled and tried to look interested as if she was hearing it for the first time. He continued talking about his estate and Grace was pleased no more was required of her, because, while he was speaking, she was far too conscious of Mr Hayward standing across the other side of the room. She forced herself to keep her focus fixed solely on the Duke and not to look in his direction, but that did not mean she was unaware of him, where he was in the room and to whom he was talking.

Out the corner of her eye, she saw a young lady join his group. Her attempt to maintain a delighted smile wavered and it took every ounce of willpower she possessed not to turn around to see who this young woman was.

He had said he was not interested in marrying, but if he did it would be to a woman who could be his helpmate, one he respected and admired. Did this young lady have those qualities? If only she could find a reason to look in Mr Hayward's direction and satisfy her curiosity.

But it would have to be a very convincing reason to look away from the Duke. Anything less than an enormous commotion on that side of the room would inflame her grandmother's wrath. After all, *Mr Hayward had served his purpose.* There was no justifiable reason why she should be at all interested in anything he was or wasn't doing, or who he was or wasn't talking to.

The dinner gong rang and the couples lined up to parade down the hallway to the dining room.

'Would you do me the honour?' the Duke said, offering his arm.

She exchanged a quick glance with her grandmother and they both knew what that meant. The honour was all Grace's. That position should have been reserved for the woman present who had the highest title and that most certainly was not Grace.

By taking her arm, he was all but declaring they were a courting couple.

Grace should be ecstatic. This was what she wanted. It was what her grandmother wanted. Her grandmother would now be so pleased with her, she might even hug Grace this time, rather than merely saying she could do so. That was something Grace had longed for all her life. So many times she had tried and failed to make her grandmother proud of her and now she was. She had always dreamed of being courted by a handsome man such as the Duke and now her dream was within her grasp. How could she not be ecstatic?

She sensed, rather than saw, Mr Hayward join the parade on the arm of the young lady he had been speaking to. Who was that woman? What was she to Mr Hayward?

Grace was tempted to turn around to find an answer to her questions or to ask the Duke, but she knew she would do neither.

Mr Hayward had served his purpose. She should forget all about him.

So instead she smiled at the Duke and placed her hand on the top of his, all the while fighting to ignore those whirling questions.

The Duke led her to the seat on his right, while her

grandmother had been assigned the seat on his left. Once again, he was letting Grace, her grandmother and the assembled guests know she was more than just another debutante. She was the one he had chosen.

The other guests lined up in front of their place names, with Mr Hayward at the far end of the table.

The footmen held out the seats of the ladies and with much rustling of silk and satin they took their places.

Throughout the twelve-course meal, the Duke continued to talk. Thankfully all he required from Grace was the occasional 'Oh, how fascinating!' or 'That is so interesting, Your Grace.' And even for her to once or twice say, 'That was so clever of you.'

At one time she had to bite her lip to stop herself from giggling, remembering her conversation with Mr Hayward when they had joked about such behaviour. With him, conversation flowed so freely, smiles and laughter came so easily. She so envied the young woman sitting next to him, even though she knew right now she would be the envy of every unmarried young woman in the room.

Despite that, she still wished to know who that young woman was at Mr Hayward's side.

'The table arrangements are simply divine,' she said to the Duke when there was a brief pause in his monologue. Under the guise of admiring the table setting, she tried to look down the table, to where Mr Hayward and that mystery woman were seated at the far end.

More than twenty guests separated them, along with a large floral arrangement in the centre of the table and several tall candelabras made even taller by their flickering candles, all contributing to thwarting her from seeing Mr Hayward's dinner companion.

And as for trying to hear what they were talking about, that was beyond impossible. Any words that might travel down the long table were drowned out by the noise of the guests talking and laughing and the clink of silverware on fine porcelain.

It was a fruitless task, so she turned her full attention once more back to the Duke, where it belonged.

The meal finally over, the ladies rose from the table and retired back to the drawing room, leaving the men to their cigars and brandies. Now she would get her opportunity. The women were all lined up in the order in which they had been seated. Dare she do something as crass as gawping over her shoulder to see which young lady was at the end of the line?

But before she could succumb to temptation, her grandmother took her arm. 'You've done it, my dear, darling child,' she whispered in her ear, barely containing her excitement.

Grace had to think for a moment what exactly she had done to make her grandmother so happy.

'You will soon be a duchess.'

Oh, yes, that. She smiled at her grandmother, wanting to share in her excitement.

They returned to the drawing room and her grandmother rushed over to join her friends, as if bursting to impart the good news and be bathed in their congratulations and envy. Grace watched the group of older women move into a chattering huddle and had no doubts that her success was the topic of their animated conversation.

The footman handed her a cup of coffee. She took a seat beside the fireplace and with gratitude used the time to relax before the men joined them and she would once again have to present herself as the ideal bride for the Duke.

She scanned the other young women in the room. Mr Hayward's companion had been wearing a cream gown, but then, so were at least five of the debutantes. Her chestnut hair had been braided and plaited and piled high on her head, but again, so was every debutante's in the room. She sighed, knowing she was unlikely to know the identity of the woman without doing something unforgivable and asking.

'I hear there is to be dancing tonight,' a young lady seated on a nearby sofa said. Grace quickly scrutinised her. She was thankfully dressed in a pale blue gown and was not Mr Hayward's companion.

'I wonder if Graceless will take another fall and

the Duke will realise that if you're born low you stay low-born.'

Grace froze, her cup halfway to her mouth, as the other girls giggled behind their fans, all looking in Grace's direction.

'It's a shame no one has yet told him what a fool she made of herself at his ball,' another added. 'Then he'd know it would be the joke throughout society that someone so lacking in grace and charm was called Grace and it would be, too, too funny for her to become a duchess and for everyone to have to refer to her as Your Grace.'

This caused the girls to giggle even louder while Grace wished she could curl up into a little ball, one so small she would all but disappear. Would she never be allowed to forget her shameful behaviour at the Duke's ball? It would seem not.

The men entered the room. The giggling ceased immediately. The young ladies all sat up straight, adopted the required polite smile, the requisite tilt of the head, and looked towards the men as if they were the sun rising over the eastern horizon.

Grace knew she should follow their example, but those cruel words were still ringing in her ears. The Duke hadn't seen her fall. If one of those girls told him, would he withdraw his attentions from her? And if he did so, would all the affection her grandmother had bestowed on her also be withdrawn? Would Graceless

Lower-Born prove herself to be just as much a disappointment as her mother had been?

Thomas returned to the drawing room with reluctance, certain he would have to endure more of the Duke's crowing. That puffed-up rooster had looked so pleased with himself throughout dinner and Thomas had not missed the looks of triumph he had repeatedly sent him while the brandy was being served.

The only way Thomas had managed to squash down his agitation was by reminding himself that everyone was close to getting what they wanted. He would get his land cheaper than he had originally asked, Miss Lowerby would become a duchess and the Duke would get a wife who was far too good for him.

He quickly scanned the room and saw Miss Lowerby, seated alone, her face dejected, her shoulders hunched. Something was wrong. He pushed past the other men crowded around the door, crossed the room and took the seat beside her without being invited.

'Grace, what is it? What's wrong?'

'It's nothing,' she mumbled.

'Is it the Duke? Has he said or done something to upset you?'

'No, no, it's not the Duke.' She looked towards the young women who had hurt her so. 'It's nothing, really.'

The chamber group seated in the corner struck up

a tune. Music filled the air and couples lined up for the first dance.

'Dance with me,' he said, offering her his hand. 'And tell me all about it.'

She quickly looked in her grandmother's direction. The old lady was watching them and with a quick nod of her head gave her permission.

'So what has happened that has made you look so sad when so far this evening has been such a success for you?'

'I suppose it's silly really, but those debutantes were laughing about my falling over at the Duke's ball and I suspect they're going to tell him that, you know, I completely embarrassed myself at his ball.'

He released an annoyed sigh. 'You know why they're doing that, don't you?'

'Because they're right. Graceless Lower-Born should never have thought she could possibly marry a duke.' She looked up at him. 'That's what they call me: Graceless Lower-Born.'

'Bullies always aim for what they think is your greatest vulnerability. Remember what I said to you at the Duke's ball? The secret is to not let them see that they have hurt you. If you do, then they will be relentless.'

'That's easy for you to say,' she murmured. 'No one would ever try to bully a man as strong as you.'

'That is where you're wrong. At school I was certainly the target of bullies.'

His mind shot back to those first days at school, to the relentless name calling and the constant threats of violence.

'What did you do?'

'Luckily for me, the bullies picked on something I cared nothing about. They thought my family's lack of a title was my vulnerability, but it was my strength. And you should be the same—make your vulnerabilities into your strength and be proud of yourself and all you've achieved.'

She stared at him with wide disbelieving eyes. 'You think I should be proud because I fell over in the middle of a ballroom?'

'Be proud that despite doing something that would be the ruin of a lesser young lady's Season, you managed to pull yourself up and go on to capture the interest of the most eligible man available this Season.'

'But I didn't pull myself up. You did. But their teasing is all so unfair. Why do they have to be so mean?'

'Because you have what they want. They might call you Lower-Born, but they weren't the ones sitting at his side at the dinner table. They weren't the one to whom he was giving his complete attention.'

'I think that is also because of you and the Duke's jealousy.'

'That's not true.'

She raised her eyebrows.

'Well, not entirely,' he added. 'But he is only jealous because he wants the prettiest, most delightful, most elegant young lady in the room as his own.'

'You certainly know how to flatter, don't you, Mr Hayward? Anyone would think you were the one who attended finishing school.'

She gave a small laugh and relief washed through him. It pained him so much to see her unhappy and he knew that was all he wanted for her. It was just unfortunate that she thought her happiness lay in capturing a man who was so unworthy of her.

'Or should I call you Thomas, now that you've called me Grace?'

He raised his eyebrows at this surprising question.

'When you asked me to dance, you called me Grace.'

'My apologies, that was forward of me.'

'You're forgiven, but only on the condition that you allow me to call you Thomas.'

'I would be honoured, Grace.'

They smiled at each other as they continued to dance, then her smile turned to a slight frown. 'Your schooldays must have been miserable if you were constantly having to deal with bullies.'

He shrugged as if to dismiss all those disagreeable times. 'They would have been, but on my first day I also made two very good friends, Isaac Radcliff and Sebastian Kingsley. They were also outsiders at the school and the three of us took great delight in being the best at everything. I suppose we were trying to prove something, to ourselves and everyone who looked down on us.'

'You're lucky to have friends,' she said, that look of sadness returning. 'But I have a friend now as well, don't I?' she added, smiling up at him. 'A very good friend who always seems to be at hand when I need to be rescued.'

'And if you ever need a friend, at any time, remember, I will always be at your service,' he said, surprising himself with this admission.

But she did deserve a friend and looking out for her was the least he could do to make up for her unwittingly being caught up in a game between himself and the Duke, even if that game did end with her becoming the Duchess of Hardgraves.

She bit the edge of her lip in that now familiar manner. 'So, who were you sitting next to at the dinner table?'

He cast his mind back, trying to remember. 'Lady Catherine and Lady Stephanie, I believe.'

Thomas hoped that was what they were called. All the debutantes tended to look alike, and their conversation was unvaryingly the same and unvaryingly dull. 'Why do you ask?'

'No reason.' She smiled up at him, her eyes glinting

in the candlelight. 'No reason at all, except I think you mean Lady Catarina and Lady Seraphina.'

'Yes, perhaps.'

The dance over, Thomas escorted a much happier Grace back to her grandmother, who was standing beside a scowling duke. Good, he should be made to work for the hand of such a worthy young lady and not expect her to be handed to him on a silver platter, the way everything else in his life had.

'I believe you promised the first dance to me,' the Duke said, that childish petulance in his voice.

'My fault entirely,' Thomas answered before she could make an apology, one the Duke did not deserve. She was not his property. Not yet. And she should not have to defer to him.

'Well, let's rectify that situation, what?' the Duke said, taking Grace's arm as if he already owned her.

He led her back out on to the dance floor and Thomas watched as he wrapped his arms around her waist and held her somewhat closer than was demanded for the gallop.

'Don't they make a perfect couple?' Lady Ashbridge said.

'Hmm,' was the only response Thomas believed that comment required.

'My granddaughter is quite smitten with the Duke.'

'Is she?' he responded, still watching the Duke and fighting the temptation to stride across the dance floor and pull him off her. His hand had moved lower down her back and was now resting on the top of her buttocks. Lady Ashbridge must have seen that and must know it was unacceptable behaviour. But she quite obviously did not care.

'Yes, quite perfect,' Lady Ashbridge continued. 'It is her dream to become a duchess, you know.'

'So I hear.'

'Good, because she will never be yours.'

He turned to look at Lady Ashbridge, who, despite her snappish tone, was smiling as if they were having a polite conversation.

'It appears, on that, Lady Ashbridge, you and I are in complete agreement.'

'Are we?' she asked, her voice still curt while her smile never faltered. 'I saw how you were looking at her while the two of you were dancing. But if you have any thoughts of trying to lead my granddaughter astray, then you can put those ideas right out of your head.'

'As lovely as your granddaughter is, I have no intentions of taking a wife any time soon. All I have ever offered her is my friendship. And as for leading her—'

'Good, then you can stop trying to bedazzle her. She is a naive, chaste young lady and a man such as yourself could easily turn her head.'

It appeared his use as bait had come to an end. The Duke's performance this evening had presumably convinced Lady Ashbridge that an offer was imminent and Thomas had become redundant to this woman's plans.

'You have no reason to fear me turning her head, Lady Ashbridge. You have convinced your granddaughter that what she wants more than anything else is to be married to a duke. After many years of being told what to think, what to want and how to feel, I do not believe anything I or anyone else could do would convince her that it is not her own dream, but one that has been imposed on her.'

The polite smile faltered and briefly turned into a grimace, before returning, just as bright and just as false as before.

'You have no right to question anything I do. All I care about is what is best for my granddaughter and I will not have you ruining my plans for her. I saw the way the two of you looked at each other when you danced together. It would be best for all concerned if you have nothing more to do with her.'

Thomas wanted to argue, but perhaps she was right. Despite himself, he had become far too involved in these people's intrigues and stratagems. This was not his world. He did not belong here. He should just get what he came for and withdraw.

'As you wish.'

He and Lady Ashbridge turned back to watching the couple dancing in the centre of the drawing room.

Still holding her far too close, the Duke leant down to whisper in Grace's ear while he stared straight at Thomas. Her eyes grew wide, her mouth opened in surprise. She looked over at Thomas, then her gaze moved to her grandmother.

Lady Ashbridge nodded her head rapidly, no longer worrying about the need for discretion or the veneer of politeness.

Grace copied the motion and gave a small nod of her head and he could see her lips form the word *yes*.

It was done. The Duke had made his offer of courtship, maybe even marriage. Thomas was tempted to rush across the room and tell her she was making a big mistake, but it was none of his business. And even if it was, what good would it really do? This was what she thought she wanted and why would she listen to him? She would now be a duchess. Lady Ashbridge would also get what she wanted and would perhaps stop treating her granddaughter simply as a means to achieve her own ambitions, but as someone who should be loved and cherished.

And Thomas would get his land at a lower price. Although right now, that felt like a very hollow victory.

Chapter Eight

Grace fought to maintain her smile while turbulent emotions swirled within her. She should be jubilant. The Season had barely begun and she already had what she wanted. The Duke had asked to court her. Well, he hadn't actually said it was he who wanted to court her. He had asked her if she would like to be courted by him, but surely it was the same thing.

She was not sure why she had hesitated and not given him an immediate yes—yes, yes, of course she wanted it, wanted it more than anything in the world. She wanted him to court her, to marry her, to make her a duchess and give her the fairy-tale marriage she had always dreamed of.

Yet, between him asking and her answering, it had not been jubilation that had coursed through her veins. And why had she looked to Thomas?

She forced herself to smile brighter. She would not think of those things, nor would she focus on the pain in the centre of her chest, or the tightness of her stomach. She was to be courted by a duke, the most eligible man available this Season. She was a success. Her grandmother would be proud of her. She was proud of herself.

'Now that that is settled,' the Duke said, finally removing his stroking hand from her arm, 'will you excuse me? I believe there is a card game in progress.'

Not waiting for her response, he gave a quick bow of his head and departed, leaving Grace to cross the room alone and impart the wonderous news to her grandmother.

Thomas was still standing beside her grandmother, watching her, and his face did not suggest he was happy with what had just occurred. But surely that mattered not. She was not here to make him happy. He had said she should do whatever it was she wanted with her life and this was what she wanted, what she had always wanted, and now it was almost a reality.

'Miss Lowerby, Lady Ashbridge, if you will excuse me,' Thomas said as soon as she joined them.

Her grandmother didn't reply, nor did she curtsy, her focus being intent only on Grace.

'Don't tell me yet,' she whispered. 'Wait until we are alone in your bedchamber, then you can tell me everything the Duke said.'

With that, she took Grace's arm, rushed her out of the room, up the stairs and into her bedchamber with as much haste as possible without actually running.

'What did he say?' her grandmother asked the moment the door shut behind them. 'Did he propose? Am I going to receive a formal offer for your hand?' She tapped her chin with her index finger in thought. 'I suppose it should be your uncle who he makes the offer to, as he is now the Earl of Ashbridge, but I am your nearest living relative, even if I am a woman.' She flicked her hand in dismissal. 'But it matters not. Your uncle will do whatever I tell him to and how could anyone turn down a duke?' She laughed at the impossibility of that idea.

'So tell me, my dear child, what exactly did he say?' She took Grace's hands, stood back and smiled at her, a genuine, warm smile that filled Grace's heart with joy. Then she did what Grace had been longing for her to do her entire life. Pulled her into an embrace. Like a child, Grace sank into her arms. As a child she had yearned to be held by her grandmother, to be cherished and loved, and now she was. All other, confused feelings evaporated. She had made her grandmother proud. She had made her grandmother love her.

'Was it a formal proposal?' her grandmother asked, in the voice of an excited debutante.

'No, not exactly.'

Her grandmother dropped her arms and took a step backwards. 'What? Well, what did he say to you then?'

The churning emotions returned as the need to have her grandmother's approval gnawed at her like a physical ache. 'He asked if I would be agreeable to being courted by him,' she said in a choked voice.

Her grandmother nodded and once again tapped her chin. 'Yes, that will do. It's not as good as a proposal, but it's the next best thing and will inevitably lead to an engagement, then marriage. There is no reason why it should not.'

The finger dropped from her chin and she smiled. 'Oh, my dear, dear child, this is wonderful, more wonderful than I could ever imagine.' She resumed tapping her chin. 'I wonder if the Prince of Wales will attend the wedding, maybe even Queen Victoria herself. After all, it's not every day that a duke marries.'

Grace kept smiling, caught up in her grandmother's excitement.

'I could tell by the way he was touching you when you were dancing that he would have to make an offer of some sort. To not do so would be a disgrace and a man like the Duke of Hardgraves would never do anything disgraceful.'

Grace's confusion once again forced its way up through her happiness as she remembered the way the Duke had held her far too close while they danced, and how he had kept rubbing his fingers up and down her arm.

'Grandmama,' she said and bit her bottom lip, as she tried to compose questions she was unsure she should ask. 'I don't really like it when the Duke touches me. Is that normal?'

'What?' Her grandmother frowned at the question. 'Yes. I suppose so. It doesn't really matter, does it? It's not your place to like or dislike him touching you. Your place is to do what he wants. Your pleasure comes from pleasing him.'

'It does?'

'Oh, my dear, you are such an innocent. I blame myself. I should have explained all this before the Season began. Sit down, my dear, and let me explain a few things to you.'

She took a seat on the sofa by the window. Her grandmother sat beside her and took Grace's hands, her expression serious.

'The Duke will have his needs and it is your duty to satisfy those needs, whatever they might be. That is all that will be expected of you. Once you are married, he will want you to provide him with an heir and you must submit to him in the bedchamber and do all that you are instructed to do in order for that to be accomplished.'

'I see,' Grace said, not entirely seeing at all and not particularly liking the sound of the words 'submit' and 'doing as she was instructed'.

'But that won't happen until we are married?' she asked, hoping that would be the case.

'Ideally, but now that the Duke has said he wishes to court you he can be granted some liberties.'

'Liberties? What sort of liberties?'

'That will depend on the Duke and what he wants. Just do as he asks. He may have a mistress and not require anything of you, merely that you perform your duties once you are wed. Then when you have provided him with an heir, he might require no more of you. It is entirely up to him.'

'A mistress?'

Her grandmother smiled as if she had said something quaint. 'Yes, men of the Duke's standing often keep a mistress, sometimes several. That is something you will just turn a blind eye to.'

'But—'

Her grandmother held up her hand to stop her objections. 'You will never question anything the Duke does.'

'So if he touches me again, the way he did tonight, that is all right?'

'Yes, and, well, whatever else he wishes to do. And if he does take a few liberties, do not screw your face up the way you did tonight. You don't have to look as if you're enjoying it, you're to be the wife after all, not the mistress, but don't at any time let him think that you find his touch objectionable.'

'I see,' Grace said, suppressing that forbidden look of horror. 'So, what sort of liberties might he take?'

'Oh, for goodness' sake, girl, stop with all these questions.'

Grace's heart lurched and her body tensed, as it always did when she upset her grandmother.

'Just do as the Duke wishes. He is the man and he is a duke. It is your duty to do as he bids.'

'Of course, Grandmama,' Grace replied, causing her grandmother to smile once again and pat her hand.

'Good girl.'

Grace smiled back at her, while questions swirled unanswered in her mind. She really did not like the Duke touching her, nor did she like the idea of him taking liberties, whatever that meant. Kissing, probably, more touching, perhaps. Thankfully, her grandmother had said she was not expected to enjoy it, because she doubted she ever could.

Her thoughts strayed once again to Thomas. If he had been the one to caress her arm, if his hand had slipped lower down her back so it was resting on the top of her buttocks, she was sure she would not object.

Heat pulsed through her body at the thought of Thomas kissing her, of his hand stroking her, of his hand moving to places it shouldn't.

'I can see by that flush on your face that you are thinking of all the ways you can please the Duke,' her grandmother said, once again patting her hand. 'Well, I will leave you alone with those thoughts and tomorrow I'm sure the Duke will be asking me for a quiet word.'

Grace had hoped for another hug, a stroke of her cheek, even a kiss on the forehead, but her grandmother departed without bestowing any of those longed-for gestures of affection.

She rang for her lady's maid to help her undress, then climbed into bed. She knew she should be thinking about this evening's joyous outcome, but all she could think about was how, if it was Thomas she was supposed to submit to, if Thomas was the one she should allow to take liberties, she would be more than willing to do so.

Chapter Nine

'I think we can unequivocally declare me the winner of this wooing duel, can't we, Hayward?' the Duke said when Thomas entered the study the next morning.

'Yes, you won. Now it's time for you to sign those papers.'

The Duke picked up his pen and dipped it in the ink pot, then smiled at Thomas.

'You were never really in contention, though, were you? You should stick to things you know something about, like business and making money, and leave courtship and gallantry to the men who were born to such things.'

'Indeed. Now if you'll just sign the papers, I'll be able to inform my bank to forward you the reduced sum for your land.' Thomas had thought that might temper the man's bluster, but it did not. He still thought he had put Thomas firmly in his place and had finally got that victory he'd desperately been seeking since their schooldays.

'Yes, when it comes to selecting a mate, women always know to go for the most superior man. It's only natural. It's what they're destined to do.'

'Indeed,' Thomas said, pointing to the line waiting for the Duke's signature.

'But you tried your best, I suppose,' he said, shaking his head as if the insult was a compliment. 'But you have to realise, you can't go chasing after a young lady like you're a tom pursuing a cat on heat. These things have to be done with finesse and that is something that can't be learnt. It is inborn.'

The man really was an insufferable dolt. The sooner Thomas could leave this house and focus entirely on building a railway through his property the better.

'I'm sure you're right,' he added, once again tapping the document.

'I'm pleased you finally can see that I am the superior man.' With that, he signed away his land and ran his blotter over the wet ink. 'Now, you can sign this.'

The Duke removed a piece of paper from his inside pocket and handed it to Thomas. He read the words and sighed. It spelt out the terms of the bet and that the winner was the one that Grace chose.

'Go on, sign it, next to the line that says loser,' the Duke said gleefully, as if the document had some value.

Thomas signed it and threw it across the desk to the

Duke, then picked up the document that was actually legal and folded it in two.

'Thank you for selling your land to me for less than I was prepared to pay.' He took great pleasure in watching the Duke's smug smile falter as doubt started to undermine his sense of superiority.

'You do realise you made a bet in which even if I lost I won, and even if you won you lost, but all in all I'm pleased to do business with you. I've now paid much less than I intended for your land and you have missed out on money that you most sorely need.'

Confusion distorted the Duke's features and Thomas could almost see the effort it was taking for him to come to the realisation that he had just squandered part of his inheritance on a ridiculous bet.

'So when will you be announcing the engagement in the newspapers?' Thomas asked and, despite himself, he could not entirely mask his displeasure.

'Oh, all in good time, all in good time,' the Duke said, eyeing him suspiciously.

'You are intending to marry Miss Lowerby, aren't you?'

'Why, Hayward, despite me winning her outright, I believe you're still hankering after the pretty little thing, aren't you?'

Thomas placed the document in the inside pocket of his jacket. 'I'm merely pointing out that for a man who puts such an emphasis on gallantry and courtliness, it would be bad form to lead the young lady on.'

The Duke's smile returned, more gleeful than before. 'You do care for her, don't you? Everything you said about not being able to lose our bet was just balderdash to cover up the fact that you lost what you really wanted. Well, you did lose and I won. You can't have her. She wants me, not you.'

Thomas was sorely tempted to plant his fist in his smug face, but that would do nobody any good. And he was right. Grace was his and Thomas could not have her.

Instead, he leant over the desk, his face mere inches from the Duke. 'You will treat her well, you cretin, or I will ruin you, do you understand?'

He shouldn't have taken so much pleasure in the look of fear that crossed the Duke's face, but then, as the man pointed out, Thomas was from a class that knew nothing of gallantry.

Having made his point, he departed, certain the Duke would take heed of his words. He had promised Grace he would always be her friend and he intended to look out for her, whether she was aware of it or not.

While it was tempting to make a quiet departure, it would be remiss of him not to say goodbye to her, so once he had given instructions to his valet to pack his bags he went in search of her.

Finding her seated in the morning room, staring out

the window, he paused briefly at the door and watched her. She did not look like a young woman in love, but one who had been abandoned on a distant shore and was looking out for a ship to come sailing over the horizon to save her. She turned to look in his direction.

'Thomas,' she murmured, then smiled forlornly. 'Won't you join me?'

He took the seat beside her. 'I have heard the news about your courtship and have...' he paused '... I have offered my congratulations to the Duke.'

She nodded and gave him a small smile. 'Thank you.'

'You now have all your heart desires,' he added, fighting to keep any cynicism out of his voice.

'Yes,' she said. 'And what of you? Did you achieve all you wished for and can now extend your railway over the Duke's land?'

'Yes,' he responded, trying to ignore the guilt over how he had achieved that wish. 'And now I intend to depart, but I did not want to leave without saying goodbye.'

'Oh, but I will be seeing you again during the Season, won't I?'

'I don't usually attend such social events. I only attended this one because the Duke left me little option.'

Her brow furrowed. 'Oh, I see. I was hoping... Well, I will miss our talks.'

'Our talks might not be acceptable now that you are to marry the Duke.'

'He didn't say he would marry me. He just asked if I would be agreeable to a courtship.'

'And you said yes—that means spending time with other men will no longer be acceptable.'

'Oh, I see.' The furrows in her brow deepened.

'Goodbye, Grace.'

'Yes, goodbye, Thomas.'

He remained seated. 'Always remember, you are a beautiful, intelligent young lady and the Duke is lucky to have you.'

She smiled at him, the first real smile he'd seen since he entered the morning room.

'You will make a perfect duchess, one who I suspect will eventually be running this estate much better than the Duke ever could. Never, ever think you are not worthy of the position of duchess.'

'Thank you,' she murmured.

'Goodbye, Grace.' And with that, he stood and departed before he said anything more that he should not.

Grace watched him go, suddenly feeling more alone than she had felt in years. If he did not attend society events, then she was unlikely to ever see him again. She blinked to flick away some ridiculous tears that were threatening to fall. She was being silly. She was about to be courted by a duke, no less. Her Season was already more glorious than she could possibly have hoped for.

She turned to look out of the window. This was where she would stay for the rest of the morning, so she could get a final glimpse of him as he drove up the gravel pathway and departed from her life.

'Is this where you are hiding yourself away?' her grandmother said from the doorway.

Grace turned towards her and tried to smile.

'Now, now, now,' she said, taking the seat beside Grace. 'There is no need to look so despondent, my dear. The Duke is a busy man. He can't spend all his time in your company and he does have other guests to entertain.'

'Yes, Grandmama.'

'Now, come and join me and the other ladies in the drawing room. We've got a lively game of whist going and I'm sure everyone is anxious to ingratiate themselves to the next Duchess of Hardgraves.'

'Have you told them?' Grace asked, shocked at her grandmother's lack of propriety. The Duke had not yet made their courtship formal.

'Of course I have done no such thing, but everyone could see the way he was looking at you and no one missed that quiet conversation the two of you had last night. You've made a lot of debutantes very jealous and a lot of mothers extremely annoyed,' her grandmother said, as if these were admirable accomplishments. 'So come along, dear, don't dally.'

Grace gave one last look out the window, before following her grandmother down the hallway and into the drawing room. She was greeted with a row of polite smiles as false as her own. But her grandmother was correct. While they chatted over the card table, everyone deferred to her as if she was a woman of high status and not the daughter of a piano teacher. Even the debutantes who had mocked her were now solicitous, asking her opinions and listening as if everything she had to say was of the greatest interest.

Was this what the rest of her life would be like? Would she never again know who really liked her for who she was and who only acted as if they did because of her title?

She looked towards the window, wondering if Thomas had left yet.

A footman informed the ladies that luncheon had been served and they joined the men in the dining room, where she was once again the focus of much smiling and looks of admiration from people who had previously shown her no interest.

When the meal finally came to an end, everyone retired to their rooms to change for their trip home. Grace's lady's maid's mood seemed as despondent as her own as she helped her into her dark blue dress, scarf and travelling coat.

Her grandmother entered her bedchamber and dismissed Molly with a flick of her hand. ‘He hasn’t had a quiet word with me yet,’ she said, scowling at Grace as if she were to blame.

Grace shrugged one shoulder, not knowing how she was expected to respond.

‘Don’t do that,’ her grandmother snapped. ‘It’s most unbecoming in a lady.’

Grace could point out it was a gesture her grandmother often made, but knew better than to do so.

‘Perhaps he’ll have a word with us as we depart. Yes, that’s probably what he’ll do. He’ll take me aside and have a quiet word with me then.’ She nodded her head, but continued to frown. ‘Well, come on, make haste, the train won’t wait and we don’t want to have to hurry our departure.’

They joined the assembled guests at the entrance way, where goodbyes were being exchanged, cheeks were being kissed and promises of ‘we must meet again, soon’ made.

The Duke was present and was fully occupied, laughing with his male guests. A line of carriages arrived, some to take those who lived nearby home, others to transport guests to the railway station. The Duke helped each young lady and her escort into their waiting carriages.

When there was only one carriage left, Grace and her grandmother walked down the steps to where the Duke was standing by the open door of the carriage.

He helped Grace in and, as he had done with all the other debutantes, lightly kissed the back of her hand. 'Goodbye, Miss Lowerby,' he said. 'It has been a delight having you as a guest in my home.'

Grace waited, expecting him to say more, but he merely smiled at her, so she climbed into the carriage.

'I believe we need to have a conversation,' her grandmother said, standing at the foot of the carriage and rather rudely taking hold of the Duke's arm.

'All in good time, Lady Ashbridge. All in good time.' Still smiling, the Duke pulled his arm away. 'I wish you a pleasant journey home.'

Her grandmother was left with no other option than to climb into the carriage and take her seat. And with that, the Duke walked away and out the window Grace could see him join a group of male friends and the sound of their loud laughter reached them as they drove off down the gravel pathway.

Grace bit her bottom lip and looked tentatively at her grandmother. She was sitting ramrod straight on the leather bench, outrage written large on her face.

'He will probably send a letter as soon as he returns to London,' she finally said as the carriage approached the small country station. 'Yes, that would be more appropriate.'

Grace chose to say nothing. She had no notion of how a courtship was to be conducted, she just wished the Duke had been more attentive to her, as she hated to see her grandmother looking so distressed.

The train journey home seemed even longer than the trip to Cornwall had been and was made even more trying by her grandmother's continued ill temper.

As she looked out at the passing scenery, Grace wondered where Thomas might now be, what he would be doing and who he would be seeing. Although he said he did not attend society events, maybe there would be a chance that they would see each other again. Maybe he would want to buy more land off the Duke, or would be in attendance when the rail tracks were laid through what had once been the Duke's land.

And if they did meet again, surely there would be nothing wrong with greeting an acquaintance. After all, they *had* been formally introduced and he *was* a friend of the Duke's, or at least had been a guest in his house.

After an interminably long journey, the train pulled into Paddington Station, the noise and bustle a shock compared to the quiet of the countryside. Trains arriving and leaving from the platforms sent out large gusts of hissing steam, a platoon of porters urgently raced up and down, countless passengers moved in every direction and a cacophony of voices and whistles filled the air.

She followed her grandmother down the platform to their waiting carriage, then travelled through the busy London streets to their quiet townhouse. Now all she had to do was wait until the Duke contacted her and their courtship could begin in earnest.

At breakfast the next morning her grandmother urgently flicked through the first post of the day.

'I didn't really expect a note from him. Not yet. He might not even be back in London,' her grandmother said, the disappointment in her voice contradicting her words. Leaving the unopened letters lying on the table, she went back to eating her breakfast.

The second mail delivery of the day also contained no letter from the Duke, nor did the third.

Days passed with no note from him. Her grandmother's temper grew worse. An unpleasant atmosphere permeated every area of the house and, like Grace, the servants walked around as if on tiptoes, their bodies tense, just waiting to be on the receiving end of some criticism from her grandmother.

A week had passed and still there was no note, no visit. Nor were there any cards, flowers, or invitations, all the things her grandmother had said one would expect from a man who was courting a young lady. It was as if the offer had never been made.

With each passing day her grandmother's rage increased until Grace could hardly bear to be in the same room. But bear it she must.

The arrival of the mail was particularly tense. It became a familiar pattern. The footman would enter with the letters on a silver tray and his sympathetic smile at Grace would tell her all she needed to know before her grandmother took the letters. There was still no note from the Duke.

When they entered the second week with no message, her grandmother finally exploded over the breakfast table, her fist hitting the table, making the cups, saucers and egg cups jump.

'He has made a fool of me,' she all but screamed, glaring at Grace as if this was all her fault. 'He has made a fool of you. He made a promise and now he has all but rescinded it.' She threw down the letters she was holding, and they scatted across the table. 'We are going to have to accept that the Duke is not courting you.'

Grace stared back at her grandmother, hardly able to believe what she was hearing. Her grandmother never conceded defeat, but she was now. She would not have to marry the Duke. That was terrible. Grace knew it to be, yet her shoulders relaxed slightly and that churning in her stomach that had been her constant companion since the Duke had whispered to her in the drawing room calmed somewhat.

There would be no more waiting anxiously for his letter, hoping it would come so her grandmother's temper would be pacified, but dreading its arrival because so much would then be expected of her.

'Thankfully society has no knowledge of your shame,' her grandmother continued, as if talking to herself. 'As far as anyone knows, the Duke still showed you special favour, but no actual offer was made.'

'Yes, Grandmama,' Grace said dutifully, all the while thinking, *It's over.*

'And there is no reason why you can't be in favour again and be favoured to such an extent that he has no choice but to make a formal proposal of marriage.'

The churning in her stomach rumbled back into life.

'And we know exactly how to get him to do that, don't we?' Her grandmother smiled at her, a smile that suggested victory was imminent.

'We do?'

'We need Mr Hayward.'

At the sound of his name, Grace's heart skipped inside her chest. 'Mr Hayward?' she asked, loving being able to say out loud the name of the man who was constantly in her thoughts.

'Yes, Mr Hayward's presence seems just the catalyst needed to remind the Duke that you are the one he wants.'

Grace placed her hands on her stomach, preparing herself to ask the difficult question. 'Does that mean I'm to encourage Mr Hayward again?'

Please, please, say yes.

'I can see you're starting to understand how this works,' her grandmother said.

Grace smiled at the compliment, not caring that her grandmother thought she wanted to see Thomas again so he could once again be used to incite the attentions of the Duke. She was going to see him again. That was all that mattered.

Chapter Ten

'A Lady Ashbridge has requested to see you, sir.'

Thomas looked up from his desk at his secretary standing by the door.

Lady Ashbridge? What could that dragon possibly want with him? But there was only one way to find out.

'Show her in, thank you, Worthington.'

The man bowed and departed and soon Lady Ashbridge bustled in, all strained smiles and false politeness, putting Thomas on his guard. He stood behind his desk and indicated for her to take a seat, which she did with much rustling and flouncing of her skirt.

'How lovely to see you again, Mr Hayward,' she said, causing Thomas to raise his eyebrows in disbelief.

'And what a delightful office you have.' She looked around, taking in the bookshelves full of bound ledgers lining the walls, the leather furniture, then back to his oak desk, with its piles of papers awaiting his attention as soon as she left.

'This looks like quite the hive of activity.'

Thomas stifled a sigh of impatience. 'And to what do I owe the pleasure of this visit?' he said as he took his seat, aware that it was unlikely to contain any pleasure for either of them.

'I believe I owe you an apology, Mr Hayward,' she said, her smile fading and an equally false look of regret crossing her usually stern features.

'Apology?' he prompted.

'Yes, at the Duke of Hardgraves's weekend party I was perhaps a tad rude to you.'

A tad. The lady was certainly one for understatement.

'Yes. I believe I told you to stay away from my granddaughter. That was very rude of me.' She sighed lightly as if unable to believe that she could do something so out of character. 'Especially as you had shown my granddaughter nothing but your friendship.'

Thomas looked at the elderly woman over his desk and made no comment, waiting to discover exactly what game she was now playing.

'My granddaughter is fond of you and I believe if you wished to continue with this friendship, then that would be acceptable.'

Thomas continued to say nothing. Lady Ashbridge moved uncomfortably in the plush leather seat.

'Very acceptable,' she added, her smile becoming increasingly strained.

He remained silent, enjoying her discomfort.

'If that is what you wish, Lady Ashbridge, then, yes, I am prepared to continue with our friendship, but I ask one thing of you.'

'Oh, and what might that be?' she asked, tilting her head as if she really did care about anything he might ask.

'Honesty.'

She all but jumped back in her chair and stared at him, her brow furrowed as if this was a concept unfamiliar to her.

'I'm assuming things have not gone quite so smoothly with the Duke of Hardgraves as you had hoped or you would not be here in my office.'

'Oh, no, my granddaughter has—'

He held up his hand to still her words. 'Honesty, Lady Ashbridge.'

'Oh, all right then,' she said, lifting her nose and pursing her lips. 'The Duke has made no contact with Grace since our return from his estate.'

A sense of relief swept over him, to be quickly replaced with concern for Grace. She must be devastated, humiliated even, that the Duke should reject her after his offer of courtship. And it was all because of that bet. This was all his fault.

'And what do you wish me to do to rectify that situation?'

'I believe if we are being honest then you know the answer to that question,' the canny older woman said.

'You wish me to what, pay court to Miss Lowerby, to reignite the Duke's interest?'

'Yes,' came her brief and undeniably honest answer.

'And I assume you then wish me to graciously bow out when she does recapture his interest.'

'Yes.'

He remained silent while he digested this outrageous request.

'And is Miss Lowerby in agreement with this?' he finally asked.

'Of course she is. Despite everything, she is a sensible girl. She could see as clearly as I could the effect spending time with you had on the Duke. And she has, well, some affection for you, so to spend time in your company will not be arduous for her.'

And he, too, had some affection for Grace, perhaps too much affection, and found her company far from arduous. Since he'd left Hardgraves's estate, he had been doing something he had never done before—scouring the society pages to see any mention of her being seen in the company of the Duke. And he had to admit he was somewhat relieved when their names were not mentioned.

But did he really want to be used in this way?

'I wouldn't ask, but this has all been so humiliating for my granddaughter.' Lady Ashbridge pulled a lace handkerchief out of her reticule and dabbed the corner of her eyes. It seemed honesty was now being replaced with play-acting.

'She had to endure that awful incident at the Duke's ball, which I believe everyone saw, and now it appears the Duke has abandoned her.' She gave a small sniff.

Despite the theatrics, Thomas knew what she was saying was correct. Both events would be humiliating for Grace and at future social events those bullying debutantes would be certain to not let an opportunity pass to further ridicule her.

'It was her dream to become a titled lady, but now that the Duke has spurned her, she is receiving no invitations, no expressions of interest from any other young gentlemen,' Lady Ashbridge pleaded. 'It has been a disastrous Season for her and she is so intensely sad.' The dabbing continued along with a few more sniffs. 'All her dreams have been destroyed.'

'You make a fine actress, at least for a melodrama, Lady Ashbridge,' he said curtly, causing the older woman to drop her handkerchief from her eyes and glare at him. 'Although I believe the sniffling was rather overdoing it.'

'Well, are you going to help or not?' she snapped at him. 'You did say you were her friend. Isn't this what friends do? Help each other out in their times of need?'

'Yes. I will do as you request.'

'Excellent,' Lady Ashbridge said, standing up. 'I'll tell my granddaughter to expect you at three o'clock this afternoon so the two of you can take a walk in Hyde Park.' Having got what she wanted, she briskly walked out of the office.

Thomas looked back down at the pile of papers on his desk. He had work to do and, unlike the aristocracy, he did not fritter away his afternoons promenading and socialising, but it would not hurt to take off one afternoon, especially if it meant seeing Grace again.

'He has agreed to escort you on a walk around Hyde Park this afternoon,' her grandmother announced the moment she arrived home.

It took every ounce of willpower Grace possessed to not react to this news and remain seated demurely on the sofa while continuing to embroider the delicate flowers on her sampler.

She was to see him again. After these long days and nights when she had thought of nothing but his laughter, his voice, the touch of his arm as they walked together, she was to see him again.

'That is indeed excellent news,' she said, hoping her voice had not revealed her excitement.

'Now remember, make the walk as public as possible,' her grandmother added as she took her seat.

'The more people who see the two of you together, the more the likelihood that it will get back to the Duke.'

'Yes, Grandmama.' She placed her sampler on the side table. 'I suppose I should change into a suitable dress and get Molly to style my hair.'

'Yes. You need to look as attractive as possible.'

Grace fought to restrain her smile when what she really wanted to do was laugh with joy and maybe even dance and sing. She would be seeing him again. It was almost impossible to believe and she had the Duke and his absence to thank for bringing him back into her life.

With as much decorum as possible, she left the drawing room, then rushed up to her bedchamber and pushed the bell to summon Molly. She then flew to her wardrobe to inspect the gowns that he had not yet seen, determined to select the most flattering.

Molly knocked on the door, entered and curtsied.

'Oh, Molly, I have to look my very best for a walk in Hyde Park. What do you suggest I wear?' she asked, pushing the gowns along the rail as she searched for perfection.

'It is good to hear the Duke has finally contacted you, miss,' Molly said as she joined her at the wardrobe.

'What? No, he hasn't. I'm to walk in Hyde Park with Mr Hayward.' She bit her lip as if she had revealed too much. 'Grandmama says it is what I need to do to once again gain the Duke's affections, so I must look my best.'

'I believe the blue-and-white-striped gown brings out the colour of your eyes.' Molly went over to the dressing table and picked up the curling tongs. 'If we have the time, I could style your hair with soft ringlets around your face and I could sweep the remainder up into a high, full bun on the top of your head and weave it with blue and white ribbons. That would look ever so feminine and sophisticated.'

Molly smiled as she waited for her answer, seemingly bubbling with as much excitement as Grace. 'Yes, let's do that,' she said, pulling the blue-and-white dress out of the wardrobe while Molly summoned a servant to heat up the tongs. 'After all, the Duke must see me at my very best,' she added in case Molly thought there was any other reason for all this fuss.

'Of course, miss.'

The two women set to work and Grace watched herself transform in front of the looking glass. Molly was as usual correct in all her choices.

'This style is perfect,' she said as Molly held up a hand mirror to show her the back of her head in the looking glass.

'Thank you, miss. I'm sure no man will be able to resist you.'

Grace smiled at her lady's maid, then suddenly remembered that Thomas was due at three o'clock. She collected her lace gloves and returned to the drawing room to await his arrival.

Her grandmother gave her an assessing look as she entered and with a nod of approval declared her suitable.

Her heart racing, her stomach fluttering, she took her seat, picked up her embroidery and attempted to give the appearance this was simply another afternoon, one where nothing of any particular importance was happening.

The footman entered and announced Mr Hayward's arrival. It was mere luck that Grace did not plunge the embroidery needle into her thumb, so shaky were her hands.

'Show him in,' her grandmother said, as Grace placed the embroidery on the side table, then picked it up again, sat up straighter, then once again returned the embroidery sample to the table.

He entered the room and Grace had to suppress a little gasp of surprise. Had he always been this sublimely handsome? Was his hair always that black? Were his eyes always that dark and intense?

Her heart did the seemingly impossible and beat even faster as her gaze moved to the angular lines of his jaw. She imagined running her finger over the dark stubble. What would it feel like? Soft? Spiky? Her fingers were itching to find out.

He strode across the room, drawing her eyes to his

strong body, his long slim legs and powerful shoulders. It was a body she remembered leaning into during their walks, a body she had been unable to stop thinking about all the time they were apart.

Her gaze remained fixed on him and she hardly heard the greeting he made to her grandmother. Then he turned to her and bowed.

'Miss Lowerby,' he said in that lovely, warm voice she remembered so well. 'It is a pleasure to see you again.'

'Yes, a pleasure,' Grace parroted, like an inarticulate nincompoop, looking up into those alluring brown eyes and that charming smile.

'Shall we?' He offered her his arm.

'You young people go off and enjoy the delightful weather,' her grandmother said as Grace stood up and placed her arm through his. 'And remember all that I said to you.'

Grace was unsure whom she was addressing, but it mattered not. She was to spend the afternoon with Thomas and she had her grandmother's blessing to once again do whatever it took to encourage him.

Chapter Eleven

'You look lovely today,' Thomas said as he helped Grace and her lady's maid into his carriage. And so she did. Had he forgotten just how beautiful she really was and the effect that beauty had on him?

She had done something different with her hair, and the loose blonde locks appeared almost golden in the afternoon sunlight, her skin almost translucent, just as he imagined an angel to look. Her delicate features and innocence made him want to protect her from all the harms of the world. Yet, when he looked at her full lips, his thoughts were not innocent, nor were they angelic.

But he was not here to think of her lips or indulge in any fantasies of kissing her or caressing her lovely, curvaceous body. He was here as a friend, to save her from the humiliation of being briefly courted, then immediately abandoned by the Duke, a humiliation that was all his fault, and to help her find the husband she and her grandmother desperately wanted. If not the

Duke, then some other titled man. And she would not find that man seated at home waiting and pining. She needed to be out in society. She needed to be seen. Society needed to know that she was not ashamed of anything that had happened, but was an attractive, vibrant young lady, that any sensible man would be pleased to call his wife.

He signalled to the driver, and they moved off through the streets of Knightsbridge, towards Hyde Park.

'It is so delightful to see you again, Mr Hayward,' she said, turning towards him and smiling. 'I could hardly believe it when Grandmama said we were to take a walk in the park together.'

'You do realise what your grandmother's game is, don't you?'

'Of course I do, but I don't care,' she said with a delighted laugh that made him smile. 'She is hoping the Duke will finally start to court me, but it matters not what her reasons are, I'm just so pleased to see you again.'

Unlike the grandmother, the granddaughter did not have to be instructed to be honest. It was yet another of her endearing qualities that he adored.

'I take it the Duke has made no attempt to follow through with the promises he made at his estate.'

'No, we haven't heard a thing from him,' she said with a shrug of her shoulder.

Thomas should be angry with the cad for leading this sweet young lady on and then so unceremoniously discarding her, but he was far from angry. How could he be angry when it had led to him spending more time in her enjoyable company?

'You don't seem particularly upset by this outcome,' he probed.

'Well, I don't really know what to feel, but I know Grandmama has been furious and that always makes me very upset.'

Thomas did not doubt that.

'Well, you're out of the house, away from your grandmother, and we're going to have an enjoyable afternoon.'

She moved in closer and he inhaled lavender and rose water, a scent both innocent and enticing, just like the young lady herself.

'Yes, we are, aren't we,' she said with a small, contented giggle.

The sudden desire to place his arm around her shoulder and draw her into an intimate embrace crashed down on him. He longed to hold her close, to feel her body against his, to taste those lips.

He moved across the bench, putting a wider space between himself and temptation. With thoughts like that invading his mind, Thomas had to wonder whether this was such a good idea after all. Would a man who was merely offering friendship really have such thoughts? That was a question Thomas knew the answer to.

He looked over at the lady's maid, staring out at the passing scenery, and gave a silent thanks for her presence. He needed to focus on the one and only reason he was here, to help Grace achieve her dream. No, make that two reasons. To help her and to soothe the guilt that had been gnawing at him since the Duke won her in that inappropriate bet.

They drove through Hyde Park's ornate wrought-iron gates and Thomas could see that almost all of society was doing what society did best, frittering away their endless time in pointless pursuits. Although, in reality, their pursuits were not entirely pointless. Like Grace, they were here to see and be seen. The young ladies were all dressed in their finery, strolling under their lacy parasols and showing off their charms to the eligible young men.

And soon he would lead Grace into that milieu, placing her on display, so the dukes, marquesses, earls, viscounts and barons could weigh her up, compare her to the other young ladies on the market and decide whether she was worthy.

Bile burned up his throat at the thought of these men who dared to judge her, who dared to want her. He swallowed it down.

That is what she wants. Remember.

And as her friend that was what he would help her achieve.

The carriage came to a halt. He jumped out and held out his hand to her. As she lowered herself down from the carriage her chest came dangerously close to his own, so close he could feel the warmth of her body, so close he could imagine her breasts against him. He swallowed a groan as he imagined what those breasts would feel like: soft, full, irresistible.

Friend. Remember.

He helped the lady's maid descend from the carriage, then took Grace's arm and they joined the parade. Thomas had to admit, it was pleasant to be out of the office, away from his work and taking in the crisp air. Although he'd prefer it if the park was not full of other people, laughing and chattering away, and all but drowning out the birds singing above them, oblivious to the artifices of the high and mighty walking on the paths below them.

'It's rather crowded, isn't it?' she said, echoing his thoughts. Their progress was halted by a couple in front of them who had stopped to chat to a group walking in the opposite direction. 'Isn't there somewhere a bit more private we could walk?'

Thomas looked down at her. What was she suggesting? That she wanted to be alone with him? If that was what she wanted, then Hyde Park on a sunny afternoon was not the place to be.

'I believe being among the crowds is the whole point. One is here to be seen as much as to enjoy the surroundings.'

'Yes, I suppose so.' Did he imagine the disappointment in her voice?

'I believe that is what your grandmother wishes.'

She sighed gently. 'Yes, I know. She's gone from being over the moon with happiness when the Duke offered a courtship, to being even more angry and disappointed in me than usual.'

'You have done nothing wrong. The fault is all with the Duke of Hardgraves.'

And with me for using you to win his land at a reduced price.

'I don't believe my grandmother sees it that way.'

'No, perhaps not, but you should not blame yourself.' He struggled to keep his voice nonchalant as he composed the questions he was burning to ask. 'And what of you? Do you still have your heart set on marrying the Duke?'

She shrugged one slim shoulder. 'It's not really up to me, is it?'

'I believe whomever you choose to marry is entirely up to you, or indeed if you choose to marry at all.'

She laughed as if he had made a joke, which had not been his intent.

'But let's not talk of my marriage.' She lowered her parasol and tilted her head towards the sun, closed her eyes and sighed. 'Let's just enjoy this glorious afternoon and the pleasure of each other's company.'

Thomas stared at her as if transfixed. She looked so content, like a woman relishing in sensual pleasure. A vision of her lying in his bed invaded his mind: her blonde hair cascading over the pillow, her head tilted back in just this manner, her eyes closed and that same smile of fulfilment playing on her lips.

He coughed to drive out that image. He was in the company of an innocent young lady, albeit an attractive and rather tempting young lady. But she was still an innocent and had to preserve that innocence until she married.

She opened her eyes and smiled at him, then caught the way he was still looking at her. He tried to look away, but failed to follow that simple command. She was so beautiful, with the sun shining on her golden hair and turning her creamy skin a soft, honey colour. Her lips parted and her teeth ran gently along her bottom lip.

Was she trying to torment him? If she was, it was working. Hungry desire raced through him. It was wrong, so wrong, but he wanted her so much, wanted to kiss her, to trace his hands over her body, to explore her with his lips and tongue, to take her entirely. He knew he wouldn't do it, but he had to admit he wanted to.

With more strength than he had thought himself capable of, he drew his eyes away, in a fervent attempt to break the spell of those bewitching lips.

'We should walk,' he said, not looking at her, determined to continue their stroll, like any other couple out enjoying the summer's day.

She walked beside him and he hoped and prayed she was so innocent she could not tell the effect she was having on him. The mere fact she was still at his side suggested she was ignorant of his thoughts and feelings. If she'd had any idea of what he wanted to do to her, what he wanted her to do to him, she would have demanded that he take her back to the safety of her grandmother immediately.

He was both thankful she was so innocent, while also frustratingly annoyed that she was.

Grace moved as close to Thomas as propriety would allow—closer, if she was being honest. She wanted to be near him, wanted to touch him, wanted him to touch her, or at the very least wanted him to look at her again the way he just had.

He had tried to disguise it, but when she had opened her eyes she had caught him staring at her with such intensity, such passion. That was not the look of a friend. That was the look of a man who desired a woman, who wanted her. It was a look that sent heat throbbing through her, had made her body yearn for him to do more than just look, but to act on his desires.

Her grandmother had said once they were courting the Duke would be free to take liberties with her. The thought of it had filled her with trepidation and not a little abhorrence, but that was not what she thought with Thomas. If he wanted to take liberties, she knew she'd be powerless to say no. If he wanted to kiss her and relieve the tingling of her lips, she would say yes. If he wanted to wrap her in his arms, she would say yes. If he wanted to caress her body, she would say yes.

Yes, yes, *yes.*

It was such an unfamiliar sensation, thrilling but tinged with a hint of delicious danger. Her body was seemingly crying out for him. Her skin was aching to feel the touch of his hands. She had never been so aware of her lips or her breasts and had never before felt that demanding throbbing tension between her legs.

She could not marry him, could not even be courted by him, her grandmother would never countenance that, but she had been told she must encourage him once again. Did that mean she should allow him to take liberties, the way her grandmother had said she should allow the Duke to do so? She wasn't going to marry Thomas, but would that really matter?

Surely, one could see it as a type of training, so she would know what would be expected of her when she did finally marry. After all, her grandmother had given her no instructions on what that would entail. She had merely said she should let the Duke, or whomever it was she married, do what he wanted with her and not screw her face up the way she had when the Duke had caressed her naked arm and placed his hand inappropriately on her buttocks.

Well, if she was to give the appropriate response and avoid making the terrible mistake of looking disgusted or surprised, she needed to be prepared for what was to come. It made complete sense. And Thomas, a man who had said he was her friend and would always be there when she needed him, was just the man to teach her what to expect.

She moved a little closer, hoping that would encourage him, but drat it all, he moved further away. He was not averse to her, she knew that. She had seen the way he had looked at her. Was it because he knew they were never to wed, that they would never be more than just friends?

Somehow, she was going to have to make him forget all about that and do what she was certain he was longing to do as much as she was.

But that was not going to happen while they were here, in this public place, surrounded by all these people. For now, she would have to be content with his company and wait for the opportunity when she could encourage him to move beyond merely looking at her with desire.

'Shall we walk to the Serpentine?' she said, keeping her tone light.

'As you wish,' he said and she smiled at the hoarse tone of his voice. He was still in the grip of that desire. Good.

In silence, they walked towards the lake, its water glistening in the sunlight. They were both still lost in their own thoughts, while the hubbub whirled around them. Grace could only hope his thoughts were travelling down the same path as her own. That he, too, was wondering how they could be alone so he could act on his passions and take those liberties she was desperate to surrender to him.

He led her to a bench and they sat under the draping leaves of an oak tree and watched the swans gliding past, the people rowing on the water and the small children playing with their toy sail boats.

'I believe Grandmama is hoping this is the first of many times we are to be in each other's company,' she said, relishing the prospect.

'She wishes you to be seen in public with a gentleman to incite the interest of titled men, particularly the Duke of Hardgraves.'

Was he trying to remind her of the real purpose of this walk, of what she was supposed to be focusing on, or reminding himself? It mattered not. Grace cared nothing for why they were to spend time together, only that they would continue to do so and hopefully not always in public.

'And it appears to be working,' he said, looking around at the people promenading past.

'What is working?'

'You have attracted many glances from men throughout the day.'

'Have I?' Grace had not noticed, but she had seen the sideways looks of many a young lady directed at her handsome companion. She should be outraged at their behaviour, but she was not. She knew exactly how they felt. How could one not look at a man like Thomas? He was so much more handsome than any other man she had ever seen. Despite now knowing he was a complete gentleman, perhaps too much of a gentleman, when she looked at him she still saw that dashing pirate she had imagined when they first met. It was that ink-black hair, those dark, intense eyes and the sculptured cheekbones and jawline that gave him such a wild, rugged look.

A delicious shiver rippled down her body. Didn't pirates have a reputation for ravishing young maidens?

'Yes, many men have tried to catch your eye,' he continued. 'I believe it won't be long before you are receiving many offers and perhaps even the Duke's interest will spark back into life.'

'Do you think so?' Grace tried to keep all displeasure out of her voice. It was what she wanted, of course it was, but not just yet. She had been promised more time with Thomas and she wanted more time, much more time.

'Of that I am certain.'

'But Grandmama said we could go to the theatre together, perhaps be seen riding in your carriage, and for us to take many more walks like this. We could perhaps attend the same balls. I know you said you don't attend balls, but as my friend, surely you will attend any that I am invited to so I have at least one person to dance with.'

Grace was babbling, her words tumbling out in a desperate attempt to make him agree to see her again, but she could not help herself. It would be terrible if this was the last time they were to be together.

'I would be honoured to escort you to the theatre and if you wish me to attend any balls to which we are both invited, then, of course, I shall do so. That is what friends are for.'

'Yes, friends,' she said, feeling rather pleased with herself.

'Now that we have been seen in public by enough people, I believe it time I return you home so you can tell your grandmother what a success today has been.'

Grace bit down a laugh. She would not be telling her grandmother about everything that happened today, nor the decisions she had come to, suspecting her grandmother would not quite understand her reasoning when it came to Thomas and the taking of liberties.

But if her grandmother really thought it through as logically as Grace had, she was sure she would come to the same conclusions. It was essential when the Duke, or some other titled man she was engaged to, wanted to take liberties that she react appropriately and not put him off the thought of marrying her. So there could be nothing wrong with encouraging Thomas to prepare her for that eventuality. Then she would know what to expect. After all, that would surely help her catch a titled man for a husband. If she did have to explain this to her grandmother, that was what she would say, but it was probably best to keep that to herself for now.

Chapter Twelve

Thomas knew he should take her home. Now. And he should not have committed to further outings, not when frustrated desire continued to rampage through his body.

It was so wrong to think of her in any terms other than as a friend. She was not his and never would be. The Duke didn't know it, but he had got his revenge. He had won that ridiculous bet after all. Thomas wanted her and he could not have her because she was the Duke's for the taking.

Anger at that undeserving buffoon surged up within him and he was grateful for its ferocity. That was what he would focus on, not her lush mouth, not her golden hair, not the tempting curves of her body.

He looked out at the Serpentine, hardly registering the quacking ducks, the colourful rowboats or the throngs promenading around its edges. All he was conscious of was the woman sitting beside him, so close they were almost touching.

'Shall we walk?' he said, standing up and not giving her an option. He had to get moving. Activity would surely quell the appalling thoughts that kept invading his mind.

'Yes, let's.' She stood up, took his arm and smiled up at him. Was her smile different? It almost had a complicit look to it, as if she was aware of what he was thinking, what he was feeling, and had no objections. No. It had to be his imagination. If she could read his mind, he knew she would not have placed her arm through his in such a trusting manner and would not be standing so close to him.

'Shall we walk over there? It looks rather idyllic.' She pointed to an area where trees and shrubberies concealed the path.

A wicked jolt of desire ripped through him at the thought of what he could do if they were alone, away from all prying eyes.

'I believe the point of this walk is for you to be seen by as many people as possible,' he said, surprised at how prim and proper his voice sounded. 'That would not be achieved by taking such a path.'

'No, but it would be fun.'

He looked down at her, wondering at the meaning of her words. Surely her thoughts were not running along the same lines as his own. No, of course they were not. She was an inexperienced young lady. He was misinterpreting her words to suit his own carnal longings.

'I suspect your grandmother would not think that.'

'My grandmother is not here.'

'But your lady's maid is and she is sure to report back.' He looked around. Where had that lady's maid got to?

'Oh, it seems Molly has wandered off,' she said with a cheeky smile.

'Be that as it may, we will remain where others can see us.' By God, he sounded like the most anxious of chaperons. And like a good chaperon he was ensuring she remained in public to preserve her virtue, because with the powerful need to feel her soft skin and to taste her lips coursing through him, he was unsure if he would be able to control himself if they found themselves alone.

She shrugged one slim shoulder. 'Some other time, then.'

He commenced walking, feeling as if he had just avoided stepping into a very deep quagmire from which there would be no escape.

'I believe it is time we returned home,' he said.

'Oh, so soon?'

'Yes.' He was still sounding like that strict chaperon. 'Your grandmother must be wondering why we have been away so long.'

Since when did you care about Lady Ashbridge? You coward.

'I suppose so,' she agreed and allowed him to lead her back to the carriage, where thankfully the lady's maid was waiting, chatting amicably with some friends and failing to do her duty in protecting her mistress's virtue.

Not before time, they arrived at her grandmother's home. He escorted her up the path, then bowed goodbye as the footman opened the door.

'Won't you come in?' she asked. 'I'm sure Grandmama would love to see you again.'

Thomas doubted that very much. He hesitated, but knew it would be rude not to at least exchange a few words with the older woman. Thomas could only hope that she did not notice the effect her granddaughter was having on him. He had accused Lady Ashbridge of dishonesty and theatrics, now he was going to have to put on a consummate performance of a man who could be trusted implicitly with her granddaughter.

He entered the parlour, but remained standing to indicate he had no intention of staying any longer than necessary.

'Did you have a nice walk?' Lady Ashbridge said, the real questions unasked. Was the Duke present?

Was my granddaughter seen by a sufficient number of the aristocracy on the arm of a gentleman?

'Yes, the park was extremely busy,' he said, causing Lady Ashbridge to smile.

'Did Grace mention that she has been just dying to see the latest play at the Savoy Theatre? I am unfortunately unable to attend, but perhaps you could escort her.'

'It would be my pleasure to escort her.' It *would* be his pleasure, perhaps too much of a pleasure, but at least they would once again be in a public place and there were no private tree-lined paths to tempt him into doing what he knew he should not. 'Now I must say goodbye.'

'Yes, of course, you'll have your business to get back to,' Lady Ashbridge said with arched eyebrows, as if to remind Thomas of something he already knew only too well: that he was not a titled man and would never be in contention for her granddaughter's hand. He was here to serve a purpose and should not see his association with Grace in any other light. And on both those points Thomas could do nothing but agree.

He bowed to Grace and her grandmother then departed.

Now that was over, he could return to his work and not think about Grace's lips, her skin, her hair and certainly not her shapely body. Nor would he remember all the images that had been unleashed when she closed her eyes and smiled so contentedly.

He groaned. That was not going to be easy, especially when all that unsatisfied lust was still pounding through his body. He could relieve his unsated hunger by visiting one of the women he often kept company with, but he would not insult them by using them in such a manner. And it was not them he wanted. He wanted Grace. He wanted her naked beneath him, writhing under his touch, opening herself up to him and giving him the release he desperately needed. He wanted to feel her loving touch on his skin, to see the ardour in her eyes when they made love, to hold her afterwards in an intimate embrace as they relished in the pleasure of having satisfied their passion for each other.

But that was not going to happen. He would have to deal with his lust in the time-honoured fashion of frustrated men, then think of ways in which he could stop acting like a lecher and remember what his role was. To be her friend, nothing more.

'Did you see him?' Grace's grandmother asked as soon as the door closed behind Thomas.

It took a moment or two for Grace to think whom she was referring to. The Duke. Of course she was asking about the Duke. 'No, unfortunately we did not see him, but the park was very busy so I'm sure he will hear I was out walking with Mr Hayward.'

'Good, good,' her grandmother said, tapping her chin. 'And the Duke is sure to be at the opening of that new play at the Savoy.' She smiled at Grace. 'He is so discerning and such a great patron of the arts.'

Grace resisted the temptation to frown and certainly resisted the temptation to contradict her grandmother. They would be attending the latest Gilbert and Sullivan comic opera. Hadn't her grandmother previously said such performances were a travesty? That they were low art that should never be allowed on the respectable stage. Grace was sure she had dismissed them as the preserve of the hoi polloi and not suitable for genteel ladies and gentlemen.

But it now seemed if the Duke approved, then they, too, would approve. If he enjoyed something, then they, too, would enjoy it.

But instead of doing something she had never hitherto done and suggesting her grandmother was being a hypocrite, she did what she always did and smiled. 'Yes, he must be a man of refined tastes if he enjoys comic operas and Gilbert and Sullivan's musicals are said to be such rollicking fun.'

Her grandmother's smile became strained and Grace could not resist teasing a bit further. 'I believe I read somewhere they are quite the satirical take on society and its manners. I wonder if that is what the Duke likes about them?'

Her grandmother's nostrils flared, even as she kept smiling. 'You will hopefully soon have a chance to ask him for yourself, but when you do, remember, do not give your own opinion. Ask the Duke what he thinks, then tell him you agree completely.'

'Of course, Grandmama,' she answered dutifully, unable to quell a satisfied smile of amusement at her grandmother's predictable answer. With Thomas she would never have to tell him what he wanted to hear. She could have her own opinions and that was so invigorating.

Her grandmother's eyes narrowed. 'I hope spending time in Mr Hayward's company is not making you wilful.'

Panic twisted in Grace's stomach. It had been a mistake to behave in such a manner. She must not give her grandmother any cause to stop her from seeing Thomas again.

'No, Grandmama,' she answered quickly.

'You are not wanting to go to this play because it will mean spending time with him, are you?'

Grace had never lied to her grandmother before, but if her grandmother felt it acceptable to not entirely tell the truth when it suited her, surely it was not wrong for Grace to follow her example. 'No, Grandmama. I am merely excited about the prospect of attending a performance where the Duke will be present and hopefully of renewing our acquaintance.'

Her grandmother said nothing, just continued to stare at her in that disconcerting manner. The silence between them stretched on and on, becoming increasingly uncomfortable.

Grace attempted to swallow down her anxiety without her grandmother seeing and fought to maintain her false smile.

'You're not developing feelings for Mr Hayward, are you?' her grandmother asked, her eyes narrowed.

'Of course not,' Grace shot back and attempted a dismissive laugh.

'That's not why you're so eager to go to this play, is it?'

'No, Grandmama, of course not, Grandmama.'

Lies were piling on top of lies. She did want to see Thomas again, yearned to see him again.

'Need I remind you that he has no title?'

'No, Grandmama.'

'His only purpose is to help you find a suitable husband.'

'Yes, Grandmama.'

'And once you are courted by another, then you will never see him again.'

Grace's hands flew to her stomach as she gasped in a breath. She knew that. She had always known that.

She had to marry a titled man. Thomas would never be anything more than a friend. A good friend.

'Yes, Grandmama,' she said quietly with lowered eyes.

'Good, and never forget it. That is the one and only reason I am permitting him to accompany you to this play.'

The turmoil in her stomach started to ease. She had her wish. She would be able to see Thomas again and the longer it took for the Duke or any other man to express his interest in her, the more she would see of him. She could only hope and pray that took a very, very long time. Not every young lady married in her first Season—some spent as many as five Seasons or longer in search of a suitable husband. There was no reason why that couldn't happen to Grace.

But she had nearly taken a misstep and ruined everything. She must never do that again if she was to continue seeing Thomas. From now onwards she must watch every word she said.

'On the night of the play you must look your very finest, as you might not get another chance to capture the Duke's heart,' her grandmother continued.

'Perhaps I can wear the sapphire-blue gown.' Grace held her breath, waiting for her grandmother's answer.

She nodded slowly. 'Yes, that would be perfect.'

Grace exhaled quietly, and the two women smiled at each other as if joined in a conspiracy. The blue gown was the most daring of her collection and one that Grace had thought she would never be so bold as to wear. It was cut lower, exposing a hint of décolletage, and the straps of delicate silk made her shoulders appear almost naked.

She knew her grandmother would see that gown as one to tempt the Duke, but there was another man Grace hoped would find the sight of her dressed in such a revealing manner a temptation impossible to resist.

Chapter Thirteen

It was obvious from the moment Thomas stepped into the drawing room of Lady Ashbridge's home to escort Grace to the theatre that her reappearance in public had had its desired effect.

'Look at all these gifts from admirers,' Lady Ashbridge said, indicating the bouquets adorning the various tables dotted around the drawing room. She picked up a card, nestled inside a display of brightly coloured flowers. 'This one is from Howard Seymour, the Earl of Whitecliff, an eminent and very suitable man.' She moved across to the sideboard and another bouquet. 'And this one is from the eldest son of Baron Morsley, such a refined young man.'

'Nothing yet from the Duke of Hardgraves?' Thomas already knew the answer to that question. If that man had sent flowers, the Earl of Whitecliff and Baron Morsley's son would not get a mention, and tonight's outing to the theatre would have been regretfully cancelled.

'No, not yet. Although I have heard from a reliable source he, too, will be attending tonight's performance.'

Thomas had heard the same rumour and knew what it meant. Grace was about to be placed on display and expected to reel the Duke back in, and Lady Ashbridge expected him to help her do so.

He was tempted to turn around and walk out the door rather than be caught up in this appalling game, but despite his contempt for the scheming and artifice of the aristocratic marriage market, he had made a promise to Lady Ashbridge and it was no more than he owed Grace after using her for his own ends in that bet. If this was the only way he could pay her back, then so be it.

She entered the drawing room and any thoughts of walking away from this evening's commitments evaporated. She was nothing short of a vision of loveliness. It was the way the blue gown matched the colour of her eyes, making them sparkle, that caught his immediate attention. Quickly followed by the plunging neckline, revealing the swell of her creamy breasts. If she was trying to gain a man's admiration, there were few ways better to achieve it than this. His own reaction was testament to that.

He had spent far too many tortuous hours speculating as to what she looked like under her layers of clothing. Now he had a tantalising hint of what reality would be like and could now see it would be irresistible.

But resist he must. She had not dressed to impress him, to tempt him or incite his desires, even if that had been the unintended effect. She was on display for the Duke's appreciation. Not his.

'Doesn't my granddaughter look like a duchess tonight?' Lady Ashbridge said.

'Yes, you look very nice, Miss Lowerby,' he replied, those words wholly inadequate in describing her enchanting appearance.

'Thank you,' she said, giving him a sweet, innocent smile and reminding him that, despite her appearance, she was a young debutante, an untouchable woman, someone with whom he would never, ever be anything more than just a friend.

'I think she's bound to catch a certain man's eye tonight,' her grandmother added in an almost coquettish manner.

Grace smiled up at him, a pretty flush tinging her cheeks. There was no denying she would catch the Duke's eye. How could she not? It was going to take every ounce of self-control Thomas possessed to stop his eyes from straying to that enticing décolletage. Somehow he was going to have to stop not just his eyes, but his mind from straying, to not think about what her breasts looked like released from the gossamer-thin silk, what they felt like cupped in his hands, what they tasted like when he caressed them with his tongue.

He gritted his teeth tightly together and dug his fingernails into his clenched hands to drive those images out of his mind.

'The Duke is expected to be in attendance tonight and I'm sure he will be enchanted,' Lady Ashbridge continued, staring hard at her granddaughter. 'That is what we are hoping, isn't it, Grace?'

'Yes, Grandmama,' she said with lowered eyes.

Lady Ashbridge turned her attention back to Thomas and narrowed her eyes. 'Grace is so excited about the prospect of reacquainting herself with the Duke.'

There was no possibility of missing the intent of her words. He was being reminded, even though it was not required, that she was not for him and there was only one reason why he was present tonight.

Lady Ashbridge continued to show what a cunning old fox she was. She had packaged her granddaughter up in this revealing manner so the Duke would be able to see what was on offer. Now she was to be sent out with Thomas, making her even more desirable to a man who couldn't bear the thought of others having what he believed was his by right.

'Shall we?' he said, offering her his arm and leading her out to his carriage, followed, of course, by her discreet lady's maid.

The moment they left the drawing room, she looked up and smiled at him. 'This is so exciting. I've never been to the theatre before. I am so looking forward to it.'

'And you'll be pleased to know that my private box is directly across from the Duke of Hardgraves's.'

'Yes, so my grandmother has informed me, repeatedly,' she said as he helped her into the carriage.

Thomas looked at her in the dim light of the carriage lamp. Her tone did not suggest this was as an exciting prospect as her grandmother had implied. Was she starting to question the wisdom of her grandmother's wish to marry her off to this Season's most eligible man?

Hope swelled up inside Thomas. Not for himself. Of course not for himself. Despite his undeniable attraction for her she was an untouchable young lady. Only one man would taste the sensual delights of those luscious lips and alluring body. The man she married and that would never be him. But she deserved a better man than the Duke of Hardgraves.

'Do I sense some reluctance regarding the Duke?' he asked, keeping all hints of expectation out of his voice.

She shrugged one shoulder, drawing his gaze to the naked skin, covered only by straps in the thinnest of sheer fabric.

'Grandmama is still certain that all the Duke needs

is a gentle reminder of what he said to me at his estate and he will make good on his promise to court me.'

'And what of you, Grace? Is that what you want?'

She turned towards him in the intimate space of the carriage. 'Well, I do want to make my grandmother happy, but I also want to experience some happiness of my own.'

'And how are you going to achieve this happiness?' he asked, staring into those blue eyes so his eyes would not stray to where they wanted to go.

'I'm not sure. Perhaps you can show me,' she stated, still looking at him with an unfamiliar boldness.

Desire ripped through his body. He wanted to show her all the ways a man could make a woman happy. He wanted to teach her how to lose herself in the taking and giving of pleasure, but he would never do so. Her words might have caused erotic images to rampage through his mind, but that was where they would remain—he would never act on them.

He flicked a look at the lady's maid, who was staring out the carriage window as if fascinated by all that was happening outside. She might not be as focused on her charge as she should be, but Thomas said a silent thank you for her presence.

'Happiness is so elusive.' He coughed to clear the restriction in his throat. 'I believe we all have to find it in our own way.'

'Oh, yes, that is what I intend to do,' she said with a mysterious smile.

The carriage came to a halt in front of the theatre. That enigmatic smile lingered on her lips as the attendant opened the carriage door. Her behaviour tonight was decidedly out of character. While he applauded her new-found determination to find happiness, he could only hope this inexperienced young lady knew what she was doing and she did not make such a request of any other man, particularly the Duke.

He had said happiness was elusive, but Grace knew he was wrong. She knew exactly what made her happy. Being with Thomas made her happy. She was all but bubbling over with that wonderful emotion and just wished she could feel like this for ever.

The bubbles deflated slightly. This would not last for ever, only tonight, or for as long as she failed to attract the attention of the Duke.

Perhaps he *was* right. Perhaps happiness *was* elusive. Once he was no longer in her life, did that mean she would never be happy again? She gave a little shake of her head. That was too upsetting to contemplate, especially on a magical night such as this, and she simply would not ruin things by focusing on the future.

She would just enjoy their time together and maybe, just maybe, she would find some way to make it last for ever, while still doing her duty to her grandmother and making her proud.

Achieving that, she suspected, would be more elusive than happiness, but she would think of that another time. Tonight she would forget all about such things and just enjoy herself.

As she stepped down from the carriage, she leant forward under the guise of lifting the bottom of her gown, knowing exactly what would happen. Thomas's eyes lowered briefly as if they were no longer under his control.

A delicious sense of power rippled through her. This, too, was happiness. Knowing he wanted her. He desired her.

She smiled at him, a smile she hoped he would interpret in the way it was intended. *If you want me, you can have me.*

It was decidedly naughty of her and she knew it, but she had nothing to feel guilty about. Not really. Her behaviour was exactly as her grandmother had prescribed.

She had instructed her that, when meeting the Duke, she was to make a very low curtsy and, rather than keeping her back straight as would normally be expected, she should lean forward ever so slightly.

'If the gown gapes open that is hardly your fault,' her grandmother had said with a wink. 'And if the Duke happens to look down at your décolletage, then by all means let him. After all, you're just enticing him with what will one day be his.'

At the time she had thought her grandmother's advice shocking, but when she had seen the way Thomas had looked at her when she entered the room, where his eyes had gone, she could see the value of her grandmother's stratagem.

It had been marvellous to have him look at her like that and she wanted him to do so again and again. And if he wanted to do more than just look, well, that, too, was something she would not object to.

She took his arm, moved in close to him and gave a little sigh at the thought of his hands moving to where his eyes had strayed.

It was such a scandalous thought, but one that sent a delicious throbbing sensation coursing through her body, as her nipples tightened against the soft caress of her silk gown.

Arm in arm, they joined the procession entering the theatre's foyer. Excitement bubbled up within Grace and she gripped his arm tighter. Being out on a night like this was enchanting, like being a princess in a fairy tale accompanied by her handsome prince. She looked up at the high ceiling and elegant chandelier bathing her and the other guests in warm, sparkling light, then gazed around at the other elegant patrons, and the smartly dressed ushers in their military-style uniforms.

'I wonder which play we will see tonight,' Grace said, looking at the posters lining the walls, showing beautiful actresses and handsome actors in an array of exotic costumes. Despite her question, she cared not the slightest what play she saw, just loving the experience of being here.

'Tonight's performance is *The Mikado*,' he said, stopping to buy a programme and handing it to her.

She clutched the memento of what she knew was going to be a glorious evening to her heart as Thomas led her up the plush carpeted stairs and along the hallway to his private box. Her lady's maid took a seat at the back against the wall and he escorted Grace to the front, where they settled into their velvet seats, overlooking the theatre below.

It was as if they were alone together, while still in a noisy, crowded room. She looked down on the other members of the audience taking their seats in the auditorium, then to the stage, hidden by a thick velvet curtain, then at Thomas. He was smiling at her, enjoying her excitement.

'This is marvellous,' she said. 'Thank you so much.'

'It's my pleasure,' he said and lightly touched her hand.

Even through their gloves, it was as if his skin was caressing hers and a small thrill moved up her arms and lodged itself in her heart.

She smiled at him again and looked back around

the room, at the crowd below and at the orchestra pit, where the musicians were tuning up, the cacophony of so many instruments playing at once failing to drown out the laughter and chatter from the excited audience.

Movement in the box directly across from them drew her gaze and she saw the Duke of Hardgraves entering his box, along with another man who had attended his weekend party, and two young ladies, one of whom was Lady Octavia, the bully who had called her Graceless Lower-Born.

She looked away immediately, her happiness dissolving, then flicked another glance over at the Duke's box. He had not yet noticed her presence, but Lady Octavia had. She was staring straight at Grace, a smirk distorting her otherwise pretty face.

As if sensing her discomfort, Thomas reached over and gently squeezed her hand. Grace sat up straighter, lifted her chin and stared across the auditorium at Lady Octavia. The lady stared back at her, her lips curling into a deeper sneer. But Grace would not be cowed. Not this time.

So what if I fell over at a stupid ball? So what if the Duke said he would court me, then turned his back on me?

She would not let Lady Octavia or anyone else think of her as Graceless or Lower-Born.

Lady Octavia shuffled in her seat, then turned to the man sitting next to her, who was paying her no attention, but laughing with the Duke. She sent a quick look at Grace, who was not going to look away until that bully knew her days of intimidation and teasing were over.

Once again, Lady Octavia squirmed in her seat, picked up her programme and lowered her head as if absorbed by its contents.

'That is all it takes,' Thomas said, giving her hand another squeeze. 'Once they know they can't hurt you, the coward underneath the bullying exterior is quickly revealed.'

She squeezed his hand back in response, letting him know she was thankful for his words of advice and encouragement, then looked back at the Duke's box with a sense of triumph.

The other man in the box was looking in her direction while talking into the Duke's ear. The Duke stopped laughing and looked towards her. But it was not Grace he stared at. It was Thomas, and the Duke did not look pleased to see him.

Grace couldn't help thinking that his sullen expression bore a striking resemblance to a child who had been denied his favourite toy. Had she seen that sulky expression before and, if so, why had she not noticed it?

'It looks like your grandmother's plan is working,' Thomas said. 'You once again have the undivided attention of the Duke of Hardgraves.'

Grace was not so naive as to think it was she who had drawn the Duke's attention. After all, she had done that before and had lost it. The Duke's only interest in her was because she was with Thomas.

'Yes, so it would seem,' she murmured.

'Don't let it unnerve you,' he said, his voice soothing in reassurance. 'If the Duke can't see that you are a young lady more than worthy of him, then he is a complete fool.'

'Thank you. I won't.' The only thing unnerving her was the thought that the Duke might renew his interest so soon and this would all come to an end. It would make her grandmother happy, but would it make Grace happy? She knew the answer to that. No. Only Thomas could make her happy. But what choice did she have? She had to make a good marriage and there were no marriages better than one to a duke.

'For now, let's forget all about him and just enjoy the performance.'

'Yes, let's,' she said, turning back to the stage as the curtain raised and the orchestra struck up a lively tune.

She moved closer to him, determined to do as he suggested and not think about the Duke, her grandmother, or anything else, and just enjoy tonight's performance.

Chapter Fourteen

Thomas knew he should heed his own advice and focus entirely on the performers acting, dancing and singing their hearts out on the stage below.

But that advice would be easier to follow if Grace was not sitting so close to him. So close her breast was almost skimming his arm. So close he was enveloped in her scent of lavender and rose water. So close he could almost feel the warmth of her body burning into him.

Drawing his eyes from the man singing about being a wandering minstrel while incongruously dressed as a samurai, he looked over at the Duke of Hardgraves. He, too, was not watching the performance, but staring straight at Thomas.

Thomas nodded his head, in a parody of greeting, causing the Duke to almost snarl his dislike.

If he needed any reminder of why he was here tonight and why Grace was almost pressed up against him, it was there, in the box across from him. This was all about luring the Duke back in and getting him to make good on his offer of courtship and Thomas would do well to never forget that.

She had said she wanted to do what would make her happy, and he knew what that would be. To do as her grandmother wished and become a duchess.

She turned to face him and smiled, her eyes glinting in the soft light, her look almost inviting.

It's all for the Duke's sake, he reminded himself as he smiled back.

He refused to let himself look over at the Duke to see his reaction to that exchange, but had no need to do so. He knew exactly how the Duke would be reacting. If he thought he couldn't have her, then he would want her. If he thought Thomas wanted her, then his desire to have her would be all the greater. If he thought he could put Thomas in what the Duke considered 'his place', then he would not miss an opportunity to do so.

But what the Duke wanted and what Thomas wanted were of no matter. All that mattered was what Grace wanted. She claimed it was her happiness and the happiness of her grandmother she wished for. The second would be achieved by marriage to the Duke, as for the first, whatever Grace thought would achieve her wish of happiness he would accept, even if it did irk that a man such as Hardgraves should be the one to win her hand.

He focused on the stage below him and tried to follow the plot which seemed to involve arranged marriages, people falling in love when they shouldn't, men being punished for lusting after forbidden women and characters getting caught up in various nefarious plots. It all sounded horribly familiar.

After a series of songs and lots of dancing, some witty banter and much running around the stage, the curtain descended for intermission and the auditorium was filled with the sound of gloved hands clapping enthusiastically.

Thomas saw the Duke stand and leave the box and he knew what he had to do, even if it was not really what he wanted to. He had to provide Grace with the opportunity to shine in front of the Duke, so the promised courtship could begin in earnest.

'Shall we take some refreshments?' he asked her.

'Oh, can't we stay here? Perhaps Molly could go and get us something to drink.'

She turned to look over at her shoulder at her lady's maid, who was rising from her seat.

'The Duke has left his box and I believe your grandmother would want us to take the opportunity to exchange some words with him.'

'Oh, yes, I suppose so,' she said, picking up her shawl and fan and taking his hand as he helped her up from her seat.

They strolled down the corridor, Grace on his arm, and still just a tad closer to him than etiquette demanded. She really was determined to arouse the Duke's jealousy. He just wished she wouldn't come so dangerously close to arousing *him* in the process.

'There you are, Hayward,' he heard the Duke's booming voice from the end of the corridor. 'Thought I saw you. Thought private boxes were reserved for the aristocracy. Didn't know anyone could buy one, what.'

The guests parted to let him through, not daring to stand in the way of a duke's progress.

'Miss Lowerby,' he said when he reached them. 'How delightful to see you again.'

She performed a small curtsy, her back so ramrod straight she was almost leaning backwards, and murmured, 'Your Grace...'

'I've been quite remiss in not visiting you since your return from my weekend party. Tell your grandmother I will be paying the two of you a visit soon.'

'Yes, Your Grace,' she said quietly, like the obedient young woman she had been trained to be.

Once again, it looked like Thomas's role as bait was about to come to an end.

Grace continued to keep her eyes lowered while the Duke smirked at Thomas, knowing that his status meant there was nothing to stop him from taking her off him if that was his wish.

Thomas glared back at him, his body tense as if readying for a bout of boxing. Hardgraves pushed out his chest and lifted his chin, his curling upper lip exposing his teeth. Teeth Thomas would so love to push down the back of the puffed-up fool's throat.

For several long seconds they remained like that while the noisy audience swirled around them.

'Well, won't keep you,' the Duke finally said, turning to the prize he intended to take from Thomas. 'And remember, Miss Lowerby, expect a visit from me very, very soon.' With another contemptuous sneer in Thomas's direction, he turned and strode off, the patrons once again parting so they would not impede the progress of the titled clod.

'I believe your grandmother will declare tonight a success,' he said once the Duke was well out of hearing distance.

'Yes, I'm sure she will,' she murmured, then turned to her lady's maid. 'Molly, will you arrange for some refreshments to be sent to Mr Hayward's box.' She looked up at him and shrugged. 'We've achieved the purpose of joining the throng. I for one would be much happier if we returned to the privacy of your box.'

'And your happiness is all I care about,' he said, taking her arm as the lady's maid rushed off in the opposite direction.

'Good,' she said, that enigmatic smile returning. 'I intend to hold you to that promise.'

They returned to their box. She took her seat and looked over towards the Duke's box, her smile disappearing.

'Is everything all right?' he asked as he took the seat beside her.

'Oh, yes, perfectly. It's just, well, sometimes this game can become a little tiresome.'

'That's one way of describing it.'

'I thought the Season was going to be such fun. I didn't realise I'd have to take part in all this pretence and intrigue. It's more complicated than all the tangled threads of this play,' she said, pointing towards the stage.

'Then I don't believe your grandmother did her job properly and explained to you what it would be like.'

'No, all she said was I had to marry a man with a title, preferably at least an earl if not higher.'

'What? A baron isn't good enough?'

She gave a small laugh. 'Well, a baron would do at a pinch, but after the Duke's offer of courtship I suspect my grandmother would be very disappointed with such a lowly title. It's almost as if it is now the Duke of Hardgraves or nothing.'

'And nothing is not an option, I suppose.'

'No, of course not.' She laughed as if this was something that would only ever be said in jest. 'Although sometimes I wish it was.'

'Always remember that, whatever you decide to do, it is your choice. You can choose whom to marry, or you can choose not to marry if you wish.'

'Yes, that's what you said to me when we were at

the Duke's estate. But what do you suggest I do? Become a piano teacher like my father?'

'Would that be so bad?'

She stared back at him with a look of incomprehension. 'Grandmama said that when my mother married my father, the shock was so bad that it sent my grandfather to an early grave. I could never do such a thing to my grandmother.'

'I suspect your grandmother is much stronger than you think and is more than capable of bearing a shock or two,' he said, certain he was speaking the truth and that tale was simply that manipulative old dragon's way of using emotional coercion to ensure her sweet granddaughter did exactly as she was told. 'You have every right to what you want even if at times it runs counter to what your grandmother wants for you.'

That enigmatic smile once again played around the edges of her lips. 'Yes, perhaps you are right.'

Molly entered the box, followed by two waiters carrying a bottle of champagne in an ice bucket, two glasses and a tray of canapes.

'Oh, lovely, but can you bring another glass for Molly,' she informed the waiter, who bowed and departed.

She really was rather special. Apart from his sister, he knew of few young women of her class who would ever consider the enjoyment of their servants.

He waited for the third glass to arrive, then poured the champagne and handed one to each of the women.

'To us,' Grace said, raising her glass.

'To us,' Thomas echoed, although he doubted that after tonight, once the Duke had visited Lady Ashbridge's home, there would be an 'us' to celebrate. But in the meantime he might as well enjoy this last evening in her company.

The curtain rose, the orchestra started playing, the cast began singing and Grace wished this evening could go on for ever. Then she could stay as she was, seated beside Thomas, champagne and happiness making her giddy.

She moved a fraction closer towards him, close enough so the naked skin of her arm was skimming his jacket, so close her thigh was all but touching his.

This was perfection. Well, almost perfection. What would make this evening perfect would be if it wasn't his jacket that was caressing her arm, but his fingers. Her arms tingled as she imagined them tracing a line up her arm, then slowly moving over her body.

She closed her eyes and sighed, pleased that laughter from the audience covered the sound.

He looked at her and smiled at something amusing that had happened on stage. She smiled back at him. His gaze moved to her lips and she willed him to do it, to kiss her. No one would see. Everyone, including Molly, was watching the play.

He turned back to watching the performance and she silently cursed his respectable behaviour.

He should kiss her. Now. Tonight.

If the Duke did start to pay her court, she knew what would happen. Her grandmother would insist she see no more of Thomas. Tonight might be the last time she was in his company. This might be the last time she would have an opportunity to discover what it was like for him to hold her, to kiss her, to feel his caresses. It was an opportunity she would not waste.

If he would not take advantage of the dark and his private box, she would have to find some other way to get him to do what she wanted and what she was sure he must want as well.

The performance came to an end. Grace joined in the rapturous applause as if the entire thing had been an absolute delight, even though her thoughts had been on other matters and she had failed to follow the story line. The cast took bow after bow. Even Mr Gilbert and Mr Sullivan made appearances and received standing ovations. Eventually, the electric house lights were turned on and it was time to go.

They left the box and joined the exuberant crowd departing from the theatre, all loudly discussing the performance and laughing at the antics of the cast.

Like herself, Thomas remained silent, as if he, too, was lost in his thoughts.

It had been a magical evening, but all Grace could think was they might never again walk arm in arm.

The carriage was waiting for them at the entrance and they drove home through the busy streets, still full of traffic at this late hour, the pavements packed with people walking under the glow of the gas lamps.

The journey was annoyingly short and they arrived home far sooner than she had hoped. This was it. She would now say goodbye to him and if the Duke made good on his promise to call, they might never see each other again.

He helped Molly down from the carriage, then held out his hand for Grace. She placed her hand in his. The strong fingers curled around hers. Was he thinking the same as she? Was he regretting the likelihood they would never again be in each other's company? Was he thinking they had to make the most of these last precious moments together?

She looked into his eyes to try to answer those questions. He gazed back at her and there was such warmth in his look, such intimacy, she was sure he was feeling the same.

She lowered herself to the ground, her body coming temptingly close to his. How she longed to know what his body felt like up against hers. She'd had hints of the strength and power of his arms and chest when they'd walked and danced together, but she wanted to know what his muscles felt like under the touch of her fingers.

'You can go ahead, Molly,' she said, not looking in the direction of her lady's maid. 'I shall be in shortly.'

The door opened, light briefly filled the path, then with a soft click the door closed. They were alone in near darkness. No one would see them now. Grace continued to stare up into his eyes. She knew he wanted to kiss her. She could see it in the intimacy of his gaze.

Do it, she silently urged.

She parted her tingling lips in invitation, her breath turning into gentle sighs.

His hand moved tantalisingly slowly up her arm, over her elbow-length gloves to her naked skin, further kindling her burning need for him. She had to feel his lips on hers, his body up against hers. She yearned for him to relieve this pounding desire for his kisses, for his caresses.

She moved in closer, closed her eyes and tilted back her head.

'We can't,' he whispered, his lips so close she could feel his warm breath feather-light on her cheek.

'Yes, we can,' she whispered back. 'It's what I want. No one will see. No one will know.'

Then his lips were on hers, hot, hard and hungry.

She kissed him back, unleashing the pent-up longing that had been building up since she had first danced with him, loving the taste of him, the feel of his rough cheeks on hers and relishing the sensation of his strong muscular chest against her soft breasts.

Oh, yes, this was what she wanted.

She wrapped her hands around his head, her fingers weaving into his thick hair, holding him tight as her kisses gave full vent to her passions.

His tongue ran along her bottom lip, causing her lips to part so she could fully experience the pleasure of that arousing touch. Kissing her deeper, holding her tighter, he let his tongue gently enter her mouth and she was sure that if he hadn't been holding her so tightly, she would have swooned with the sheer sensual thrill of such intimacy.

His masculine taste was so intoxicating, the feel of his body pressed against her was maddingly enticing, but it was still not enough. She wanted more than his kisses. She wanted his caresses. Her breasts yearned to feel the touch of his hands, the throbbing between her legs demanded release, a release only he could give her.

His kisses moved to the sensitive skin of her neck and she pressed herself against him, silently urging him to continue in his exploration of her body.

'Miss… Lady Ashbridge insists you come inside, now,' Molly said, her voice urgent.

He all but jumped backwards.

Grace had not heard the door open, nor the arrival of her lady's maid, and as fond as she was of Molly, she cursed her for her unwanted interruption.

'I'll be in shortly,' she said.

'Yes, miss.' The door opened and closed and they were once again alone, but he remained standing frustratingly apart from her.

'You must go inside before Lady Ashbridge comes looking for you,' he said, his voice a hoarse rasp.

Grace released a sigh of exasperation. 'Yes, I suppose you're right,' she said, but did not move.

'I'm sorry, Grace. That should never have happened.'

'You have nothing to be sorry for,' she whispered back.

'You have my assurance that no one will ever know.'

She shrugged. 'I don't care if everyone knows.' Why should she care if everyone knew about something that had given her so much pleasure? Surely the world should be allowed to share in her joy.

'Yes, you do,' he said, his voice surprisingly stern. 'You do not want your grandmother to know. You don't want anyone in society to know. You will be ruined. Your chances of marriage will be destroyed.'

Again, what did she care?

'Go inside, Grace,' he said quietly. 'We'll talk of this another day.'

'Yes, yes, you're right, I suppose,' she said, her voice full of disappointment. 'Thank you,' she added, unsure what she was thanking him for: for bringing her back to reality or for kissing her and showing her what true pleasure was like. But she knew he was right, she had to go.

'Goodnight, Grace,' he whispered.

'Yes, goodnight, Thomas,' she replied and continued to stare up at him, until he opened the door for her and she knew she had to depart.

The door closed behind her and she released a long, euphoric sigh. That had been more captivating than she had imagined kissing a man could possibly be. She had thought she would not know what to do, but it had all come so naturally, as if they were made for each other.

And she would be seeing him again. He said they would talk of this another day, but she did not want conversation, she wanted more of his delicious kisses.

Smiling to herself, she walked down the hallway towards the drawing room where her grandmother would be waiting, expecting to hear of everything that happened tonight.

She would tell her grandmother the Duke planned to call. That was what she wanted to hear, but she certainly would not be telling her grandmother anything else that had occurred. That was to be her secret. Her delicious, glorious secret.

* * *

Thomas climbed back into his carriage as if in a daze and signalled for the driver to take him home. He could hardly believe he had done something so forbidden. He had kissed a debutante. No man in his right mind did such a thing. But he hadn't been in his right mind when he'd looked down at those tempting lips. He hadn't been in any mind at all, right or wrong, as he'd been incapable of thinking. He had just wanted. Wanted her so fiercely it drove out all rational thought. He had wanted to feel her lips on his, wanted her soft body pressed up against his and wanted more, much more than he was entitled to. He had longed to explore every contour of her shapely body with his hands, his lips, his tongue.

Thank God they had not been in a private place, as he had doubts that he would have been able to stop himself from doing what he really wanted to do, lifting her up, parting her legs and finding release deep within her soft feminine folds.

He put his hands on his head and groaned. He could not believe the depths of his moral decay. She was an innocent debutante, a young lady who knew nothing of the world and nothing of men, and she was expected to remain that way until she was married.

Yet she had made it clear she wanted his kisses and the way she had reacted did not suggest she was quite as unworldly and naive as he had assumed. A vision of her beautiful face before he kissed her appeared in his mind. With her lips parted in invitation, her body arched towards him, her head tilted and her eyes closed, she gave every impression she was offering herself to him. And he had been incapable of resisting the irresistible.

But it was still wrong, so wrong as to be unforgivable, and nothing could justify what he had done. Under normal circumstances such behaviour would have to be followed by an immediate proposal of marriage, but Grace did not want marriage to him and Lady Ashbridge most certainly did not want him to marry her granddaughter. She had set her sights much higher than Thomas and after tonight was likely to get her wish.

And once the Duke did come courting again, Thomas's role as Grace's escort would come to an end.

He groaned again at the memory of her lips, at the feminine taste of her, of the spicy, womanly scent under her floral fragrance. Now that he'd experienced her kisses once he wanted them again, wanted more than just her lips on his, but that could never be.

His carriage pulled up in front of his townhouse, but he signalled to his driver to take him to his club. He did not need the quiet of his home, where he would spend what remained of the night being tormented by what he had done. What he needed was a stiff drink, several stiff drinks, and some raucous masculine company to divert his mind from his appalling behaviour.

Arriving at his club, he walked up the stone stairs towards the highly polished black doors as if approaching a sanctuary. Only men could be members of the Eldridge Club and, while his sister and her friends constantly railed against such institutions, tonight he gave thanks for it.

He nodded to the doorman as he entered and headed across the foyer, his footsteps muffled by the deep crimson carpet. He entered the dimly lit bar and was pleased to see his two oldest friends seated in an alcove, sharing a bottle of claret.

'Thomas, where have you been hiding out?' Sebastian called out while Isaac signalled to the waiter to bring another glass.

Thomas sank gratefully into a leather chair. This was just the diversion he needed.

'No, I haven't been hiding. It's just been business as usual.' He poured himself a glass of wine, downed most of the contents and poured himself another.

His friends exchanged looks at his uncharacteristic behaviour, but thankfully made no comment.

'I heard you had bought a sizeable chunk of Hardgraves's land,' Isaac said with a satisfied smile.

'Yes, and I got it for much less than I was prepared to pay.' Thomas took another large sip of the claret and forced himself not to think of how he managed to make such a good deal.

'I saw him tonight, at the theatre, looking as pompous as ever,' he continued, then cursed himself. He did not want to think about tonight. Not the theatre and not that kiss. Definitely not that kiss.

'You weren't at The Elysian,' Isaac said with mock disapproval, referring to the music hall of which he was the manager.

'No, I was accompanying a debutante, so I don't believe The Elysian would have been appropriate.'

Sebastian and Isaac looked at him with raised eyebrows, their lack of comment speaking volumes.

'I was merely doing her grandmother a favour,' he said, hoping that was enough of an explanation.

The eyebrows were not lowered.

'Hardgraves was there as well,' he added, desperate to change the subject.

'I hope you were at a pantomime,' Isaac said. 'I doubt if that buffoon would be able to follow anything more complicated.'

Thomas smiled at the jest, while inwardly cringing that Isaac was talking about the man Grace might end up married to. She deserved so much better than Hardgraves. She deserved a man who would cherish and appreciate her. That would never be Hardgraves.

He took another long swallow of his claret while the others laughed about all the times Hardgraves and the other aristocrats had tried to get the better of the three of them when they had been schoolboys. They had arrived at school at the same time, three lost young boys. They instantly found they were all outsiders and soon became firm friends. A friendship that continued to endure to this day.

Isaac and Sebastian were both sons of aristocrats but were still seen as 'not up to snuff' by the other boys, Isaac because his mother was an actress and Sebastian because his family had been tainted by scandal for several generation, scandals he chose not to discuss. That had always mattered more to the other pupils and the schoolmasters than the boys' academic achievements or their sporting prowess.

Talk of school soon moved on to other topics and it wasn't long before they were laughing loudly as Isaac regaled them with ribald tales from his music hall. Thomas said a silent thanks for having such friends, who could so easily divert his brooding mind from what he should and should not have done, and what he should and should not do in future.

They were saving him ruminating, at least for the moment. He knew as soon as he left the club he was going to have to do some serious thinking about what had occurred tonight and come to some important decisions. But for the rest of the evening he would just drink and laugh with his friends and try to forget about everything else.

Chapter Fifteen

Grace had hardly been able to stop smiling from the moment she left Thomas on the doorstep. She had gone to bed with a silly grin on her face, had spent the night revelling in the most glorious of dreams and had woken still smiling with delicious contentment. Then continued to smile as she joined her grandmother in the breakfast room.

'You're in a very good mood today, my dear,' her grandmother said, looking at her over her teacup. 'I take it that seeing the Duke again has put that smile on your face.'

'Yes, Grandmama,' Grace replied dutifully with the only response her grandmother ever wanted from her.

The footman entered the room with an enormous bouquet of flowers.

From Thomas?

Grace could only hope their kiss had affected him as deeply as it had her and these were a token of his affection.

She jumped up from the table, rushed over to the footman and removed the note. She forced herself to keep smiling as she saw the crest. 'They're from the Duke of Hardgraves.'

'Oh, my dear, darling girl,' her grandmother said, rushing to join Grace, taking the embossed card from her fingers and placing her hand over her heart. 'This is wonderful, wonderful news.' She looked back down at the card. 'And he wishes to call on us this afternoon. This is it, my dear, this is it. You're about to become a duchess.'

Grace should be dancing with joy. She should feel as if she was floating on air. She should be tingling all over as if unable to contain her happiness. She should be feeling how she felt last night as the memory of Thomas's kiss played out repeatedly in her mind. What she should not be doing was having to force herself to keep smiling, nor should she be thinking of ways to get out of this afternoon's visit.

'Should we invite Mr Hayward as well?' she said quietly. 'So, well, so the Duke doesn't think he's got things all his own way?'

Her grandmother looked up from the card, still smiling, then placed her finger briefly on her chin, before shaking her head. 'No, I believe that man has served his purpose. You won't need to see him ever again.'

A heavy weight descended on Grace, making her shoulders slump. Her legs suddenly seeming incapable of carrying her. She wanted to cross the room and collapse on to the nearest dining chair. This could not happen. To never see Thomas again would be torture. She simply *had* to see him again. It was as if her very life depended on it—certainly her happiness did. It was imperative that her grandmother change her mind.

'But wouldn't it be better to continue to make the Duke jealous? I mean to say, he has shown me such favour before and withdrawn it. Perhaps he will do the same again this time.'

'We will just have to make sure he doesn't,' her grandmother said, lightly stroking Grace's cheek. 'You will have to do everything in your power to make sure he doesn't. And I mean, everything.' It was a gesture of affection Grace always longed to feel, and under normal circumstances it would be enough to make her do and say exactly what her grandmother wanted, but not this time. This was too important. She could not lose Thomas, not now.

'Grandmama, I have something I have to tell you.'

'Hmm, what is that, my dear?' Her grandmother placed the card back in the flowers and took her seat at the dining table.

Grace joined her, pleased that she was finally able to sit.

'Last night…' She gasped in a breath to give herself strength.

'Yes, last night?' Her grandmother signalled to the footman to pour another cup of tea.

'Last night I kissed Mr Hayward,' she said, forcing her words to come out in a rush before her constricted throat prevented her from speaking.

'Leave us,' her grandmother barked at the footman.

Grace clasped her hands together in her lap to stop them shaking. She was tempted to lower her head in shame, knowing how disappointed her grandmother would be in her, but how could she be ashamed of kissing Thomas? She had wanted to do it. She had encouraged him to do it and wanted him to do it again.

She breathed in deeply to try to slow her racing heart and looked across the table at her grandmother, who was glaring at her with dagger-sharp eyes, seemingly speechless with rage.

'It wasn't Mr Hayward's fault,' she rushed on. 'I encouraged him. I wanted him to kiss me.'

'Did anyone see you?' her grandmother said, her voice ominously quiet.

'No, we were outside the house, the entrance was in darkness and there was no one in the street.'

'Good.' Her grandmother looked towards the door, then picked up the silver bell beside her plate and gave it a vigorous ring.

The footman appeared immediately. 'Samuel, I have decided to increase your wages. I have always appreciated your discretion and loyalty and believe it needs to be rewarded. Do you understand what I am saying to you?'

'Yes, my lady,' the footman said with a bow. 'Thank you, my lady.'

'But I also believe in punishing disloyalty and indiscretion. Should I, say, hear that the servants are gossiping about something they should not, then I would have no hesitation in sacking the culprit responsible for spreading unfounded rumours and throwing him out on to the street without a reference. Do you still understand what I am saying to you?'

'Yes, my lady,' the footman said with another bow.

'Good, you can leave us now.' With that, her grandmother turned the full focus of her displeasure back on Grace.

'No one saw what happened. No one knows what happened. No one needs to know what happened. I will make sure Mr Hayward says nothing. You've been a stupid, stupid girl, but it should not harm your prospects.'

'But—'

'No buts. We will never mention this again and, of course, you will never, ever see that man again.'

'But—'

Her grandmother held up both hands to stop her words.

'But I love Mr Hayward,' Grace blurted out before she even had the chance to think about what she was going to say. But it was true. She did love him. She loved being with him, loved the way he made her feel, loved the way he made her laugh, loved the way she could rely on him, loved everything about him.

A smile spread across Grace's lips, a glorious, blissful smile. She was in love with Thomas. Of course she was. That was why the world seemed like a better place the moment she saw him. That was why she thought of him constantly. That was why she felt complete when she was with him.

She was in love with Thomas Hayward. And she wanted to spend the rest of her life with him. Not the Duke, not any other man. To marry another would be a travesty, for herself and for the man she did not and never could not love. It had to be Thomas, only Thomas.

Surely even her grandmother would be able to see that.

'Don't be ridiculous,' her grandmother all but snarled back at her. 'You don't know the meaning of the word love. The man was just using you.'

'He was not. He's not like that,' she said, defiance welling up inside her at this unfair criticism.

'Oh, isn't he? He kissed you last night, didn't he? He took an enormous liberty that no man should take with a debutante, but did he send you a bouquet of flowers this morning?'

Grace looked over that the enormous bouquet from the Duke.

'No,' her grandmother answered for her. 'When he kissed you, did he ask for your hand in marriage, as any real gentleman would?'

'No,' Grace whispered.

'Or did he take what he wanted, then run off into the night feeling pleased with himself that he had taken liberties with a silly debutante?'

Grace chose not to answer.

'He did, didn't he? Then he probably went and boasted to his friends as to how you had all but thrown yourself at him and he had merely taken what was offered.'

Heat rushed to Grace's cheeks at the memory of how she had indeed offered herself to him, desperate for his kisses.

'And is he here today, offering for your hand in marriage, making right on the wrong he committed?'

Again, Grace did not answer, the pounding of her heart and the burning of her cheeks making thinking all but impossible.

'No. The man does not love you, Grace,' her grandmother said in a softer tone. 'He could just see that you are a stupid, naive little girl who could be taken advantage of. You're just lucky that a kiss was the only thing he took.' She narrowed her eyes and stared at Grace. 'That is all he took, wasn't it?'

Grace nodded, trying to take in all her grandmother had said. There *was* no bouquet from Thomas and certainly there had been no mention of marriage, except when he had first told her he had no plans to do so. Could her grandmother be right? It seemed there was only one thing for it, she would have to ask him herself.

'And you can put any thoughts of trying to contact that man again right out of your mind,' her grandmother said as if reading her thoughts. 'If you do see him again or write to him—and believe me, if you try such a foolhardy action I will hear about it—then I will cut you off. You will have nowhere to live and no money to live on. Then you really will find out whether your precious Mr Hayward is actually enamoured with you or was just taking advantage of your stupidity. You will discover whether he is prepared to take in a waif with nowhere else to go. You'll know for certain whether that one kiss was enough to make him want to take you as his wife.'

Grace gripped her hands tightly in her lap, her heart racing, her stomach tying itself into ever tighter knots.

'Or you can continue to live in my home, where nothing more is expected of you than to marry well.'

Grace made no reply.

'And this afternoon you can show me just how grateful you are for all that I have given you by being charming to the Duke so he knows that it is he, and he alone, that you wish to wed.' She narrowed her eyes again. 'And you will never, ever mention that kiss again or speak Hayward's name in this house. Do I make myself clear?'

Again Grace made no reply.

'Or do I need to show you what life is like for a young woman such as yourself who is thrown out of her home after shaming her family? Do you think you will actually be able to survive out there?' She pointed towards the window. 'Can you imagine what would have happened to you if I had not taken you in and given you a home and the best of everything?'

Grace looked down at her trembling hands.

'Good. Then we will pretend that this conversation never happened.' With that, her grandmother rang for the footman. 'Samuel, my tea has gone cold,' she barked at the young man. 'Make another pot.'

The footman took the teapot and hurried out of the room.

'I believe you can spend the rest of this morning in your bedchamber, thinking about all I have said, while Molly helps you prepare for your important visitor. Tell her the lavender gown will be appropriate. You should be dressed in a manner suitable for receiving an offer.'

Grace remained quiet, staring down at her hands.

'Right, you are excused.'

She stood up and moved away from the table.

'And remember,' her grandmother added, stopping

Grace just as she took hold of the door handle, 'you will smile throughout this visit. You will let the Duke know you are flattered by his renewed interest and you see him as the most charming, most intelligent, wittiest man you have ever met, or you will face the consequences. Do I make myself clear?'

'Yes, Grandmama,' Grace said as she walked slowly out of the room on legs seemingly made of lead. Her entire body ached as if she was coming down with influenza and even in her childhood, she had never felt more confused and alone that she did right now.

While Molly took to her hair, backcombing, curling, sweeping it up, pushing in pins and flowers, Grace stared at her reflection in the looking glass and chewed on her bottom lip in thought.

Her grandmother was wrong. Thomas had not used her. She had to be. He had not seen her as a silly, naive debutante and taken advantage of her. Well, she *was* a silly, naive debutante, but that was hardly her fault. She knew nothing of the world. She'd been cloistered away in her grandmother's homes for the last eighteen years. Her only experience of life was at the social events she had attended during the Season and there had been woefully few of them, and what she had seen out the window of their carriage.

But her grandmother was right about one thing—many of the sights she had seen as they had travelled through London had been grim indeed. Even in the wealthier areas she had seen some shocking sights, children begging on the streets, people dressed in rags, desperate women trying to sell flowers, blind men selling trays of matches.

She would never survive if she was tossed out into that world. But nor did she want to stay in this world, one where she had to marry a man she did not love and hardly knew and see nothing of the man she did love.

If only she knew how Thomas really felt about her. If only he had sent her a note declaring his love. If only he had asked for her hand in marriage. If he did love her as much as she loved him, they could wed and she could still have her fairy-tale ending. It might not be what her grandmother wanted, but it would still be glorious, and maybe, just maybe, when her grandmother came to see what a remarkable man Thomas was, she, too, would come to see how perfect such a marriage could be.

She released a loud, slow sigh. That would never happen and there was no point pretending it would. Thomas did not have a title. It did not matter how perfect he was, the possession of a title was all that mattered to her grandmother.

Her hair styled to perfection, Molly helped her into the lavender gown her grandmother had insisted she wear. It was a gown Grace had simply adored when the dressmaker had presented it to her, but now it felt like she was being clapped in irons rather than adorned in satin, and being taken to her execution rather than receiving a visitor for afternoon tea.

'You look lovely, miss,' Molly said. Despite the compliment, her lady's maid's voice reflected Grace's sadness.

'Thank you, Molly,' she said, releasing a low sigh.

Molly hesitated, as if there was something she wished to say, then curtsied and departed. Grace waited until she was summoned. Then, with a heavy heart, walked down the stairs and entered the drawing room, where she found her grandmother and the Duke of Hardgraves seated on the sofa, their heads close together as if deep in conversation.

The Duke stood as she entered and smiled at her. She flicked a quick look at her grandmother, who glared at her, then sent her a false, beaming smile. Grace knew she should imitate her grandmother's expression, but her lips refused to move.

'Your Grace,' she said with a curtsy, then kept her eyes lowered as she took her seat. Hopefully, that was all that would be required of her for the rest of the afternoon.

The Duke asked whether she had enjoyed last night's play and how she was enjoying the Season, which she responded to in as few words as possible.

He then went on to discuss the changeable weather and how much he was looking forward to the hunting season once the social Season was over. To which Grace made the required non-committal responses.

'I am aware that you have been keeping company with Mr Hayward and believe you have developed a certain fondness for the man.'

At the mention of his name, Grace's gaze fixed on the Duke, both interested and wary as to where the conversation would now go.

'I believe I would be remiss in my duty if I did not inform you as to that man's true character,' the Duke said, shaking his head slowly and frowning.

'Really, Your Grace?' her grandmother said in mock surprise. 'We were under the impression that Mr Hayward was an honourable gentleman and he has been so attentive to my granddaughter.'

'Yes, he no doubt was able to deceive such a trusting soul as yourself,' the Duke said, the furrows in his brow deepening. 'But I should inform you that, unfortunately, that man is neither honourable nor a gentleman.'

Grace stiffened and forced herself not to blurt out that he was both. He had been the one to restore her dignity when she had fallen so ignominiously at the Duke's ball. He had given her the strength to stand up to that bully Lady Octavia. And his behaviour towards her had always been honourable. Some might say he should not have kissed her, but that had been what she wanted so he could not be criticised for such behaviour. And, yes, perhaps he should have made an offer of marriage, but, well, maybe he just hadn't had the opportunity to do so yet.

'Is he not honourable?' her grandmother said, placing her hand over her heart and tilting her head, as if hanging on the Duke's every word.

'Yes, I'm afraid the man is quite disreputable and I can tell you things that perhaps a young lady should not hear.'

'It is good of you to spare my granddaughter's delicate feelings, Your Grace, but it if is something she needs to hear for her own protection, then I believe you should tell her all that you know.'

Grace was beginning to wonder if this was a discussion they had already had and were now merely putting on a performance for her benefit.

'Mr Hayward is a covetous man who always wants what other men have.'

To Grace this sounded like one of those occasions her old nanny would have described as the pot calling the kettle black.

'He knew that I had, shall we say, an attraction for you,' he continued and gave a small smile. Her grandmother tittered behind her hand while sending Grace a steely gaze of disapproval, a look that Grace returned.

'That is why he appeared to be so interested in you at my weekend party.'

'Appalling, simply appalling,' her grandmother said,

shaking her head in disapproval as if this was something about which she was unaware and not something she had orchestrated as part of her plan to capture the Duke.

'But it is worse than that, I'm afraid.'

'Oh, surely not,' her grandmother said with a gasp of feigned shock.

'Yes, the man had the audacity to suggest to me we use Miss Lowerby in a shameless wager.'

Grace's gaze shot to the Duke, her body suddenly numb, even as her heart thumped loudly in her chest.

'Yes, it's true,' the Duke added, looking in her direction. 'And I'm ashamed to say, I accepted his bet, but only because I knew that I would win.'

Her grandmother tilted her head once again, as if to say, please go on, and despite herself, Grace also wanted to hear what the Duke had to say, even though she suspected, or hoped, it was all lies.

'He challenged me in a contest to see who could woo Miss Lowerby and gain her affections, and, in his words, to make things more interesting, that we should bet on the outcome.'

Grace covered her mouth with her hand to stop herself from crying out, *No, he would not do that.*

'I took the bet because I knew just how greedy the man was and because, well…' he shrugged and smiled at her '… I was intending to woo you anyway.' He pulled his face into a more serious expression. 'But I told him that if he won he would have to pay me more for the land I no longer required, the land he so desperately wanted for that railway thing of his, but if I won, I would sell it for a lower price.'

Grace stared at him, her heart pounding hard, as the ramification of that bet crashed down on her. Hadn't Mr Hayward informed her when they were out walking that he expected to get the Duke's land at a lower cost? She had enjoyed that walk so much, but was he merely playing a role? It could not be true. It simply could not be. Surely she would have known if he had been merely toying with her. The fun they'd had together, the way they had laughed and teased each other, that could not have all been artifice. Could it?

'I can see you are now starting to understand what sort of man he is,' the Duke said, shaking his head in disapproval. 'I knew he would merely go through the motions of wooing you, but let me win so he could get my land off me for less than he had originally offered. That's the sort of man he is. One who only cares about business and will do anything to get what he wants. Whereas I was prepared to sacrifice my land for a lady's honour.'

'Oh, Your Grace,' her grandmother said, both hands over her heart. 'That was so noble of you. And dare I say rather romantic?'

'Well, I did have my own selfish reasons.' He smiled at Grace. 'I actually wished to win the fair maiden.

That was much more important to me than land or money ever could be.'

Her grandmother sighed loudly, while Grace tried to take in all that he had said.

'I don't believe you,' she seethed, finally finding her voice.

'I can understand that,' the Duke said, once again shaking his head dolefully. 'It would be hard for a young lady as kind and gentle as you to believe someone's behaviour could be so disreputable, but I have the altered contract and a written document that attests to the bet if you wish to see it.'

'I'm sure that won't be necessary,' her grandmother said as Grace continued to stare at the Duke in disbelief. Could it be true? Had Mr Hayward used her so he could buy the Duke's land at a reduced cost? Was that all she had ever been to him? A means to advance his own business interests?

He had mentioned his expectation of making an even more advantageous deal than he had expected, that she must be his lucky star and would be the one to make it happen. She had felt so flattered at the time. Had he been making fun of her? Had it all been just one big joke at her expense?

'I'm so sorry you have had to hear this and I can see it has been a shock for you,' the Duke said. 'But people are not always what they seem.'

Grace gave a small, mirthless laugh. That was becoming increasingly obvious.

'But even though I lost the bet I feel like a winner,' he continued. 'And that is why I am here today. I hope I will continue to be a winner.' He turned towards her grandmother. 'At my weekend party I asked if your lovely granddaughter would be amenable to a courtship. To my delight she said yes. Now I wish to ask whether she would be equally amenable to my offer of marriage.'

'Oh, Your Grace,' her grandmother said. 'Of course my granddaughter would be amenable, more than amenable.' She laughed as if this was all so amusing. 'Wouldn't you, Grace?'

They both looked at her and Grace knew she had no option. She had thought she loved Mr Hayward, but he was not the man she thought he was. She didn't love the Duke and suspected she never would, but as her grandmother said, what did she know of love? Nothing.

There was no point pursuing the foolish dream of being with Mr Hayward. In fact, there seemed no point in anything. It was time to accept her fate.

'Yes, I accept your proposal,' she said, her dreams of happiness as shattered as her heart.

Chapter Sixteen

Thomas had received no response to the note he had sent Grace containing a clumsy attempt at an apology for his outlandish behaviour. He had not gone as far as to offer his hand in marriage, but he had made it clear he would do whatever was required to make amends.

When another day had passed and he had still received no reply, his concern continued to mount. Had Lady Ashbridge intercepted the letter and destroyed it? Or had Grace received it, but not replied? Had he offended her by not immediately proposing marriage? Would his presence at her home be welcomed or rebuffed?

It was a bizarre situation in which he found himself. He did not obsess over women. Apart from the occasional pleasant reminiscence, he gave his romantic encounters scarcely a second thought. Yet he couldn't get Grace out of his mind, nor could he stop wondering why he had heard nothing from her and speculating over what she might be feeling.

* * *

By the third day he resolved to visit her and find out for himself what she was thinking and feeling. When a letter arrived in the morning post bearing an unfamiliar feminine handwriting, he opened it with relief. Finally, his questions would be answered.

But that relief soon turned to dismay when he read the contents.

It was not from Grace, but Lady Ashbridge, informing him that Grace had accepted the Duke's proposal of marriage and their engagement was soon to be announced. She went on:

My granddaughter confessed all regarding your deplorable indiscretion and has my full forgiveness. Under the circumstances, it is advisable for you to have no further contact with my granddaughter and, if you care anything for her well-being, you will act as an honourable gentleman and do or say nothing to jeopardise her future with the Duke of Hardgraves.

He reread the letter, hardly able to believe the words, then crumpled it into a tight ball and threw it on to the table.

It was done. The Duke had finally made good on his offer. Grace and her grandmother had achieved their goal. Thomas had served his purpose and was no longer needed.

He stood up and paced the room, angry energy making it impossible to remain seated. Had this all been just a ruse? Had that kiss meant nothing at all? Was it merely a bit of fun before she committed herself to marriage? A goodbye gesture, perhaps?

Whatever it was, it mattered not. It was over.

He shot an angry glare at the note and went back to pacing. Instead of being angry, he should be thanking Lady Ashbridge. He had kissed a debutante, but there would be no demand for a proposal, quite the opposite. She had given him his freedom.

His life could return to the way it was before Grace had tumbled into it. And that was what he would do. He would put her behind him, forget all about her and let her get on with her life with the Duke.

He stopped pacing, picked up the note, smoothed it flat and read it yet again. The words remained the same, but he wondered as to their real intent. It was from Lady Ashbridge, not Grace. Was this what she really wanted or was it being forced on her?

Was she at home now, waiting for him to save her from this terrible fate?

The way she had kissed him had not been that of a young woman set on marrying another. Nor had it felt like just a bit of fun, or a goodbye kiss. It had contained real passion. It had been obvious in her response she was yielding to a powerful desire, a desire that had mirrored his own surging need.

And yet she was now to wed the Duke of Hardgraves.

This was surely happening against her will.

Clenching his fist, he crushed the letter in his hand.

If she was being forced to marry the Duke against her will, he would not stand for it. He would not take Lady Ashbridge's letter at face value. He had to hear from the young lady herself that she was willingly entering into this marriage. And if she wasn't he would… he would… He resumed pacing the room, a tumult of thoughts churning in his mind.

He stopped walking. What would he do? Would he offer to marry her himself?

He looked down at the tightly crunched paper in his hand.

Would that be such a bad thing?

He had never considered marriage before, but then, he had never met anyone like Grace Lowerby before. He'd never met a young lady who could cause him to forget himself in the way she did. The idea that he might one day kiss a debutante would not so long ago be ludicrous. And yet he had done so, knowing where that must lead.

Marriage.

Every man knew the consequences of kissing a debutante. He had known it when he kissed her and that had not stopped him. Was it because that was what he really wanted?

Of course he had wanted her. His body ached for her, his dreams were full of her. When they were apart she was all he could think of. And that kiss—by God, that kiss had been like nothing he had experienced before. It wasn't just the sensuality of such an intimate act, it was more, so much more, something that transcended the mere physical.

But marriage?

It would mean spending every day with Grace, waking up to her each morning, going to bed with her every night. He smiled at the prospect. She would be in his life permanently. He would see her smile every day, hear her lovely voice, her laughter.

They would be husband and wife, lovers, friends, companions for the rest of their lives.

He smoothed out the letter, folded it up and placed it in the inside pocket of his jacket. His mind was made up.

The first thing he would do was find out what was really happening, and if, as he suspected, she was being coerced into this marriage and it was not what she wanted, he would offer for her hand.

He patted his jacket pocket where the letter sat over his heart and smiled to himself.

The smile faded. But what if she was doing this willingly? He released a long sigh through flared nostrils, then dismissed that idea.

It was extremely unlikely. A woman who wishes to

marry another does not kiss with such ardent passion and surrender so fully and fervently.

Did she?

If he wanted that question answered, and he most certainly did, he was going to have to ask the lady herself. And if she did tell him she was entering into a marriage with the Duke willingly he would wish her every happiness in her future life as the wife of the Duke of Hardgraves. Then he would follow Lady Ashbridge's demands and do or say nothing to endanger her future with the Duke.

But he knew that outcome would be unlikely.

Grabbing his gloves and hat, Thomas took his carriage over to Lady Ashbridge's townhouse to have a conversation he would once have thought he would never have. One where he would soon be an engaged man, a man about to make an innocent debutante his wife. A man who was surprisingly not just resigned to the idea, but rather pleased by the prospect. More than pleased. And if she consented to be his wife he was sure that pleasure would turn to euphoria.

His carriage pulled up in front of their home. He rushed up the path, rang the bell and composed himself, trying to think what one says in these circumstances.

When the door opened, he handed his card to the footman who returned a few moments later to inform him that Lady Ashbridge was not at home to him.

Ignoring the man, he pushed past him, entered the drawing room, and was faced with a furious Lady Ashbridge.

'I believe I told you—'

'Grace,' Thomas interrupted Lady Ashbridge and strode across the room where she was seated beside the window, embroidery clasped in her hands. 'Your grandmother has told me that you have accepted a proposal from the Duke. Is this true?'

She lifted her chin and met his gaze with steady eyes. 'Yes, it's true,' she stated clearly.

Thomas paused, his unformed words dying before they could be uttered. This did not sound or look like a woman who was being coerced.

'But is it what you want?'

'Yes, it is.' She continued to stare at him without coyness or artifice. 'The Duke has won my hand, fair and square.'

Thomas remained staring at her, trying to make sense of her words.

'Are you sure? Have you been forced into this?' He looked over his shoulder at a now preening Lady Ashbridge.

'No. I have not been forced. I am to marry the Duke of Hardgraves,' she continued. 'He has won my heart.'

'I see,' he said, not really seeing at all. He wanted to ask, so why did you kiss me with such passion? She was such a chaste young lady he could not imagine she would do so for any flighty reasons. It had to mean something. Didn't it? Surely her words did not mean what they were saying. There must be a hidden message in them. Somehow they had to be a cry for help, to be rescued, but he couldn't for the life of him see how her words could be interpreted in any other way than an admission that she actually wanted to marry the Duke.

'Is it really what you want?' he asked again.

'I believe I have made myself clear, Mr Hayward,' she said, her tone becoming terse. 'The Duke is my champion. He is the one who values my affections above everything else. He took a chance on winning my love and he secured his prize.'

'But, Grace—'

'My granddaughter has answered your questions repeatedly, Mr Hayward, and made her feelings very clear. Now, would you please leave my drawing room. You were not invited and I would rather not have to call my footmen to eject you.'

'If that is what you want, Miss Lowerby, then I wish you every happiness with the Duke,' he said softly and bowed to both ladies. 'I promise you will see no more of me.'

He had expected a reaction from her, something, anything, but she kept her head high, and stared straight ahead, not even looking at him.

There was nothing for it. He had his answer. It was time to go.

Lady Ashbridge followed him out the room and grabbed hold of his arm as he reached the front entrance.

'I'm assuming that despite that reprehensible display to which you have just subjected my granddaughter, you are still capable of being a gentleman and will give me your promise that you will forget about anything that may or may not have happened between the two of you, and never, ever mention it to anyone.'

'You have my word I will discuss nothing of what occurred between myself and your granddaughter,' Thomas said, giving the only promise he was capable of keeping. While he would say nothing, he could not honestly say he would never think of the kiss they exchanged.

'Good, then I will say goodbye to you, Mr Hayward.'

With that, he left, the footman closing the door behind him with a decisive thud.

Now it really was over. She had stated clearly that none of this was against her will. It was what she wanted and it seemed she even had a strange affection for the Duke, seeing him as her champion who had won her heart. It was difficult to believe, but believe it he must.

He should be relieved that she was not being coerced and was doing what she wanted. And he supposed he should be pleased. He was once again free. He had never wanted to marry. He had never wanted to kiss a debutante and put himself in such a perilous position. But as he drove back to his home it was not a sense of freedom he was experiencing.

Nor was it relief. She wanted that buffoon, the Duke of Hardgraves. She had kissed him, but she wanted the Duke. She even saw the Duke as her champion. As if that imbecile could be a champion at anything. He had despised the Duke since he was a boy of seven, but never so much as he did now.

How could she believe herself to be in love with a man who was so beneath her?

Anger surged up within him. The Duke was beneath her in every way except one. He was a man with a title.

She was about to do what countless generations of aristocratic women had done before her, marry one of her own kind.

And there was nothing he could do about it. He could not capture her, run off with her and marry her against her grandmother's and, so it would seem, her own wishes. He would simply have to accept her decision.

He called out to his driver to take him to his office. It was time to get back to his old life and put this entire episode behind him and he knew the best way to do that. He would bury himself in his work and forget all about Miss Lowerby, Lady Ashbridge and the Duke of Hardgraves. Compared to the scheming and double-dealing of the aristocracy in search of marriage partners, the affairs of business seemed so much more straightforward.

'Well, of all the nerve,' Grace's grandmother said, taking her seat. 'Barging into our home like that. It shows an appalling lack of manners and breeding.'

Grace chose not to answer and continued staring out the window, not seeing anything of the garden.

'Thank goodness you'll never have to see him again. Believe me, I let him know what's what before he left. We won't have to put up with displays like that ever again.'

'Yes,' she murmured, sure that her grandmother was correct. What was the point of seeing a man who lied to her and used her in such an outrageous manner? She should be angry, offended, hurt at all he had done.

Instead, she felt nothing, as if all feeling had died. The man she was certain she loved was not who she thought he was. He was a man who could use her as part of a callous bet. And she had just given him enough opportunity to tell her she meant more to him than just a means to get a better deal on the Duke's land. But he had not taken that opportunity.

Why hadn't he said *he* was her champion, that he wanted to win her heart, that he prized her above everything else, including that damn piece of land? But he had said nothing of the sort. Merely accepted that she was now to be the Duke's.

'But you conducted yourself admirably, my dear,' her grandmother continued. 'You put him in his place and let him know how things stand. He now knows the Duke has won you fair and square and is the champion of your heart. It's all perfect.'

'Yes,' she responded automatically, still staring out the window.

'You'll have to tell the Duke what you said. I'm sure he'll get a lot of pleasure in knowing you gave that upstart a good telling off and let him know he will never measure up to the Duke of Hardgraves.'

'I thought you said we were to never speak of Mr Hayward again?' she said, turning to look at her grandmother.

'Well, yes,' her grandmother spluttered. 'Yes, I suppose you're right. There's no point bringing him up and we most certainly wouldn't want the Duke to get the impression Hayward means anything to you.'

Her grandmother narrowed her eyes. 'He doesn't mean anything to you, does he?' Her stern expression made it clear there was only one correct answer to that question. 'All that ridiculous talk of love is forgotten now, isn't it? You've come to your senses, haven't you?'

'Yes. He means nothing to me.'

'Good. And you're right. We should never talk of him again. You can just put all thought of him and the very short time you unfortunately spent in his company completely out of your mind. It's time to focus on the future. Your future as a duchess.'

Grace turned back to the window. Never talking about Mr Hayward was going to be easy. She was hardly going to want to discuss him with her grandmother or the Duke, but as for never thinking about him, that was going to prove more difficult.

She lightly stroked her lips.

'We've got so much to do in preparation for your forthcoming marriage I believe there will be no time to think of anything else.'

'Yes, Grandmama,' she answered, hardly knowing what her grandmother had said, her mind completely taken by the memory of that kiss and how it had made her feel. Would the imprint of his lips on hers ever leave her? Would she ever forget how it felt to have his arms encasing her, holding her tightly in an impassioned embrace? Heat erupted deep within her at the memory of the burning passion they had shared. She ran her tongue along her bottom lip, remembering the masculine taste of him and how it had set off a desperate throbbing need throughout her body.

Would she ever feel like that again?

Kissing him had transported her to such an ecstatic state it was hard to believe it all meant nothing to him.

She had merely been someone he had played with. Her grandmother had been right. She was a stupid, naive little girl who had no idea what love was and knew nothing of men and the world.

And it had taken the Duke, of all people, to open her eyes to what he was really like. Mr Hayward was a businessman who thought only of profit, success and winning.

'Grace, Grace,' her grandmother interrupted her thoughts. 'Have you heard a word I have said?'

'Sorry, Grandmama, what were you saying?'

Her grandmother smiled benevolently at her. 'You were thinking of the Duke and your wedding day, no doubt. It's perfectly understandable that you should get a bit distracted.'

Grace made no response.

'I was saying that the days leading up to your marriage are going to be the most exciting of your life. Well, the most exciting days until you are actually married and become a duchess.' Her grandmother placed her hand over her heart and smiled. 'You really are the luckiest of young ladies and you are going to have the most wonderful life imaginable.'

Again, Grace made no response, merely turned back to stare out the window.

She had agreed to do her duty, after all, what choice did she have, but it would be asking the impossible for her to actually enjoy doing so or to see it as the most wonderful life imaginable. She could easily imagine a more wonderful life, but that was one denied to her, one that had never really existed.

Chapter Seventeen

As he did every morning, Thomas strode up the stairs towards his office like a tiger seeking sanctuary in his lair. That was where he was comfortable. Not in the ballrooms mixing with society, not in drawing rooms taking tea with the ladies, but in his place of business where he knew the rules and how to always come out the victor.

Thank goodness for his work, he muttered to himself. He had plenty to keep him occupied now that he was no longer involved in helping Miss Lowerby achieve her dreams. Now he could focus on what was important to him. And there was one project demanding his immediate attention—the surveying and construction of a railway line on the land that was once the Duke of Hardgraves's.

He entered the reception area and came to an immediate halt. Seated on one of the leather chairs in the waiting room was his sister, Georgina. It seemed he was not going to be able to take immediate refuge in his work after all.

'Georgie, how lovely to see you again,' he said, kissing his sister's cheek. 'I hope you haven't been waiting long.'

'That is all right. Mr Worthington and I have been having an interesting conversation while I waited.'

He looked at his secretary, whose face remained professional and impassive, although Thomas suspected the poor man had just been disturbed from his work and subjected to a long monologue from his sister on whatever topic was presently fascinating her.

'Shall we go into my office?' He placed his hand gently on his sister's back and escorted her through the open door, smiling as he spotted a sign of relief cross Worthington's face.

'Tommy,' she squealed with delight as soon as they were alone in his office. 'What are all these rumours I've been hearing about you?'

Thomas cast a look at the solid oak door and hoped the squealing had not carried through to the outer office.

'How are things with the Duke of Ravenswood, and with the children?' he asked, hoping to divert the subject away from himself.

'Fine, fine.' She waved her hand in circles to indicate she would not be distracted from what she really came to talk about. 'So, what is this I hear about you being seen round town with a certain young lady?'

It was Thomas's turn to wave his hand as if it was nothing. 'I was merely escorting a young lady to a few social events as a favour to her grandmother.'

'That's not what I heard.' There were few things his sister enjoyed more than a good gossip. Usually Thomas remained unaffected by this, seeing it as one of her silly indulgences, but then he was not usually the subject.

Georgina settled herself on the leather couch and sent him an enormous smile, her hands clapping lightly together as if unable to contain her excitement.

'What I heard was you danced with Grace Lowerby at the Duke of Hardgraves's ball, that you were seen walking together at his estate. Alone.' At this, Georgina raised her eyebrows as if to underline the importance of her statement. 'That you were spotted walking in Hyde Park together, and…' she paused, presumably for dramatic effect '…you escorted her to the Savoy Theatre and were seen drinking champagne in the family's private box. All and all, this indicates you are courting. So why do I have to hear about this from my spies? Why have you not introduced her to the family?'

'Because I am not courting her and the young lady in question will be soon announcing her engagement to the Duke of Hardgraves.'

'No,' Georgina squealed even louder, as if he'd just announced they were about to face a life-altering catastrophe. 'Oh, Tommy, you must be heartbroken.' She rose from her chair and started to approach him. He waved his hand back at the sofa. The last thing he wanted was his sister's condolences.

'I know how that feels,' she said, thankfully taking her seat once more. 'It's devastating. And, yes, I can see that you are suffering.' She paused and tilted her head, her lips turned down in sympathy.

'So, how can I help you win her back?' she added, once again becoming animated. 'I'm very good at doing that. I've helped all my friends and they're all happily married now.'

Thomas couldn't help but raise his eyebrows. He doubted that Georgina's friends had benefited from any of her help, which tended to run to outrageous plans that caused more problems than they solved.

She continued to look at him, with that eager expression he had seen many times when they were children, the one that usually came before she was about to indulge in an act of mayhem.

'I am not heartbroken and I do not need your help,' he stated as emphatically as possible, hoping against hope she would listen to him.

'Of course you're heartbroken. What you need to do is declare your love to her in a heartfelt manner, preferably accompanied by a magnificent and sincere gesture that she cannot ignore. That always wins over a young lady.'

She stood up and began pacing the room, her brow furrowed in thought. 'Adam made a grand, if rather dangerous, gesture when he declared his love for me. I was so touched I just couldn't resist him.'

Thomas found it hard to believe the sensible Duke of Ravenswood would do anything dangerous, but under Georgina's influence anything was possible.

'You could challenge the Duke to a duel. No, that might be a bit much,' she added before Thomas had a chance to tell her what a ridiculous, not to mention illegal act that would be.

'Maybe you could serenade her under her window.'

Thomas released a low groan.

'Yes, you're right. You've got a terrible singing voice. You could write her poetry.' She stopped walking and turned towards him. 'Do you know how to write poetry? You've never really seemed like the poetic type, too busy with ledgers and all of that.' She indicated the books open on his desk, books he was desperate to get back to.

'Stop, Georgie,' he said, louder than he intended. 'I do not need to make a sincere and magnificent gesture of love. I do not need to win the young lady's heart for the simple reason I am not in love with her. I was merely helping her capture the man she really wanted, the Duke of Hardgraves. He was one of those bullies from school who always resented the fact that someone from my background achieved so much more than him. I was merely making him jealous so he would see Miss Lowerby as a desirable marriage prospect.'

Georgina stared at him, her mouth open, but for once not speaking, her eyes boring into his. 'How could you possibly be so heartless?' she finally said.

'What? Heartless? I was being gallant. I was helping a debutante achieve her dreams.' Thomas knew that was only half the story, but there was no point giving Georgina the full details. She would only react in her usual dramatic fashion and make more of this situation than it deserved.

'You have fobbed her off on a man you describe as dim-witted and a bully. How could you?'

'She had her heart set on marrying a titled man and that is exactly what she is going to do.' He strove to keep the bitterness out of his voice. 'It's what they all do.'

They might toy with the lower orders, they might kiss them, but they marry to advance their position in society.

'The Duke may be a dim-witted bully,' he continued while Georgie stared at him wide-eyed, 'but he is a duke—that makes him a highly desirable catch as far as any debutante is concerned.'

'Nonsense. Love transcends such things.'

He sighed at his sister's romantic fantasies. 'Whatever you might like to think, the Duke is the man she wants to marry.'

'Well, you need to show her she is making a mistake.'

He stared at his sister as if she was the dim-witted one.

'Don't look at me like that, Tommy. I've known you long enough to be able to read everything you are thinking.'

Georgina might think that was the case, but she was deluded.

'You have feelings for Miss Lowerby, strong feelings. I can see it in your face. And if my spies are correct, she most certainly has feelings for you. I was told she was sitting so close to you at the theatre she was almost in your lap.'

'I believe that is an exaggeration.' He was certainly pleased her so-called spies had not seen them on the doorstep outside Miss Lowerby's house.

'No, no exaggeration. I never exaggerate.'

Thomas merely shook his head at this delusion.

'So what are we going to do about this situation?'

'*We* are going to do nothing about a situation that only exists in your head. *You* are going to go and do whatever it was that brought you to London. *I* am going to get back to work.'

'No, you have to tell her how you feel. You can't let her marry the wrong man.'

'Don't you have some shopping to do, or something?'

'Yes, and I'm meeting my friends for afternoon tea, but first we have to sort out your problems. So, what do *your* friends think of what has happened? What have Sebastian and Isaac advised? Whenever I have a problem I always talk it over with my friends and get their advice.'

Once again, Thomas shook his head in disbelief. 'Unlike you, I do not get together with my friends to discuss my love life.'

'Ah ha.' She pointed her index finger at him. 'You admit it. It is your love life we are discussing.' She resumed pacing before Thomas could counter this claim. 'But Seb and Isaac would be of no help anyway. They're as useless with women as you are.'

This time, Thomas shook his head and rolled his eyes at his sister's ignorance. The only problems Isaac and Seb had when it came to women was dealing with the large numbers they had in and out of their beds, but that was not something he wished to discuss with his sister.

'I can see it is going to be all up to me to solve this problem.'

'There is no problem. Nothing needs to be solved and, as I have already said, I do not need your help.'

He stood up, crossed the room and opened the door. 'But thank you for coming. Now, I won't keep you from joining your friends and give my regards to your husband and my love to the children.'

Georgina was about to say something more, but he sent her a warning look and tilted his head towards Worthington seated in the outer office, as if to say he did not wish this to be discussed in front of his secretary. To his immense surprise, she did as she was bid.

'Goodbye, Georgina, it was a pleasure as always.' He kissed her cheeks and guided her towards the stairs.

'I'm not finished with you yet, Thomas Hayward,' she said in a voice she no doubt used when calling her stepchildren into line, but one entirely wasted on her brother.

'Goodbye, Georgina,' he repeated, and with relief watched her walk down the stairs.

Thomas returned to the sanctuary of his office, where under normal circumstances no one discussed love, courtship, magnificent gestures, or any other frivolous matters. He picked up his pen, then lowered it and stared out the window.

His sister was wrong, as usual.

He had not been courting Miss Lowerby, far from it. If it hadn't been for her falling over at the Duke's ball, he would never have even considered talking to a debutante, never mind dancing with one. If the Duke hadn't made that ridiculous bet and if he hadn't been tempted by the chance of getting the land at a more advantageous price, he would not have spent so much time in her company. If her grandmother had not come to him with that request to be seen in public with her, and if he hadn't been feeling uncharacteristically guilty over that bet, he would not have escorted her out in public.

That was the truth of the matter. Not all this romantic rubbish his sister was spouting.

Well, not entirely the truth. Yes, Georgina was right that he did have feelings for Miss Lowerby. And, yes, he had kissed her, which he would never do with a debutante if he hadn't been irresistibly attracted to her and, yes, it had crossed his mind to offer his hand in marriage as a result of that kiss, but it mattered not one iota. She was to marry the Duke of Hardgraves and that was the end of it.

He picked up his pen one more time and stared at the contracts in front of him. This would be his focus from now onwards, the uncomplicated world of business, not love, romance, grand gestures or any of that other baffling nonsense.

Chapter Eighteen

Her dream had come true, but like all dreams it was all an illusion. Grace was now engaged to a duke. Her grandmother couldn't be happier and showered her with praise and affection as if she were a princess. She had craved such attention when she was a child with a desperation that had made her ache. Now she had it. It should be making her content.

You should be happy, she had told herself yet again.

She had everything she had ever wanted. And surely, if she had never met Mr Hayward, she *would* be happy. But she *had* met him and he had ruined everything.

'Not long now,' her grandmother said over breakfast, having once again counted down the days until Grace would be married.

'Yes,' Grace responded with the only answer possible. It would not be long. The engagement had been announced, the banns had been read. Soon she would be walking up the aisle in her beautiful white gown, for which no expense had been spared.

'I don't suppose I will be seeing the Duke again today,' Grace added, stating something else that did not need to be said.

'It's of no matter.' Her grandmother took a sip of her tea, then resumed smiling. 'You are engaged. It's been announced in all the papers. He cannot back out now. You will soon be a duchess.'

'And married to a man I never see.'

'Some women would see that as a blessing.' Her grandmother gave a little laugh. 'I've already explained all that to you, my darling child. All that is to be expected of you is to do your duty and provide an heir and maybe a spare. Once you have done that, then the two of you can live separate lives. That is the way it has been done for countless generations and will continue to be done for countless more.'

'Good.' That at least was some consolation, although the thought of actually providing the required heir and spare was something Grace would prefer not to think about.

Her grandmother studied her over the top of her teacup. 'I can see the thought of being a duchess is already starting to change you. You are becoming so much more confident and self-assured. It won't be long before you are someone completely suited to being at the very pinnacle of society, someone to whom all others have to defer.'

She gave another little laugh, like an exuberant child. 'When you do become a grand lady I hope you don't forget your dear old grandmama and all she sacrificed for you so you could achieve everything you ever wanted.'

Grace took a sip of her tea, wondering who was actually doing the sacrificing.

'Anyway, if you are missing the Duke, you will see plenty of him when we visit his estate.' Her grandmother sighed. 'Soon to be your estate. Then you will have the chance to show him how much you have missed him.'

A shudder ripped through Grace. She just hoped the Duke continued to treat her with the same indifference he had of late. She would hate for him to take those liberties her grandmother said she should now grant him.

Once again that kiss she shared with Mr Hayward invaded her mind. She drew in a long, deep breath in an attempt to slow her suddenly racing heart. She could almost feel his lips on hers, his arms around her, his body pressed against hers. Her fervid imagination could all but taste him, and that taste was intoxicating.

She shook her head lightly, to drive out that image. She would not think of him. She would focus on the future, not the past. Yes, he kissed her. Yes, he made her feel things she did not know it was possible to feel. Yes, she had thought herself to be in love with him. But it was all a mirage. He was not the man she thought him to be.

Whether she was having reservations or not about marrying the Duke, it mattered not a bit. She was now engaged. It was official. There was no getting out of it now. It might not be the fairy tale she had imagined as a child, but she was not a child any longer. She was an adult. A woman about to become a bride and one day a mother. It was time to put aside all childish fancies and do her duty.

Forgetting about Miss Lowerby was proving far harder than Thomas had imagined, harder than anything he had done before. Especially as his working day now started with a ritual that doomed him to failure, scanning the society pages of the newspapers for any mention of the Duke and Miss Lowerby.

Thomas never read such tittle-tattle in the past, but as the weeks passed he found himself reading the goings-on of society with increasing focus. The Duke and Miss Lowerby did not feature as often as he would have expected and, when they did, it was a disappointment. The journalist always failed to mention how she appeared. Was she happy, sad, excited, regretful? Nor was there any mention as to whether the Duke was treating her well and acting in the correct manner of a man courting a lady. Instead, there were gushing descriptions of what she was wearing, as if that was all that mattered.

He had read the announcement of their engagement and, with trepidation, each day he braced himself for the announcement of their forthcoming marriage.

Despite these preparations, when it came, the impact winded him like an unexpected punch to the stomach.

He gripped the paper tighter as he reread the words. Their wedding was to be held at the local church near the Earl of Ashbridge's property, in one month's time, with the wedding breakfast to follow at the Earl's estate. Thomas threw the paper across his desk, not needing to read any further about the distinguished guests from the highest echelons of society who were expected to attend. Nor did he need to read how it would be the wedding of the Season between a beautiful young lady and a man of illustrious standing.

It was all but done. She was almost a duchess. She was to get the prize that every other young debutante had been seeking this Season. At least she would have well and truly put those bullying debutantes in their place. That provided some satisfaction, he supposed. But not much.

And the Duke was wasting no time in getting his fiancée up the aisle. If he was worried that Thomas might sweep in and steal her away, he was misguided. Or was it the thought of the dowry that was prompting such haste? Thomas placed his head in his hands and refused to believe they were actually in love and desperate to be man and wife.

He stood up and paced around the office, unspent energy coursing through him and refusing to let him settle. He should be pleased it was now a done deal. He could now do what he had been trying to do these past weeks, put her firmly in the past where she belonged and get on with his life.

He paced back to his desk, picked up the newspaper, screwed it up and threw it into the rubbish basket.

It was time to get back to work and stop wasting time on things that no longer concerned him.

He sat down. Stood up, paced over to the window and looked down at the busy London street below him, then paced back to his desk.

This would not do. He could not stay cooped up like this, pacing back and forth like a caged animal. He had to be outside. He had to be active. He had to be working, doing something physical to burn off all this unspent energy.

'Worthington,' he called out to his secretary. 'Send a telegram to the works manager. I'm heading down to Cornwall to inspect the progress on the construction of the new rail line.'

'Very good, sir,' came the reply.

While his secretary was off organising that, Thomas stuffed the papers he was supposed to be working on in a leather folio and stormed out of the office. He took a cab back home to pack some essentials, then headed for the train station.

As he travelled through the countryside, he tried to focus on the documents he had taken with him, but found himself staring at the changing scenery outside the window, unable to get his wandering mind to focus.

The telegram had obviously arrived as a carriage was waiting for him at the station. As he travelled up the recently laid track on what was now his land, he ignored the overbearing presence of the Duke's house and focused instead on the work site ahead of him.

When he saw the gangs of men hard at work, he released a satisfied sigh. This was where he needed to be, among men dedicated to achieving physical goals and as far away from society events and white weddings as it was possible to get.

In the previous weeks, the land had been changed beyond recognition from the way it had looked when he had escorted Miss Lowerby around the Duke's estate.

Large carts carrying metal railway tracks and wooden sleepers were parked beside makeshift workers' camps. Teams of labourers armed with pickaxes were levelling the land, others were laying the sleepers, while a group of burly men were hammering the tracks into place.

Thomas could see his input was not necessary, but it was good to be out in the open, among the noise of industrious men. But it was not enough to just watch. He had energy to burn off. Energy that *had* to be burnt off.

'We're making great progress,' the manager shouted over the noise of men's voices and the clanging of hammers on metal.

'I can see that. I hope you don't mind, but I feel the need to do some physical labour.'

Surprise crossed the manager's face, and Thomas felt the need to explain. At least, to explain as much as the manager needed to know.

'When I first joined the family business my father made me spend some time doing labouring work, so I would know the business from the ground up. Sometimes, when I'm stuck in my office, I miss it and feel the need to get my hands dirty again.'

He expected the manager to continue to look at him as if he was insane, but instead he smiled. 'Yes, sometimes you just have to get back on the tools, don't you? Well, we could do with someone to help with driving in the spikes.'

'Perfect.' Thomas took of his jacket and shirt and tossed them to one side, picked up a sledgehammer and joined the line-up of men, rhythmically driving in the metal spikes.

Yes, this was exactly what he needed. He could not think of Miss Lowerby when he was working up a sweat and using every muscle in his body in hard physical toil.

The day passed quickly, Thomas's muscles becoming satisfyingly tired with each passing hour, his mind mercifully fixed on work that demanded his full concentration.

In the afternoon he heard the familiar sound of coach wheels crunching over gravel. He paused in his work, wiped the sweat off his brow and looked across the fields to see a parade of carriages rolling up towards the Duke's home.

He turned his back and continued pounding in the spikes with increased vigour. It mattered nothing who the Duke planned to entertain at his home. If it was Miss Lowerby, he would think nothing of it.

He was on his own land, engaged in his own work. He had no need to see or speak to the Duke while he was here. And thank goodness for that. The last thing he wanted to see was that churl's gloating face.

'And to think, all this will soon be yours,' Grace's grandmother said, not for the first time, as the carriage made its way up the drive towards the Duke's country home.

'Just one more month and you will be the Duchess of Hardgraves,' she added, as if this, too, was something she had not repeated more times than Grace could count.

'Last time we were here you were just one of many debutantes attending a weekend party,' she continued, smiling fit to burst. 'And you outshone them all to win the man every other young lady had set her heart on.'

Grace shuddered, wishing her grandmother would not use words like 'win'. Not when it reminded her of what had really taken place the last time she had been at the Duke's Cornwall estate.

She looked out the carriage window as memories of that weekend party flooded her mind. She had driven up this same path full of nervous excitement and trepidation, as if about to embark on an adventure. It was a far cry from the resignation she was now feeling.

She glanced up at the grand, imposing house, remembering all that had happened, the euphoria of walking and dancing with Mr Hayward, the despair of being yet again the victim of bullies, the sense of security that came when Mr Hayward saved her from their taunts, and then the confusion of the Duke's offer of courtship.

But so much more had gone on that weekend of which she had been unaware. There had been that bet. That terrible bet. The one where she was pitted against a piece of land.

At the time ignorance had been bliss and she had thought Mr Hayward was spending time with her because he was her friend and, dare she admit it, was interested in her romantically. She had naively been flattered and delighted. But the only thing he had been interested in was building a rail line so he could increase the profitability of his coal mines.

She quashed down her anger, determined not to let it consume her.

'And you will have the Duke completely to yourself this weekend,' her grandmother prattled on.

'Yes, that will certainly make a change.' Whether it would be a good change or not Grace was yet to discover. They had barely spent time in each other's company since his proposal. It had become increasingly obvious the Duke much preferred gambling and consorting with his rowdy friends. That should be making Grace miserable, but strangely it did not.

She knew the real cause of her despondency. Mr Hayward. Despite her determination to forget all about him, that man was constantly in her thoughts and had even taken to haunting her dreams. Everything that happened in her life, she imagined talking over with Mr Hayward. Every time she dressed in her finery for another social event, she could picture him looking at her the way he had when they had attended the theatre, with such admiration and desire. And as for that damn kiss, when was it going to stop tormenting her?

It was beyond ridiculous to be so obsessed with a man she despised. He had used her in such a cavalier manner. He cared nothing for her and had made a complete fool of her. The anger she had been fighting to control welled up inside her, along with an overwhelming, infuriating wish to see him again.

'There's no need to be nervous.' Her grandmother patted her knee, completely misinterpreting Grace's feelings. 'I'm sure the Duke will behave like a perfect gentleman this weekend.' She sent Grace a coquettish smile. 'And if he doesn't, it matters not. You'll soon be his wife and he's entitled now to show you a little of what will be expected of you.'

Grace couldn't help but grimace.

'Now, don't be like that,' she said, wagging her finger in a playful manner. 'There is nothing wrong with the Duke taking a few liberties now that you are so close to being married. In less than a month you'll be his. It won't be a liberty then. It will be your duty.'

Grace fought to pull her face into a more impassive expression.

'I know, my dear,' her grandmother said, once again patting her knee. 'You are such an innocent and this is all going to be a bit of a trial for you. But just accept it as your lot in life and think of what you are getting in exchange.' She returned to looking out the window as they pulled up in front of the house. 'It's more than worth the sacrifice.'

Grace was not convinced. Her grandmother had told her what would be required of her so she could do her duty and produce the necessary heir. She had described what went where in a clipped tone, her nostrils flared, as if it was all too distasteful to discuss, let alone do.

The main instructions Grace had been given was to lie back, give her body to the Duke and submit to whatever he wanted to do. As she spoke, all Grace had been able to think about was doing so with Mr Hayward, of giving her body to him, of letting him do whatever he wanted. But that was something she knew she must never think of again, not if she was to end this self-inflicted suffering.

The footman helped them down from the carriage and once again the Duke was not waiting to greet them, and once again her grandmother chose not to mention this lapse in etiquette.

'Make haste, dear,' her grandmother said as the footman helped them out of their travelling cloaks. 'We do not want to keep your future husband waiting.'

'No, that would be terribly rude, wouldn't it?'

Her grandmother raised one eyebrow as she registered Grace's sarcasm, but said nothing.

They retired to their bedchambers to change out of their travelling clothes. Molly removed an ornate day dress from the trunk, one of the excessive number that had been packed for the two days they were to be at the Duke's house.

With a sigh, Grace surrendered to being trussed up in an even tighter corset, weighed down with layers of fabric and having her hair pulled, combed and braided into the ornate style her grandmother deemed suitable for a future duchess.

When Molly was finished, she held up a hand mirror so Grace could see the back of her hair, but she waved her lady's maid away, rose and joined her grandmother. They descended the stairs together, her grandmother's elevated head and stately posture suggesting she felt this grand house and estate already belonged to her.

They entered the drawing room to find the Duke staring out the window, looking out over his estate. He did not turn around when they entered. Even when the footman announced their presence he did not greet them.

'That damn man is here,' he said, still staring out the window, his fists clenched behind his back.

Grace sent a quick look in her grandmother's direction. She abhorred cursing, seeing it as something only the lowest tradesman would do, but she made no reaction to the Duke's words, merely tilted her head as if in concern.

'Who is present, Your Grace?' her grandmother asked.

'That man Hayward.'

The mention of his name sent heat rushing to Grace's cheeks and caused her heart to jump.

'He's actually out there working on my land, like a common labourer,' the Duke continued.

Grace could mention it was not the Duke's land any more. He had lost it in a bet and had won her instead, but his angry posture suggested that right now he did not see that as much of a victory.

Instead, along with her grandmother, she crossed the room and joined him at the large sash windows. In the distance she could see a group of men laying the rail tracks and one of them was undeniably the tall, strongly built figure of Mr Hayward.

Grace stifled a gasp before it escaped. He was not wearing his shirt. Desire and panic warred within her as she watched him rhythmically pounding the ground with a large hammer. She should look away and end this anguish, but she remained frozen at the window, staring at him, as if under a spell.

'I know exactly why that man is here.' The Duke finally turned from the window to address Grace and her grandmother. 'He must have known my intended would be here this weekend and he thinks he can still win her. The man has no decency and was never able to accept when he had lost.'

Win her? Why would he still think he could win her? He had his land and that was all he ever wanted.

'Well, he *has* lost,' her grandmother said. 'But you are right, Your Grace. The man is beneath contempt and this display merely demonstrates that despite his wealth he is little more than a peasant.'

As their disparaging words whirled around her, Grace continued to watch Mr Hayward as he worked beside the other men. Even from this distance she could see the whip-like strength of his body as he lifted the hammer high over his head and brought it down with considerable force.

'Well, he needs to be taught a lesson, yet again. Miss Lowerby, will you accompany me on a walk?'

Grace tore her gaze away and looked at the Duke, who was offering her his arm.

'What? Now? Where?'

'I merely want to inspect my land and make sure those ruffians are causing no damage to my estate.' He sent Grace a knowing smile.

The last thing she wanted was to be anywhere near Mr Hayward. She looked towards the window, her teeth nibbling lightly on her bottom lip.

But as he now owned the land adjacent to the Duke's it was inevitable that at some stage their paths would cross. Perhaps it was better to get it over and done with. And if she was on the arm of the Duke, if she could show him that she had what she wanted, he would see that his winning that appalling bet had not been his victory, but hers.

Yet it would still mean seeing him again and ensuring she made no reaction. She could not let him see she harboured even the slightest regret that he was no longer in her life. That would be beyond mortifying.

'What a good idea.' Her grandmother's words cut across her confusion and somehow she managed to both smile at the Duke while glaring at Grace. 'Go for a nice walk and stretch your legs after that long journey.'

'Of course,' she finally acquiesced, taking the Duke's arm.

At a rapid pace, he led her straight out the house and across the fields towards where the men were working, all the while muttering curses about Mr Hayward. That was what Grace assumed they were from his tone. Whatever it was he was saying, they were expressions she had never heard before and ones she suspected even those tradesmen her grandmother looked down on would be loathe to use, especially in front of a lady.

As they drew closer, Grace fought to keep her heartbeat and breathing steady. She did not want Mr Hayward to see that he affected her in any manner, but she was still curious as to how he would react to seeing her again and on the arm of the man she was to marry.

Would he have any reaction? Would he even care?

They reached the work site and came to a halt. Mr Hayward looked up from his work. Grace froze, her breath caught in her throat, as his gaze moved from her to the Duke and back again. Then he resumed his work, pounding in the metal spike with increasing vigour.

She had her answer. He didn't care. She meant nothing to him.

'Hayward, I see you've reverted to type,' the Duke called out, causing Mr Hayward to stop once more and wipe the sweat off his brow. Grace knew she shouldn't, but she couldn't stop her gaze from moving over his naked chest, taking in those lean, hard, sweat-slickened muscles.

He cares nothing for you. Look away. You were just a means to gain this land he is now working on.

It would be so much easier to follow those commands if he wasn't so potently masculine or if her fingers would cease aching to run themselves over those powerful, naked muscles. Her gaze followed a trickle of sweat as it ran down his chest and over his firm stomach. A shocking image entered her mind of her tongue tracing its path.

She forced her eyes to do as her mind demanded, returned her gaze to his face and adopted what she hoped was an imperious look, while she fought to ignore the burning heat consuming her body.

It would be so much easier to maintain that haughty pose if loneliness wasn't gnawing at her resolve. The time she had spent with him was the happiest of her life, even if it had all been pretence. She had felt cherished and admired. They had talked so freely, had laughed together so easily and she had enjoyed every minute she was in his company. She had even foolishly thought she loved him. She *had* loved him, at least, loved the man she thought he was. Even if it had all been an illusion it had felt so genuine and it was hard to turn off those feelings just because they aren't real.

'I believe congratulations are in order,' he said, lowering the sledgehammer and taking a step forward. It took Grace's muddled brain a few moments to realise he was congratulating the Duke on their engagement.

'That is almost gracious of you, Hayward,' the Duke said, placing his arm around her waist and pulling her close. She pulled against him, mortified that he should act in such a familiar manner in front of this group of men.

'I hope you are very happy together,' Mr Hayward said with a look of derision.

'Yes, we will be. I can promise you that.'

Before Grace knew what was happening, the Duke pulled her into a clinch and his lips smashed hard against hers. Grace gasped in horror, her mouth opening, giving the Duke the opportunity to plunge his tongue inside.

He was kissing her. In public. In front of these workmen. In front of Mr Hayward.

She struggled against him, but he held her tighter.

His hands cupped her buttocks, pushing her hard against his hips and he rubbed himself against her. It was as if he was going to take her, here, in public.

This was unconscionable. A gross indecency.

Wedging her hands between them, she gave his chest a hard push.

He flew backwards with more force than she thought herself capable. Gasping in mortified breaths, she watched as Mr Hayward's fist landed in the middle of the Duke's face and he fell to the ground, blood streaming from his nose.

The Duke was instantly on his feet. He took a step towards Mr Hayward, his clenched fists raised. Then, registering the anger burning in his eyes, the coiled fury in his taut muscles, he took several steps backwards. The men had all stopped their work and were watching the scene unfolding before them as if it were entertainment provided for their benefit.

'You will treat Miss Lowerby with the respect she deserves,' Mr Hayward seethed, his words as tense as his body.

'She's mine and I'll do whatever the hell I want with her,' the Duke said, his voice muffled as he tilted his head backwards and tried to staunch the flow of blood.

He took another step towards the Duke, his fists raised, his breath coming in loud, rapid gasps. 'You will treat her with respect, you blackguard, or you'll pay the consequence.'

'I'll treat her anyway I want,' the Duke said, taking another step backwards. 'She's to be my wife. I won her fair and square and you lost. Just accept it, Hayward.'

That bet.

They were still arguing about that offensive bet.

Grace looked from one man to the other. That was all she ever was to both of them, a prized possession to be fought over, a possession made all the more valuable because they thought the other wanted it. But neither really wanted her. They just wanted to get the better of each other and she had been caught up in the middle of their rivalry.

She was the one who had been insulted and subjected to a gross act, yet they both appeared to have forgotten all about her. All they cared about was their hatred of each other and this senseless feud.

Well, she would leave them to it. With that, she turned and strode across the field back to the house.

Chapter Nineteen

Thomas was tempted to chase after Grace, to make sure she was all right, but the Duke was correct. She was his and would soon be his wife. It had been her choice and it was not Thomas's place to comfort her. It was this sorry excuse of a man who was nursing a much-deserved bloody nose who should be rushing to her side and trying to make amends for that unforgivable affront.

But he looked as though he had no intention of doing so, so it was up to Thomas to teach him where his duty and responsibilities lay.

'I don't care if she is your fiancée and will soon be your wife,' he seethed. 'You will treat her with the respect she deserves and will continue to do so once you are married.'

'Or what? You don't frighten me.'

Thomas took a step towards him and the Duke quickly took several back. 'You should be frightened of me. You have debts up and down the country. All

I have to do is buy those debts and I could take more from you than just the land to build this railway. I could ruin you.'

The Duke smiled in triumph. 'And in the process ruin Miss Lowerby and cause her to live in poverty. Is that what you want?'

Thomas drew in a slow, deep breath and fought not to let this witless churl see how right he was. He would do nothing to harm Miss Lowerby.

The Duke's smile turned into a sneer. 'I knew it. You're in love with her. You're in love with the woman I will marry. My God, I really have beaten you, haven't I.' The sneer became a leer. 'That's going to make my wedding night even more enjoyable. Every time I bed her I'll have the additional pleasure of knowing that I'm having her and you're not.'

Thomas's fist flew out again and with a satisfying crunch connected with the Duke's face. He raised his fists again, but several firm hands on his shoulders prevented him from doing what he longed to do and giving him a beating he would never forget.

As he attempted to shrug off the workmen, the Duke turned tail and literally ran back to his house.

He knew he should respect Miss Lowerby's choice, but how could he do so when it was so obviously the wrong choice? Surely that display had shown her what sort of man he was, a man she could not tie herself to, a man who would treat her appallingly at every chance he could, if for no other reason than to torment Thomas.

She could not marry him and Thomas had to stop this outrage before it was too late.

'You're back sooner than I expected,' her grandmother said as Grace strode into the house. 'And where's the Duke?'

Ignoring her grandmother, she continued walking towards the stairs.

Her progress was stopped when her grandmother grabbed her arm. 'What has happened? Did you see that Mr Hayward again?'

Grace shrugged off her grandmother's arm, but nodded, her rage making words impossible.

'Oh, my poor, dear girl. I can see you're upset. Tell me all about it.'

Grace doubted her grandmother could offer her any comfort, but she allowed her to lead her into the drawing room.

Her grandmother indicated the chairs beside the unlit fireplace and Grace collapsed into one, suddenly more exhausted than she had ever felt before.

'So, what did that terrible man do?'

'He kissed me and rubbed himself up against me.' Shame washed through Grace at the memory of that appalling encounter.

'What?' Her grandmother screeched, standing up,

her hand flying to cover her mouth. 'This is an outrage. I hope the Duke dealt with him in the manner he deserved.'

'What? No. I mean the Duke kissed me and rubbed himself up against me, in front of all the men working on the railway, including Mr Hayward.'

'Oh, I see.' She lowered her hand and once again took her seat. 'That is rather unfortunate behaviour. I can see why you are upset, as any well-brought-up young lady would be.'

She nodded and placed a comforting hand on her roiling stomach. 'It was disgusting.'

'Hmm, but we have already had this conversation. The Duke is to soon be your husband. You have to take your lead from him, even if sometimes it makes you feel, well, perhaps a little uncomfortable.'

'A little uncomfortable?' Grace repeated, her voice growing loud. Had her grandmother really just dismissed something so offensive, something that was impossible to tolerate, as a little uncomfortable?

'Did you not hear what I said? He was rub—'

'Yes, I heard what you said.' She held up her hands as if pushing the words away. 'It does not need to be repeated.'

'He was trying to prove to Mr Hayward that I was his possession and he could do whatever he wanted with me. Even kiss and fondle me in front of him and all those other workmen.' Surely even her grandmother could see this was behaviour unacceptable from any man.

'I see. Well, that explains it. The Duke is right. You are his now and it is time that Mr Hayward realised it.'

She stared at her grandmother in disbelief. It was one thing to allow the Duke to take liberties before they were married, but for him to do something so obnoxious, to treat her in that manner in front of other men, was beneath contempt. How could her grandmother possibly condone such behaviour?

Her grandmother smiled at her, as if that was to be the end of it, causing Grace to shake her head slowly from side to side, words being inadequate to express her contempt at what the Duke had done and at her grandmother for not seeing it as unforgivable.

It was obvious her grandmother was never going to side with her. No matter what the Duke did, her grandmother would accept it and expect Grace to do the same. Like the Duke, like Mr Hayward, her grandmother only saw her as a means to an end.

'But you should not allow yourself to get so upset,' her grandmother said in a soothing voice. 'Perhaps you should retire to your bedchamber for a while and have a lie-down to compose yourself.'

Grace gave a mirthless laugh.

A lie-down? Did she really think this could be cured with a lie-down?

'I'll send Molly up to you with a sedative to calm your fit of the vapours.'

Without responding, Grace flew out of the room and stormed up the stairs to her bedchamber, then commenced pacing, fury coursing through her. Her grandmother had shown her true colours. She cared nothing for Grace and probably never had. She expected her to submit to anything in order to marry a duke. Well, she would not do it. She would not marry him. She would not let that odious man near her ever again.

Molly soon arrived with a glass of warm milk and a cloth soaked in lavender oil.

'I don't need any of that,' she said, louder than intended, startling her lady's maid. 'I'm sorry, Molly,' she said in a calmer voice. 'But I don't think warm milk and cool cloths are going to solve anything.'

'No, but it might help,' Molly said, placing them on the table. 'And shall I loosen your corset? You are quite flushed.'

Grace doubted that loosening her clothes would help to alleviate her agitation, but she did as her lady's maid suggested, and with the corset removed her rapid breathing was eased somewhat.

'I am so sorry to see you upset, miss. Shall I brush out your hair?'

Grace suspected that would not help either, but allowed Molly to lead her to the dressing table.

With soothing fingers, Molly undid the clips from

her hair and brushed out her long tresses. Under the lady's maid's gentle strokes her agitated state began to dissipate slightly.

'You do deserve to be happy,' she said, her voice gentle.

'Thank you, Molly, that's very kind of you,' Grace said, closing her eyes.

Molly drew in a breath and paused in the rhythmic brushing. 'I never knew your mother, but some of the older servants did and they say she, too, was a lovely young woman. They were all so pleased she married for love, rather than marrying the man your grandmother had chosen for her.'

Grace's eyes flew open at this revelation.

'As was your grandfather,' Molly added.

'What?' Grace spun round on the stool and faced her lady's maid. 'No, Grandmama said the shock of her bringing such shame on the family sent him to an early grave.'

Molly shook her head sadly. 'That's not what the older servants say. They say he was pleased his daughter had found such happiness and it was her sudden death in the carriage accident that broke his heart and caused his rapid decline.'

Grace turned back to face her reflection. Had her grandmother really lied to her all her life? And if she lied about that, what else had she lied about? 'Have the servants said anything else about my mother and father?'

'Well, everyone remembers what a talented pianist your father was.' Molly smiled. 'They also say he was so kind to your mother and everyone adored him. Well, everyone except your grandmother. She was so angry when your grandfather gave them his blessing along with your mother's dowry. And when you were born he made provisions so you, too, would never have to worry about money.'

Grace stared at a reflection she hardly recognised, her face drained of blood, her jaw tight. She gripped the edges of the stool. 'I have money of my own?'

Molly shrugged. 'That's what the servants say.'

Her grandmother had lied to her, repeatedly. She had lied about her parents, lied about her grandfather's death. And lied when she said that without her grandmother giving her a home, Grace would be living on the street and trying to fend for herself. This was almost more than Grace could take in. She'd spent her entire life trying to make up for the so-called sins of her mother, had tried desperately to repay her grandmother's generosity, and all because she was being deceived by a woman who she had desperately wanted to please, a woman whose love she had ached for and had constantly been denied.

'Will there be anything else, miss?' Molly said quietly when she had finished brushing out her hair.

'No, thank you, that will be all,' she said in little more than a whisper. She turned on her stool to face her lady's maid. 'And thank you, Molly, for everything.'

Molly nodded and departed. Grace stared at her reflection, fury once again boiling to the surface.

She would love nothing more than to confront her grandmother and throw her lies in her face, but it would do no good, and might do a great deal of harm. Her grandmother would know this revelation came from the servants, and Grace knew how her grandmother treated staff she considered to be disloyal.

But it did mean everything Grace had thought about her parents, all she had done to make amends for the shame her mother had brought on the family, had been for nothing.

She thought of that painting in the attic, of that woman with the gentle eyes and kind smile, and couldn't help but wonder what her life might have been like if she had been raised by two loving parents instead of a woman who cared nothing for her.

She continued to stare at her reflection. She really had been naive. Everyone she thought cared about her had been lying to her and like a gullible fool she had accepted those lies and did exactly what the liars wanted her to do, allowing them to sacrifice her so they could achieve their goals.

So what did she do now? One thing her grandmother

was correct about. She did need to calm down before she made any decisions about her future. To that end, she climbed on to her bed and placed the lavender-scented cloth on her head, trying to digest all she had been told.

The Duke's behaviour, the fight, her grandmother's reaction and Molly's revelation spun round and round in her head, making rest impossible.

She climbed off the bed and paced backwards and forwards, trying to walk off her rising anger, but that was as fruitless as resting. What she had to do was face the people who had caused her wrath, to let them know she would no longer be a pawn in their manipulative games.

She left the room and all but collided with her grandmother, who was standing outside her bedchamber about to enter her room.

'You did not tell me Mr Hayward had assaulted the Duke,' her grandmother hissed, as if it had been Grace who had thrown the punch. 'This is outrageous and, instead of sulking in your room, you should be offering comfort to your future husband.'

'Don't be so absurd. Of course I won't comfort that despicable pig of a man.'

Her words caused her grandmother's mouth to fall open in a manner that would almost be comical if Grace felt like laughing.

She pushed past her grandmother, strode down the

stairs and walked past the open door of the drawing room, where a young maid was tending to the Duke, wiping away his blood.

She humphed her disapproval and headed out the front door, determined to walk and walk until she had walked off her anger and had composed the words she needed to say to these people. Words that would make it clear that things had changed irrevocably and they were just going to have to get used to it.

What she would do then she had no idea, but first she needed to get this surging anger out of her body so she could think more clearly and decide what she was to do with her future.

Her walk took her past the fields where the railway tracks were being built. Mr Hayward dropped his hammer on the ground, grabbed his shirt and, pulling it on, raced after her.

'Miss Lowerby, wait,' he called out.

Curiosity caused Grace to halt her progress. She turned to face him, anger still coursing through her, but wanting to hear what he had to say.

'I'm sorry,' he said when he caught up with her.

That was a good start, but hardly enough to quell her anger at him, at the Duke, at her grandmother, at the entire world.

'What exactly are you sorry for?'

'For punching your beloved in the nose.' The small

smile that quirked at the edges of his lips made a lie of that apology.

'He deserved it. It's just a shame I wasn't the one to deliver the blow.'

Just like her grandmother, his look of surprise was almost comical, then he laughed. She had forgotten how lovely his laugh was, warm and comforting, and despite herself she smiled back at him.

'That I would have paid anything to see. Do I take it that he can no longer be described as your beloved?'

'I believe we both know that term could never be used when describing our relationship,' she countered, her anger once again bubbling up inside her.

'I am truly sorry,' he repeated. 'You deserve so much better than him.'

That was something Grace was starting to see. She had done nothing to deserve the way she had been treated. All she had tried to do was make others happy and to do her duty like an obedient young lady.

'Yes, I do,' she stated emphatically.

'So the marriage is off?'

'Of course it is off.'

He released a long breath and nodded. 'Good.' He looked over her shoulder and frowned. 'And it looks like you're about to get the opportunity to tell him so yourself.'

She turned towards where he was looking and saw

the Duke striding across the field, followed by her irate grandmother.

'What is the meaning of this?' her grandmother called out. 'Get away from that man and come back to the house immediately.'

'It looks like the Duke is not the only one who needs telling of your change of heart,' Mr Hayward said.

'Miss Lowerby, as my betrothed I forbid you from consorting with this man,' the Duke said the moment they reached her. He puffed up his chest and attempted to look formidable, but his quick, nervous glances at Mr Hayward undermined that stance.

'I'll consort with whomever I choose,' Grace shot back.

'You will not. Not if you are to be my wife.'

'Well, that is easily solved if I'm no longer your betrothed,' Grace said, surprised by how calm her words sounded.

'Stop this at once,' her grandmother screeched. 'I don't know what's got into you, but you know better than this,' she added in a slightly quieter tone. 'Return to the house, now, and we will forget all about this peculiar behaviour. Won't we, Your Grace?' she said, smiling obsequiously at the Duke.

Grace released a long sigh of exasperation. 'No, Grandmother. I have no intention of doing anything you order me to do ever again.'

Once again, her grandmother's mouth fell open in

that comical manner before she slammed it shut, to the sound of teeth hitting teeth, and glared at Mr Hayward. 'This is all your fault. You've put these ideas into my granddaughter's head. Shame on you.'

'Perhaps you should, for once, listen to what your granddaughter has to say,' Mr Hayward said, turning to Grace with a smile of approval.

'Well, what have you got to say for yourself, and I want none of your nonsense,' her grandmother said, her glare of disapproval moving between Mr Hayward and Grace.

Grace took in a long breath as she tried to order her thoughts. 'Grandmother, I appreciate everything you have done for me in terms of giving me a home when my parents died, giving me shelter, clothing and an education.'

'Well, for goodness' sake, show that appreciation. Come back to the house and stop behaving like a spoilt brat.'

'As I said, I have no intention of following your orders ever again. While I appreciate what you have done for me, I will no longer be manipulated or taken advantage of by you or anyone else. I will not be used so you can elevate your position in society. I will not be used so you can right the supposed wrong you think my mother committed by marrying for love. I will not be sold into a loveless marriage to a man who cares nothing for me and just sees me as a way to get the better of a man who he knows is in every way his superior.'

'Now, see here,' the Duke spluttered. 'I will not allow you to—'

'Shut up and listen,' Grace said, surprising herself as much as the Duke and her grandmother. They both stared at her with matching bulging eyes, horrified that anyone, especially a powerless debutante, would dare to speak to them in such a manner.

'I was used by you, just as much as I was used by my grandmother and I will not stand for it, not for a moment longer. You're a despicable man who lacks even a modicum of honour and that obscene display in front of the workmen proved it.'

'What? What?' he gasped, his lips flapping like a fish who had just been pulled out of the comfort of the water.

Mr Hayward smiled at her in approval and clapped his hands in admiration of her performance. 'Well said, Grace, well said.'

She turned and glared at him. 'And I don't know what you're smiling at. You're no better than either of them.'

As expected, the smile died, the clapping stopped, and he, too, looked taken aback by her words.

'I know all about that bet you had with the Duke, the one where I was in competition with that piece of land. It was despicable.'

She pointed across the field to where the workmen had stopped in their labours and were looking in the direction of the commotion. 'That was so unforgivable I barely have words to express how repugnant it is. You used me to get a better deal on this land. You didn't care that I'd be married off to a man who only wanted me because he thought *you* wanted me. You led him on so that he would want to marry me even though you knew exactly what my marriage to him would be like. You had no reservations when it came to selling me off to this buffoon so you could increase the profitability of your business.'

His look of shock now matched that of the Duke and her grandmother. It was obvious he, too, did not expect to be spoken to in this manner, nor did he expect to be called to account for his behaviour, and especially by someone as powerless as herself.

All three started talking at once, the Duke to declare he was not a buffoon and as a duke would not tolerate such lack of respect, her grandmother to desperately attempt to reprimand Grace and call her to order and Mr Hayward to repeat his empty apologies.

'Well, I've had it with the lot of you,' she said, cutting across their babble. 'I want nothing to do with any of you, ever again.' With that, she strode off across the field, determined that it was all over and she could now start a new chapter in her life. One where she made her own decisions, ones that suited her and no one else.

Chapter Twenty

Thomas watched her retreating figure, awe, amazement and a sense of shame waging a war within him.

'This is all your fault,' Lady Ashbridge spluttered. 'You've put these outrageous ideas into her head.'

'All I can say is thank goodness I found out what the chit is really like before I married her,' the Duke added. 'Wouldn't want a wife with a temper like that. Lucky escape, I say.'

Thomas was tempted to once again plant his fist in that oaf's face, but this was not time to think of what he wanted to do. It was more important that he talk to Miss Lowerby, to ensure she was all right. He needed to reassure himself she knew what she was doing and to apologise with all his heart for what she had rightly called his despicable behaviour.

To that end, he left Lady Ashbridge, trying to soothe the Duke and convince him that Miss Lowerby's outburst was just some sort of pre-wedding nerves and her granddaughter would very soon come to her senses, while the Duke put on a familiar display of petulance.

Entering the house, he stopped a passing footman. 'Which room is Miss Lowerby staying in?'

The man looked him up and down, obviously reluctant to answer.

'It is vital I see her. She is in a state of distress.'

His plea had no effect on the man, who continued to scrutinise Thomas, taking in the mud on his trousers and the inevitable dishevelled appearance that followed hard physical toil.

'I am Thomas Hayward and am a guest of the Duke of Hardgraves.' Thomas was stretching the truth somewhat, but needs must.

'Of course, Mr Hayward,' the man said. 'I'm so sorry I didn't recognise you. You were at His Grace's recent weekend party, I believe.'

'Yes, I was and please excuse my present appearance. So where would I find Miss Lowerby?'

'She's in the second room after the first corner at the end of the hallway. If you wait here, I'll get her lady's maid to—'

Thomas did not hear the rest of the sentence, but rushed up the stairs two at a time and all but ran down the hallway, determined to find her room within this maze.

He passed an open door and saw her standing beside her bed, pushing gowns into an open trunk.

Without knocking, he entered, stood in the middle of the room and tried to compose what he was to say.

'I suppose you've come to give me a lecture as well,' she said, not stopping in her task.

'No, I have come to make sure you are all right and to once again apologise.'

She pushed another pile of silk, satin and taffeta into her trunk. 'You can save your apologies. I have no need of them.'

'So where do you plan to go? What do you intend to do?'

'I have no idea. All I know is I want to get as far away from this house and everyone who has ever used me.' She punched a silk gown that was refusing to sit neatly in the trunk.

'And do what?'

She picked up a lace shawl, bundled it into a tight knot and glared at him. 'I have no idea, not yet, but weren't you the one who told me women have choices nowadays? Didn't you say they don't have to marry if they don't want to?'

'Yes, but they usually have a plan.'

'I might not have a plan, but I'm not completely useless. My training to make me an ideal wife for a man such as the Duke means I can speak four languages fluently. I could teach. I could give piano lessons like my father.' She shrugged one shoulder. 'All I know is

I will survive and no one will ever use or manipulate me ever again.'

'Good.'

She stopped her packing and stared at him. 'Good?'

'Yes, you deserve to live your own life the way you want to and you are an intelligent woman who has just proven herself to be strong and determined. I am sure you will be successful in whatever you choose to do.'

'I will,' she said, resuming stuffing gowns into her trunk. 'Anyway, I've recently discovered my grandfather left me some money, which my grandmother neglected to inform me about. Perhaps I'll start my own business. I don't know, but I'll think of something.'

'But before you leave, I have to say I am sorry. Truly sorry for what I did.'

'Yes, so you said, but what are you sorry for really? For taking that bet or for being caught out?'

'Yes, you're right, for both if I'm being completely honest. And I deserve your condemnation. I wanted the land, but I should never have agreed to the Duke's proposition.'

She stopped in her packing, a silk gown crunched in her hands. 'The Duke's proposition?'

'Yes, when he suggested that offensive bet, I should have said no. I knew it was wrong at the time and yet I still agreed. That was unforgivable.'

'The Duke made the proposition?' She tilted her head in question. 'What exactly was the proposition?'

Thomas's jaw clenched tightly. He did not want to spell it out to her. His behaviour was too shameful.

'Tell me the truth. You owe me that much, surely.'

He exhaled a long breath. 'The Duke challenged me to what he called a wooing duel. If I won your affections, I would have to pay more for the land than we had agreed. If the Duke won your affections, then I would get the land at a cheaper rate.'

Her hands clasped more tightly around the gown. 'It was the Duke's idea?' she asked quietly.

'Yes, and I should have said no. I should have told him it was an outrageous thing to do. To have not done so was unforgivable and you have every right to be angry with me.'

'You're damn right I have. You had a choice, me or cheap land. You chose cheap land.'

Thomas flinched as her words hit him. 'I'm so sorry. At the time I let our childish rivalry blind me to what I was doing and I tried to justify myself by saying no one would be harmed. I told myself you would get what you wanted. Marriage to a duke.'

'You thought no one would be harmed?' she said, her eyes enormous as she shook her head in disbelief. 'You thought I would not be harmed if I married a man like him? You thought I would not be harmed if I married a man who never really wanted me, just didn't want you to have me? You thought I wouldn't be harmed if I married a man capable of behaving the way he did out in the field? You knew what he was like and you happily let me be courted by him all so you could get that land at a better price.'

His muscles clenched tighter with every word. She was right. What he had done to her was appalling and he deserved no less than her wrath and disdain.

'I am so, so sorry. I tried to justify it to myself by saying that it was what you wanted, but I was fooling myself. I was wrong, so very wrong.'

'Why didn't you tell me what he was like?' she said quietly. 'Why didn't you try to stop me from marrying him?'

'Yes, I should have. That, too, was unforgivable.'

'Yes, it was.' She stuffed another dress unceremoniously into her trunk. 'But the Duke had told me the bet was all your idea. That was why I agreed to marry him, because I thought you had betrayed me.'

'He lied.' Thomas took a step towards her. 'It was never my idea. You have to believe that.'

She shrugged as if it made no real difference and she was right. It didn't.

'But I should never have agreed to it. After the Duke announced you were courting I thought that would be the end of it. Then your grandmother encouraged me to see you again.'

'She only did that to pique the Duke's waning interest.'

'Yes. She told me you wanted the Duke desperately,

that it was your dream to be a duchess, and his jealousy was the only way to capture him.'

She snorted. '*My* dream? That's what she said, was it?'

'After that bet I felt so guilty I thought I owed you, that it was my duty to help you achieve your dream.'

She snorted again and shoved the crumpled silk dress into the trunk.

'No, that's a lie,' he added. 'That was what I told myself at the time. I did feel guilty over the bet, but I agreed to what your grandmother asked because I wanted to see you again.'

She stopped pounding the dress so it would fit in the trunk and looked up at him.

'You did?'

'Yes, and the brief time we spent together has been the happiest time of my life.'

'It was?'

'Yes.'

She ran her teeth lightly along her bottom lip. 'I suppose I have an apology to make as well.'

He shook his head. 'You have nothing to apologise for.'

She waved away his objections. 'I knew my grandmother was using you to renew the Duke's interest. I knew it was wrong, but I did nothing to stop it because I, too, wanted to see you again.'

She looked down at the trunk, then back up at

him. 'And you are right. As stupid as it now seems, I thought I did want to become a duchess. I thought that was what would make me happy. I thought it was what would make my grandmother love me.'

'Oh, Grace, you never deserved to be treated this way, by anyone. Your grandmother should have loved you for who you are, a lovely, kind, clever young lady, and not seen you as merely someone to further her own ambitions.'

He paused, wondering whether he could say what was really in his heart. 'She should have let you marry for love, to a man who appreciates you for who you really are.'

She gave a mirthless laugh. 'That was never going to happen. My mother married for love and she never forgave her, even though my father was apparently a good man who loved my mother and made her happy.'

'It sounds like your mother was a strong woman, just like her daughter, and followed her own path.'

She looked up at him, unshed tears making her eyes sparkle. He so wanted to take her in his arms and comfort her, but he had proven himself unworthy of her and had no right to do so.

'I so wish I had known her,' she said. 'I so wish I hadn't made such a mess of everything.'

Despite his command to not comfort her, he moved closer and took her hands in his. 'You have done nothing wrong. You were trying to do what your grandmother wanted, what you thought was your duty. All I was doing was trying to get the better of the Duke and increase my family's business assets.'

This might be the last time he would ever see her, so he knew he had to be completely honest or he might never get another opportunity. 'When I made that bet I thought getting the better of the Duke was all that was important and I could not see beyond making a fool of him and getting a good deal on the land I wanted. Now I know that neither of those things mattered. There is only one thing that is important. You.'

She looked up at him, blinking rapidly as if trying to make sense of what he was saying. He stepped closer to her, desperate to make her see that these were not idle words.

'Now I know there are more important things in life. You showed me that. And I no longer want the Duke's land, not when it reminds me of how I hurt you. I'll give it back to him and be done with it.'

'Don't do that. Why should that man profit from any of this?'

'Then I'll give it away to a rival railway company. I don't care. I don't want it. Not when it reminds me of how callous I have been.'

He lightly stroked the back of her hand. 'I mean what I say. You have made me see that there are more important things in life than petty revenges and acquiring more and more money. You've shown me that love is so much more important.'

'Love?'

'Yes, love. I love you. And all I want is for you to be happy and to live an independent life that will allow you to be who you really are and not the person you think other people want you to be.'

It was Thomas's turn to be surprised when she lifted herself up on tiptoes and kissed his lips. The sweet taste and gentle touch of her lips drove out all other thoughts. If this was to be their farewell kiss and the last time he had her in his arms, he wanted it to be a kiss to remember. He gently wrapped his arms around her shoulders and held her close to him, loving the feel of her soft feminine curves against his body and kissed her back.

If she wanted him to stop, he would do so and be grateful for this one, sweet parting kiss. But he hoped she did not. Not yet.

Her lips parted, making it clear she wanted him to continue. He gladly accepted the invitation and ran his tongue along her full bottom lip. She released a soft sigh and he entered her mouth, holding her close, loving the way she moulded herself into him, as if this was where she belonged.

Then to his immense disappointment, she pulled back from him. But that, too, was something he was going to have to accept. It was all over. He had hurt her. He did not deserve her forgiveness and he certainly did not deserve her kisses.

'You said you want me to be happy,' she said, looking up at him, still in his arms. 'This is what makes me happy. Being with you. Being in your arms. I had thought that being with the Duke would make me happy. I had thought that giving my grandmother what she wanted would make me happy, but it didn't. And you are the only person in my life that even cares whether I am truly happy or not.'

'And that is all I care about,' he whispered as he pushed a stray lock of her long blonde hair off her face.

'I love you,' she whispered back. 'I love you so much I never want to be away from you.'

He stared down at her, hardly believing what he was hearing. 'Then marry me,' he said, the solution so obvious. 'You can still live the life you want to live. You can still be the independent woman you want to be. Gracie, you can be anything you want to be, but I would love to be part of your life.'

She nodded, giving him hope.

'I'd love to be part of your life because I love you, everything about you,' he said, encouraged by her smile. 'I think I've loved you from the moment I saw you sprawled out on the ballroom floor.'

This caused her to laugh lightly.

'I could see how much we were alike even if I hadn't

realised it at the time. We are both outsiders, both people who have to fight for our place in the world.'

'But it was you who taught me how to fight back and stand up for myself.'

'No, I think you learned that all by yourself,' he said with a laugh.

'I did, didn't I,' she said with a cheeky smile. 'And I intend to keep standing up for myself for the rest of my life. You had better take that into account if I'm going to be your wife.'

'I would hope for nothing less, but does that mean you accept? That you will marry me?' he asked, hardly able to believe it could be true.

She nodded.

'Oh, Gracie, I love you.' Those three words hardly enough to describe the strength of the feelings rushing through him.

'And I love you.'

She stepped back from him and sent him another wicked smile. 'My grandmother has said, many, many times, that once a man has agreed to marry you, he's allowed to take liberties.' She gave a small laugh, walked over to the door, closed it and turned the key in the lock. 'And, as you know, I always follow everything my grandmother says.'

He took her in his arms and kissed her waiting lips, knowing this was what he wanted. What he had always wanted.

Chapter Twenty-One

Grace could hardly believe it was actually happening. It was what she had dreamed of since she had first met him and those dreams had only become more intense since he had first kissed her.

Now she was back in his arms, his lips were on hers. This was where she had to be and where she intended to spend the rest of her life, in love and married to this glorious man.

Her entire body aching for his touch, she moulded herself against him, loving the feel of her breasts hard against his chest as she kissed him back, unleashing a burning desire that had been smouldering within her since they had last kissed.

'Oh, God, I want you so much,' he murmured, as his lips left hers and he kissed a line down her neck. 'But if you want to wait until we are married, I understand.'

She shook her head, shocked that he could say such a thing. 'No, I want you now,' she said, her voice raspy with desire. 'I need to have you now.'

His kisses left her neck and he smiled at her, a smile that sent tingles of anticipation rippling up and down her spine.

'And you have me, my love, heart, mind and soul.'

'And body,' she added.

'Yes, and body, definitely and body.'

And that was what she wanted as well. She wanted to feel his body against her, his warm skin against hers. She needed to be out of the restricting clothes that were creating a barrier between them.

Her trembling fingers moved to the buttons of her gown and she tried to release herself from the restricting fabric.

'Allow me,' he said, removing her hands. 'I want to unwrap you like the precious gift you are.'

He undid the buttons down the front of her dress and slipped it off her shoulders. Kissing each shoulder, he pushed it lower over her hips where it dropped to the ground. His lips returned to hers, and through the fabric of her chemise, her body moved against his, the friction turning her nipples hard and sensitive. Throbbing anticipation mounted inside her, rising to an almost unbearable pitch as he continued to kiss her with ravenous longing.

'Lift your arms,' he murmured. 'I want to see you naked.'

She did as he commanded. He lifted her chemise over her head, tossed it to one side and pushed her drawers down over her hips. She stepped out of them and looked up at him. She was standing in front of him dressed only in her silk stockings and garter belts, as he slowly looked her up and down. She could see the raw desire sparking in his eyes, intensifying her own pounding need for him.

He desired her. He wanted her. He was going to take her. And she wanted it with an all-consuming wildness that was intoxicating and thrilling.

'You are perfect,' he said, his voice a husky rasp. 'You are even more beautiful than I had imagined.' He smiled at her. 'And believe me, I have a vivid imagination.'

His hand lightly stroked across her breasts, a feather touch on her nipples. She released a soft sigh and closed her eyes, focusing on that touch.

'Yes,' she murmured, that one word saying so much.

He scooped her up into his arms and carried her across the room, placing her in the middle of the bed. She lay back on the feather mattress, loving the way she was offering herself to him, loving the intensity in his gaze as he feasted himself on her body while he ripped off his clothes.

With the shedding of each item she watched as more of his body was exposed to her hungry gaze. He was perfection, like a marble statue of a Greek athlete, all sculptured muscles and sinews, and the promise of sensual pleasure.

She reached out her hands towards him, wanting to touch that hard, muscular body, to run her hands, her lips, her tongue over his skin.

'I love you so much,' he said, looking down into her eyes.

'So prove it,' she said, her breath coming in short gasps as her heart pounded hard within her chest.

He smiled down at her. 'My pleasure,' he said as he joined her on the bed and took her in his arms. Then he kissed her again. Warm naked skin against warm naked skin, his lips were on hers, hot and ravenous.

She kissed him back, giving expression to her fervent, untamed desires. Her hands ran down his strong back, loving the feeling of those rippling muscles under her fingers.

His lips left her lips, gliding to the sensitive hollow under her ear and tracing a slow line down her neck. She writhed under him, every inch of her body alive, every inch craving his touch.

His lips moved lower, tracing a line of kisses across the mounds of her breasts. Grace released a sigh of exquisite pleasure as he cupped each breast, kissed each tight bud in turn, then took one in his mouth, his tongue and lips tormenting the aching peak.

She took hold of his head, her hands running through his thick black hair, her breath coming in louder and louder gasps, his caressing tongue sending surges of ecstasy cascading through her.

As she released a loud sigh, pleasure shot through her, leaving her gasping in its wake. His lips were once more on hers and she kissed him back, unable to believe that his lips and tongue could give her so much pleasure, but desperate to know how much more this magnificent man could show her.

His hands exploring her body, she arched towards him in longing and expectation. His hands swept over her breasts, down her stomach, over her mound to the cleft between her legs. Not thinking, just reacting, she parted her legs, showing him where she wanted his caressing hands to move, letting him know how much she needed him to relieve the tight, throbbing tension that was once again mounting within her.

His hand moved between her legs. She released a *yes* on a soft sigh as his fingers parted her and slowly, gently entered her.

He lifted himself up off her, and she opened her eyes. Surely he would not be so cruel as to stop now?

'Are you sure, my love?' he asked, his voice gentle.

'Oh, I'm more than sure,' she said, placing her hand over his and urging him to continue.

'If you want me to stop at any time, just tell me.'

'Don't you dare stop,' she said, causing him to smile slightly before he kissed her again.

His lips moving to the soft skin of her neck, he cupped her feminine folds and rubbed against her sensitive spot, his fingers entering her deeper with each rhythmic stroke. Her gasps of pleasure matched the rhythm of his hand, growing louder and louder as raw need surged up within her. His hand moved faster, the pressure harder, taking her higher and higher, until exquisite pleasure crashed over her. Calling out his name, she collapsed back on to the bed.

He kissed her again, his body blanketing hers, and her desire for more of this glorious man was instantly sparked back into life.

'That was divine, but isn't there more that we can do?'

He laughed slightly and held her closer. 'Are you sure? Don't you want to wait until your wedding night? Then we will be husband and wife and in our own bed.'

'No. I want to be your wife right now. We can get those bits of paper later.'

'You really do know your own mind now, don't you?' he said, smiling down at her.

She rubbed her inner thigh against his leg and watched the effect on his face. 'I certainly do,' she said, smiling back at him.

He gently placed his hand on her inner thigh and she did what she knew he wanted, parted them wider and wrapped her legs around his waist.

'If this hurts, tell me and I'll stop,' he said. She nodded and felt his tip against her opening.

'Promise me you will let me know if I hurt you.'

She looked up into his eyes. 'I promise you.'

Gently, he pushed himself inside her. She gasped at the unexpected feeling of him stretching her, filling her up. He instantly withdrew.

'No, don't stop,' she said, sliding her hands down his back and cupping his firm buttocks so he would not escape her.

'Are you sure this is what you want, my love?' he whispered.

'Yes, I'm very sure.'

He pushed further into her and Grace released a long, slow sigh. This was perfect. They were joining together as one. He was hers. She was his.

Slowly, he withdrew and pushed inside her again, again and again, each time her body relaxing further into the heavenly feeling of having him inside her. The thrusts became faster. They penetrated deeper until Grace lost herself in the throbbing of her body as her gasping breaths matched his thrusts.

Gripping his buttocks tightly, she wrapped her legs further up around his waist so he could enter her deeper, harder and faster, taking her higher and higher with each thrust. Pleasure mounted up within her, like an ever-rising wave. Just as she thought she could bear no more, it crashed over her, sending intense euphoria flooding through her body as she cried out his name in passionate ecstasy.

'Oh, Grace, my darling Grace,' he said as he reached his own release and collapsed on to her.

She lay back panting, residual shivers of pleasure rippling through her as he held her tightly.

'You are now mine, for ever,' he said before once again kissing her still-gasping lips.

'And you are mine. For ever,' she murmured as he nuzzled her neck.

When his heartbeat finally slowed down and the fog of passion lifted, the reality of where he was and what he had done dawned on Thomas. He was in the Duke's house, in bed with the woman the Duke was expecting to marry, the woman Thomas loved and would soon make his own wife.

While it mattered nothing to Thomas what the Duke or anyone else thought, that did not mean Grace would be as equally relaxed about such a scandalous breach of etiquette.

He rolled on to his side and gazed at her. Had he ever seen a more beautiful sight? No, he knew he had never seen anything so wondrous as the woman he had just made love to. She was perfect in every way and she was his. He didn't know what he had done to deserve such good fortune, but he would be eternally thankful that fortune had smiled on him and granted him this precious gift.

He picked up a coil of her long golden hair, spread

out over the pillow, just as he had imagined it so many times, and wrapped it around his finger.

'I doubt if we're going to be welcome in the Duke's house,' he said, causing her to give a small laugh. 'I can go and tell the Duke and your grandmother we are to marry and while I'm facing their wrath you can continue packing. Then we can make a hasty retreat.'

She rolled on to her side. 'No, let's tell them together.'

He lightly kissed her shoulder. 'Are you sure? I doubt if your grandmother is going to be pleased.'

'I've spent my entire life trying to please my grandmother and all that's resulted in is me being completely miserable.'

He lightly stroked her cheek. 'Are you certain? I don't think she will take the news of our marriage at all well.'

She laughed. 'I *know* she won't take it well, but the sooner we get it over and done with, the sooner we can leave this house and the sooner we can marry.'

He smiled at her, his brave, independent Grace.

They climbed out of bed and he helped her to dress, then tried as best he could to help her knot her hair up into a bun. As he did so, he had to resist the temptation to kiss the back of her neck again. He knew where that would lead—straight back to bed—and she was right, the sooner they were out of this house, the sooner they would be married.

Hand in hand, they walked down the stairs and into the drawing room, where they found the Duke standing in the middle of the room, his nose raised high in the air, his lips pursed and his arms tightly crossed over his chest, still muttering about what an outrage this all was, while Lady Ashbridge tried to reason with him.

They both looked towards the door as Thomas and Grace entered. Both sets of eyes grew enormous and two mouths fell open as conversation ceased mid-sentence. If those two hadn't both behaved in such despicable ways, Thomas would almost feel sorry for them, they looked so stunned.

'Grandmother, Thomas and I wish to inform you that we are to marry,' Grace stated in a clear voice. 'I will be sending you an invitation to the wedding and you will be most welcome to attend.'

Lady Ashbridge's eyes grew even larger and she stared at her granddaughter as if she could hardly understand the language she was speaking.

'No,' she gasped out, placing her hand over her heart and staggering towards the nearest chair. 'You can't do this to me.'

'Yes, I can. I intend to marry for love, just as my mother did.'

'You'll get nothing,' Lady Ashbridge said, pointing a finger at Thomas. 'I'm sure you're aware of how generous my granddaughter's marriage settlement is, but you will not get your hands on one penny of it.'

'I care nothing for that,' Thomas said, giving Grace's hand a gentle squeeze. 'I'm marrying Grace because I love her, love her with my heart, mind and my soul.'

'And your body,' she whispered beside him, causing him to smile.

'Never wanted the chit anyway,' the Duke added, his nose once again lifting high into the air. Thomas took a step towards him, but was stopped when Grace placed a hand on his arm.

'He's not worth it,' she whispered. And she was right. The man was bitter and angry. And as he was responsible for bringing his lovely Grace into his life, in a strange way Thomas owed him a debt of gratitude.

'That's all we came to say,' Grace added. 'We will take our leave now.'

'No, Grace, you can't,' her grandmother cried out. 'You've ruined your chances with the Duke, but there are other suitable men. There's the Earl of Whitecliff and Baron Morsley's eldest son.'

They left the room while her grandmother continued listing men she deemed more suitable than him to wed her granddaughter.

Thomas arranged with the footman to have her trunk loaded on to one of the carts used on the railway site and for the retrieval of his own possessions, then they climbed aboard and headed off to the local train station.

'When we get to the station, I'll buy you a first-class ticket,' he said and looked down at his rough attire. 'But dressed as I am I'll have to join the other workmen in the third-class carriage.'

'No, you won't. We'll both travel third class. Don't the marriage vows say for richer or poorer, for first class or third class?'

He laughed loudly and wrapped his arm around her shoulder. 'You are precious. But this is hardly the most auspicious start to our life together,' he said as the roughly built cart rattled and creaked through the countryside.

'Yes, it is. It's perfect,' Grace responded with a smile. 'This is everything I have dreamed of since I was a child,' she added, leaning her head on his shoulder. 'I always pictured myself running away with my handsome prince, knowing that he loved me as much as I loved him.'

Thomas kissed the top of her head. She was right. This was perfect and like a dream come true.

Epilogue

No wedding could be more like a fairy tale, of that Grace was certain. Just as she had always dreamed of doing, she had won the love of a handsome prince. He didn't have a title, but in her eyes, Thomas was every inch her prince charming.

And soon he would be her husband.

On the arm of her uncle, the Earl of Ashbridge, she walked up the aisle of the small stone church near Thomas's family estate in Somerset as an organ played the wedding march. Unlike her grandmother, her uncle did not see this marriage as a travesty and, when asked to give her away, had been delighted. 'Your mother would be so happy for you, as would your grandfather,' he had said. 'And it would be my honour to stand in for your father and grandfather, two men I admired greatly.'

Each member of the congregation smiled at her as she passed, reflecting her happiness. Even the old stone church seemed to radiate joy, with the pews bedecked with ivy and white roses, and colourful floral bouquets adorning every corner.

She reached the altar and her uncle handed her over to her husband-to-be and took his seat in the front row next to Thomas's parents.

His parents had made her feel so welcome and Grace now felt as if she finally had the loving family she had always wanted and a place where she belonged. From the moment she stepped down from the carriage when she first arrived at their estate they had taken her into their fold.

'Me dear, I am so pleased to have another daughter, one I am sure is going to make my son so happy,' she said, encasing her in a warm hug, as Thomas's father shook his hand and offered his congratulations.

'I knew one day a lovely lady would capture your heart,' he said before turning to Grace and kissing her on the cheek. 'Welcome to the family, Grace.'

Then Thomas's sister also hugged her.

'This is simply splendid,' Georgina had gushed. 'I just know that you and I are going to be the best of friends, but you're going to have to tell me, how did Tommy finally win your heart? Did he do as I told him and challenge the Duke to a duel? Did he serenade you and shower you with love sonnets?'

She had looked towards Thomas, who was smiling and slowly shaking his head in amused disbelief.

'No, but he proposed in a manner that did make

me very, very happy,' she had said, sending Thomas a quick wink. 'Happier than I had realised it was possible to be.'

'Good, and he better continue to do so or he'll have me to answer to.'

'Believe me, I intend to make my new wife just as happy again and again, at every opportunity,' Thomas had said with a devilish smile, causing Grace to blush slightly.

And soon he would make good on that promise. Soon she would be his wife.

'You look like a princess,' he whispered as she smiled up at him through her lace veil.

Throughout the ceremony, Thomas held her hand and Grace tried to adopt a suitably solemn expression as the vicar took them through the service, but it was hard to keep that ecstatic smile off her face. And every time she looked up at Thomas, he, too, was smiling with unrestrained joy.

Finally, the vicar told Thomas he could kiss the bride. Gently, he lifted the veil, leant down and kissed her lightly on the lips. Grace closed her eyes and released a gentle sigh, and heard the congregation sigh along with her, basking in the sight of two people in love.

Still holding her hand, he led her back down the aisle to the sound of joyous church bells, and the moment they were on the threshold of the church they were showered with rose petals.

It was all so magical and Grace found herself both laughing and crying, until Thomas once more took her in his arms and kissed her, much to the pleasure of the assembled guests and villagers who had come out to witness the happy occasion.

A flower-bedecked carriage awaited them and, as they drove off to their wedding breakfast, Thomas once again kissed her. Now they were alone, the kisses were longer and deeper, heightening her excitement of the wedding night to come.

Flowers decorated the house and, when they pulled up in front, the servants were all waiting outside, baskets of rose petals in their hands, and they were once again showered with those delightfully scented flowers.

Hand in hand, they rushed up the stairs. Thomas pulled her behind one of the pillars and kissed her deeply, taking the opportunity before the other guests arrived.

'I love you with all my heart,' he whispered before kissing the soft skin of her neck.

'And I love you,' she gasped back. As much as she was looking forward to sharing the joy of her marriage with their guests, she couldn't wait for the wedding breakfast to be over so they could be alone together and start their life as husband and wife.

Georgina and Thomas's two closest friends, Sebastian and Isaac, were the first to arrive. Georgina had been right when she had said they would soon become the best of friends and had bubbled with excitement when Grace had asked her to be her bridesmaid.

'It will be the fourth time I've been a bridesmaid,' she had declared. 'I'm obviously very good at it.'

Sebastian and Isaac had performed their roles as best man and groomsman admirably, even if they had been unable to completely hide their surprise when Thomas had told them he was to marry.

The rest of the family, including her grandmother, were next to arrive. Grace had been surprised she had accepted the invitation to the wedding. She wanted to see it as her grandmother finally accepting her choice of husband, but suspected it had more to do with her grandmother discovering that Thomas was the brother-in-law of the Duke of Ravenswood. But whatever the reason, Grace no longer cared. Her grandmother had hurt and bullied her throughout her life and she knew that no one would ever do that again. She was now married to a man who loved and cherished her, a man who had shown her how to be strong and independent, and nothing would ever change that now.

As the wedding party were walking up the stairs, Thomas smiled down at her. 'I love you, Mrs Hayward,' he said.

'And I love you,' she responded with all her heart.

Georgina paused at the top step, sighed and placed her hand over her heart, while Isaac and Sebastian gave small, embarrassed coughs.

'Don't be so cynical,' he called out to his friends, laughter in his voice. 'Love is the best thing possible. It makes the world a better place. It makes you a better man.'

Instead of replying, both men rolled their eyes, linked arms with Georgina and led her inside.

'I think those two need to be alone together,' they heard Seb say as he walked into the entranceway.

'Agreed. There's only so much of this lovey-dovey business I can take,' Isaac added, causing Thomas and Grace to laugh.

'They will learn,' he said, looking over at his retreating friends. 'And when they do, they'll discover how love can sneak up on you in the most unexpected of places and steal your heart.' He looked down at Grace and smiled. 'And then you become it's happiest, most willing captive.'

With that, he kissed her again and Grace was certain her parents were smiling at the happy occasion, pleased that, just like them, she had married for love.

* * * * *

MILLS & BOON®

Coming next month

ONE NIGHT WITH THE DUCHESS
Maggie Weston

'And you're here because…'

She exhaled a deep breath. 'I've come because…'

'Yes?' It was a single word, a simple word, but it left Matthew's lips weighted with anticipation.

'May I ask a favour?'

'You may ask,' he countered, 'but I will most probably refuse.'

'I would like you to bed me.'

Having become somewhat used to people expecting such behaviour from him, Matthew smiled grimly. But, in spite of that, when he said, 'No,' the word left his lips tasting bitter.

*

Isabelle was startled at the abrupt answer, issued from Lord Ashworth with no hint of doubt. 'You're not even going to *think* about it?'

The giant man standing in front of her grinned, his white teeth flashing wolfishly. He ran one large hand through his unstylishly shaggy hair.

'There's no need. I don't *bed* virgins. I don't ruin reputations—'

'That is not what I heard.'

Matthew ignored her comment. 'And I certainly will not be led by the nose into a situation where you could hold any sort of power over me. I'm not the man you're looking for, *Duchess*.'

Isabelle couldn't help the slightly hysterical giggle that worked its way up her throat. 'You… You think that I would trick you into *marriage*?' she asked, somewhat stunned by the notion. 'Have you not been listening to anything I've said?' She waved both hands down towards her heavy black dress. 'I'm in *mourning*. I will be for *years*!' she practically shouted. 'And even if I wasn't, marriage to you is the *last* thing I'd want!'

Because she felt hot and flustered by his looming presence and the entirely inappropriate conversation they were having, she started to pace.

She lowered her voice. 'I'm a *duchess*. I don't need your title. And marrying again before my mourning period is over would cause a scandal that would be completely antagonistic to my main goal—helping Luke.' When he only raised his eyebrows, she continued, 'Moreover, I have no *desire* to get married again.'

'But you're not a duchess—technically. And am I just supposed to trust whatever you say?'

Isabelle turned abruptly to find that he'd closed the space between them, and that instead of looking at his face she was staring at a patch of tanned skin where his collar lay open. She slowly craned her neck back, shifting her eyes away from his chest to his steel gaze.

'Do you honestly believe that I'd be here with any other motive? That I'd want to lose my—' she lowered her voice '—my *maidenhead* to a stranger whose name I picked off a list?'

Lord Ashworth did not try to fight his grin. 'You have a list?'